if i could

Daniela has lost everything and is all alone in the world…or is she? After her son loses the battle with leukemia and her mother passes away unexpectedly, life begins to unravel.

Does the mysterious brown box in her mother's closet hold the answers to her mother's past…and Dani's future?

acknowledgments

To Lindsay McDonald and Cynthia Rose
Thank you for taking this journey with me, once again! Your editing/covers/formatting/graphic design – make me who I am. I only write the story!

To my children and grandchildren
I love you more than 'the zillion stars in the sky!'

To my dear ladies in the UK, Sue Ward
and Philomena Callan
From my first book Bishop Street, to this new one, you have been such a major support. You keep me creating and moving forward with each new book. Your devout devotion to all the Indie authors is so valuable and humbling.

To family, friends, reviewers, bloggers, and readers
You carry a special place in my heart—you know who you are and I sincerely appreciate the support and encouragement. Thank you! Please never stop! Without you this journey would not be possible…nor would it push me to write these heartwarming stories.

A Special Note to Stephenee
As a blogger, reviewer and friend, you've been on this journey with me from the very beginning. I'm humbled to be your friend. I also watched from a distance and know that sometimes life doesn't seem fair. Unexpectedly, you lost your brother and I know the pain is almost unbearable. We don't know why they are taken, but we continue to struggle looking for those answers.
Let it go…celebrate him and all those beautiful and funny memories he brought to your life.

Definition of Alone:

'Alone' stresses the objective fact of being by oneself....

Lonely, loneliness, desolate, abandoned

1. Lonely: destitute of sympathetic or friendly companionship.
2. Loneliness: depressed or saddened because of the lack of family and friends.
3. Desolate: feeling unconnected and implies inconsolable grief at loss or bereavement.
4. Abandoned: suggests sadness and a sense of loss ~ death of a parent, child, family member, or friend.

There are times in our lives where we actually feel like we are alone. Either a lack of family and friends or the death of a loved one will create this feeling of isolation. Language...has created the word loneliness to express the pain of being all by yourself. But I think there is a tremendous difference between alone and loneliness. Loneliness is a deep and powerful yearning to find a place where we fit in...alone is whether or not you chose to embrace being by yourself...as you will see in this story of Daniela Vaduva.... Is she really alone?

chapter one

THE SUN HAD ALREADY GREETED THE DAY AND WAS resting high in the sky, and yet, the room was still pitch black. The only way Daniela Vaduva could detect any light was through a small hole in the left corner of the blackout shade. This was the only window in the small bedroom and the only source of natural light. The tiny hole the size of a nickel was a steady reminder of the better times in her life, moments filled with laughter and happiness. Nowadays, this dark room had become her cave—a place to hide. It was her prison, filled with pain and sorrow, slowly sucking the life from her once vibrant youth. At twenty-eight years old, Dani had been through enough.

A loud pounding on the wall let Dani know it was time to wake up. Dani grinned when he knocked again. It was her quirky next-door neighbor who always kept an eye on her. Over the past year he had become her human alarm clock. During that year, not once had he failed to pound the wall to wake her up, so she would be on time for work. It was almost like he had taken on the responsibility and accountability of where her mother had left off. He was her guardian angel, and for that, she was grateful. Except—those days she wished she didn't have any responsibilities; that she didn't have to go to work and could frivolously sleep forever in her dark, quiet cocoon.

Anton Petrescu, her neighbor for twelve years now, had silently watched her fall into a deep depression over the past year. With no family, and few friends, she was spiraling down a deep, dark hole. The only hand that had reached out for her—was his. During those years he was always around with an open ear and a few good words of advice, but he never overstepped his welcome or pushed his way into her life. He just always seemed to appear when she was walking on the edge of her self-imposed tightrope.

Anton was a loner himself, but much older than Dani. He was well into his seventies—although most would not know it. He had once been a very handsome young man—and was still considered attractive, only in a more debonair way. His hair had become almost white and his face was lined from his years in the sun. He was considered on the tall side at six-foot, and he carried an admirable physique. His spry and exuberant behavior always made him seem younger than his years. Complete with his foreign accent and charm, he had always kept Dani fascinated and in awe, along with a few other older women in the neighborhood.

He had gotten along splendidly with Dani's mother, Ema. They were both from the same European culture that carried along old, valued traditions. Even though she was years younger, they would talk for hours about places they were familiar with from their childhoods, though they never talked about their pasts or families. Ema kept her childhood buried deep, never to be known by anyone—not even Dani.

No matter what happened in Dani's life or Anton's—their quirky little friendship was what kept them both taking two steps forward. Just knowing that made Dani a little more resilient and secure, now that her mother was gone.

The knocking continued until Dani lifted her arm out of the warm covers. She knocked back. This was their signal that she was up and getting ready for work. Dani rolled onto her back and stretched her arms over her head and yawned. She knew she had a full day ahead of her and nothing was going to stop her from getting everything done. Not even the two buses she took to work nor her antagonistic boss.

She was a very responsible young woman, and had been from a very young age. Ema Vaduva had taught her more than enough skills to survive in a world that was filled with constant unpredictability. They had worked hard together as a team while she was growing up. Things were never financially easy, and although her mother worked two jobs, their lives were always without the extras. Dani didn't care. Her gift in life had been her adoring mother. She felt lucky and happy to have such a devoted mother who worked very hard just to give them the basics. Never once had Ema complained or drawn any hostility from their sometimes difficult struggles.

Dani considered herself very blessed that her mother had decided to forfeit everything to start a new life in America. It wasn't easy as a single parent. The financial struggles were difficult, but Ema always maintained a happy and solid environment for her daughter. Ema was the center of Dani's universe. They did everything together. Even though Ema worked such long hours, she always made time for them to do something special every weekend. Whether it was going to the park, or the zoo, or taking a leisurely walk downtown—it was their time together. Ema always knew how to make Dani feel special and loved.

From the very beginning, Ema was Dani's only family and source of stability. Mother and daughter had lived alone for as long as Dani could remember.

Ema had come to America when she was nineteen, alone, and pregnant. For years Ema had strived to make sure her daughter never went through what she had endured in Romania.

What little family Ema had was scattered about. Ema's mother had died giving birth to her. With four other children at home, her father had callously handed her over to his only sister to raise. Maria was not pleased with having to feed another child. She had struggles of her own. With six children in a small two-bedroom house, they could barely pay the rent and food was sometimes infrequent. The economy in Romania had hit a crisis level in the late 1970's and into the 1980's. This had imposed a precipitous decline that left many homeless, jobless, and staving. Maria's husband was an alcoholic who worked very few hours. He didn't bring home enough money to feed the family—let alone another hungry mouth. The day she had turned eighteen, holding her meek belongings in a small paper bag, Ema had been asked to leave the only home she had ever known. Horrified, she was sent out into the cruel world to survive on her own.

She was very lucky that day. Through a referral from a teacher from her school, Ema found a position as a servant to a very wealthy family in Bucharest—the Borsacks. For a year she lived in their servant quarters in a private building built behind the main house. She shared a room with three young staff members and they became friends. It wasn't a big room. It could barely fit two bunk beds and a small three-drawer chest for each young woman. Ema was used to sharing a room with a lot of children, so this was not a sacrifice, and getting her own chest of drawers was a luxury. One small bathroom in the hall was shared by the entire staff. Their privacy was scarce; the timing had to be synchronized so everyone had their own personal time for use. Nobody complained, because jobs were hard to come by. To be supplied with room and board was practically unheard of in the large city filled with so many homeless souls.

Bucharest was only sixty-two miles from where she was raised in the countryside, just outside of Calarasi and along the bank of the Danube River. Her hometown was a small place that showed no signs of affluence, nor did it have anything to boast. Ema had never been to

Bucharest and had never seen or experienced life in a big city—filled with wealth. Bucharest was a melting pot of diversity. Ema, on occasion, would tell Dani stories of her days working for the wealthy family as a servant and quickly working her way up to the position of the nanny. The Borsacks' excess dalliances of spending money and wasting food could still cause Ema's stomach to churn. The three Borsack children were spoiled rotten beyond belief, so the parents had abandoned them to the staff.

Dani's mother shared many interesting stories over the years, each one different, and each one with a significance or a moral to live by. The only story Ema never shared was why she had left her job to come to America. Occasionally, when Dani would ask questions, Ema would refuse to answer or impulsively walk out of the room in avoidance.

No matter how hard Ema had tried losing her accent—it was hopelessly impossible. This only made Ema constantly encourage Dani to master the perfection of the English language in school. Her daughter's education was really important to her. Ema continually pushed Dani to the limit, controlling her social activities and making sure that Dani made excellent grades. Ema didn't have a solid education and had only made it through her fourteenth year. The lack of schooling had forced her to take minimum-wage jobs. She wanted more for her only child. She wanted Dani to become financially successful so she wouldn't have to struggle like her, working two or three jobs at a time. It was heartbreaking for Ema to watch Dani take a job as a waitress the day after she graduated college at the top of her class. Unfortunately, with a downsized economy in the throes of a recession, there was nothing she could do. Jobs were scarce, and with inflation on the rise, Dani did what was needed—she found a job so she could help out.

Dani smiled at her memories—they were all she had left. She had taken more than enough time just lying there, remembering the good times. That indulgence had now thrown her off her schedule, a timetable that was driven by each minute, in order to catch the needed bus to get her to work in Los Angeles. Grudgingly, she reprimanded herself for taking those few special moments this morning. She shifted her legs off the side of the bed and stood up. She wasn't terribly tall at five-three, and her slender body and pale white skin was barely covered by her old t-shirt with Marilyn Monroe screened on the front. With her long, dark hair flowing down her back, she walked across her small bedroom and went into the bathroom to take her shower and get ready for work. Once she was done with her daily routine in the bathroom, she put on a pair of worn-out jeans, a white t-shirt, pulled her hair back in a ponytail, and slipped into a pair of loafers. She walked over to the window, pulled up the blackout shade, and smiled gently. With her full backpack secured in her hand, she grabbed an apple off the small dinette table and walked toward the door. When she opened the door, she immediately looked down and noticed a small brown bag that was folded over tightly at the top. Dani rolled her eyes, as she always did, picked it up, and walked toward the lobby of her old apartment building.

chapter two

DANI JUST MADE IT TO THE STOP AS THE BUS ARRIVED. She climbed the two steps and stopped to hand the bus driver her prepaid ticket.

"Thanks for slowing down for me, Harry. I surely appreciate that. Over the years, you've been so kind," Dani said. Then she flashed him a big smile.

Harry looked up from his seat and stretched his arm to take her ticket. His large protruding belly was resting on the steering wheel, making it almost impossible for the seat to move. He tipped his hat with his two fingers and said, "Not a problem. I knew I was a few minutes ahead of schedule today. I expected you would be here, so I just slowed down the bus a little, until I saw you running toward the bench! Which stop you going to, missy?" His big, round face was dripping with sweat and he wiped his brow with a dirty rag hanging near the steering wheel.

"The first one, Harry, as usual on Sundays." With that said, Dani walked down the aisle as the bus started to jerk forward. Immediately she grabbed ahold of a pole to steady herself. Once securely anchored, she looked around for a seat, and moved toward a young woman two rows back.

She sat down on the corner edge of the seat next to the pretty, young Hispanic girl. Dani smiled and placed her backpack on her lap. As always, she quietly observed her surroundings and waited for the bus to get to her first destination. Thirty minutes later, the bus stopped. Dani picked up her backpack and got off. She turned around just as the bus was closing the door and yelled, "Have a nice day, Harry!"

He gave her a wave and the bus drifted off into the fast moving traffic. Dani turned and began walking down the street with a slight hop in her step. It was a beautiful sunny California day as always. Dani inhaled the air that was filled with a mixture of bus exhaust and other chemical fumes—then she began to cough.

When she got to the flower shop she stopped and sat down on the curb. She took out the coin purse from her backpack and counted out some change. Satisfied, she stood up and walked toward the small flower shop that was filled with beautiful flowers and interesting, crafty merchandise. She swung the door open again and waited for the bell to ring, letting the proprietor know someone had entered. Dani walked into the shop, closed her eyes, and inhaled the light floral fragrance. It made her forget about the last deep breath she had just choked on as the bus drove off. "I love the smell of spring flowers," she mumbled out loud as she slowly walked around the store.

The young girl behind the counter turned around and squealed in surprise, "It's been a little while, Dani. We missed you here. Where the hell have you been?"

Dani smiled at 'crazy' Paige. "Oh...I've been here. I just couldn't afford the flowers, Paige!"

Paige shook her head, as her eyes drilled Dani's face. "You know we would give you a flower or two for nothing. How many times have we told you that?" The grimace on her face let Dani know she was not happy with her answer.

Dani leaned over and lightly touched Paige's hand and said, "I know. You guys have been so kind. It's just hard for me to take from anyone, especially when the shop is small and struggling to make it. I don't feel comfortable taking your beautiful flowers without paying."

Paige smacked Dani's hand. "Why not? The older flowers we just throw away. So, why not give them to someone who would be able to enjoy them? You fry my ass sometimes, missy." She pointed a finger inches from Dani's face and swung it back and forth.

Dani started to laugh. "You're the second person today that's called me 'missy'! Harry, the bus driver, calls me that all the time!"

Paige started to giggle. "That's probably because his brain is fried from breathing all that polluted air from those old buses. I have no excuse—mine is 'just fried!'"

Dani looked at her with questioning eyes and broke out into laughter. "You think his brain is really fried from those buses?"

Paige laughed. Then she came around the counter with a serious look on her face and hugged Dani. "I'm sorry. I know you have been struggling with everything lately. Come here." She took Dani's hand and began to tug her forward. "Pick out anything you want."

Dani walked along the pathways lined with large, white five-gallon plastic buckets that were filled with every flower imaginable. When she got to the bouquets of wildflowers, she picked one out and held the arrangement to her chest and closed her eyes. "I want these. How much are they?"

Paige looked at Dani's sad face and said, "They are free today. I was just about to throw them away. Go…get out of here before you're late to work."

Dani took the flowers and headed toward the door. On the way out she took her handful of change and placed it on the counter. "See you next week, Paige. Thanks for the flowers. They are perfect!"

Paige waved and blew her a kiss goodbye. Dani continued down the street and when she got to the open gates, she closed her eyes and took another deep breath. With sheer determination, she kept walking forward and then began to climb up to the small grass knoll. When she finally reached the exact spot, she looked down and sighed. It was always the same spot on Sunday mornings. She dropped her backpack on the grass and looked around at the beautiful view. Her favorite spot was slightly shaded by a small tree that would eventually turn into a towering Cedar. With no hesitation, she sat down on the grass that was still damp from the morning dew, but Dani didn't care. She was nestled between her two most loved people in her entire world. They were both marked with simple brass plaques. One plaque read: 'Ema Madalina Vaduva.' The other: 'Levi Christopher Vaduva.'

Very gently she leaned over and wiped off the metal inscription of her mother's plaque. She closed her eyes, as she had done a thousand times, and dredged up that horrible day that she had lost her mother. It was one of the blackest days of her life when she got that hysterical call from her mother's friend at work. It was cold and rainy, and the sky was filled with a darkness that she had never seen before. Her cellphone had continued to ring at work, leaving her annoyed. When she finally realized it was from Ema's work, she immediately picked it up. "Hello?" she said, wondering why her mother would call. Rarely did Ema ever call Dani at work.

Carol was hysterically screaming into the phone. Through her shrieks and broken words, Dani knew something was drastically wrong. The only word Dani could make sense of was her mother's name—Ema.

"Where's my mom?" Dani kept repeating. "I want to talk with her, Carol!" Dani felt these slow fingers of dread begin to creep up her spine as she pleaded over and over to the panic-stricken lady at the other end of the phone. Then she finally heard a male's calm voice finally say through the phone, "This is county paramedics," his voice said. "I'm sorry to tell you this, Ema Vaduva has passed away. We tried all that we could, but nothing worked. She was sitting at her desk and we think she had a heart attack. We don't know exactly what happened, but when we got here, there was no reviving her. Please go to County Hospital—that's where we are taking her." With all those words ringing in her head, Dani let out a wail and slowly slipped into oblivion.

Even today it had brought a sharp pain pumping through Dani's heart. Nothing in the past six months could erase her guilt of not being able to say goodbye. From that day forward, nothing in her life would ever be the same again. She bent down and whispered, "I wish I was there. I wish I could have told you how much I loved you. I wish...."

Dani looked at the next plaque and then with the same gentle sweep of her hand, she wiped it off. A slight grin turned up her lips as she thought about those wonderful nine months of pregnancy and all the joy she had experienced day-by-day. It didn't matter to her that a one-night stand had produced this living and growing baby she now carried in her belly. She had, long before, let that go. Her days had been filled with jarring movements in her enlarged 'bump.' She was filled with wonder about this new life she was about to bring into the world. It was the beginning of her new family. Someone new and loved to bring into her and Ema's tight circle.

She had so many things to do and get ready for. Thrift stores and secondhand shops began to fill her off hours with Ema as they prepared for this baby, the crib, blankets, and all the joy he was bringing to their world. She vowed that she would never ever allow anything to erase the contentment and pleasure this baby was going to bring. Nothing.

Then one day she felt the first pains of labor. She had just gotten off work, and was about to leave, when she sat down on the floor in the bathroom. Everything had caught her off guard as she held her belly and gasped for air. If it wasn't for the quick thinking of her friends at work, she would have never made it to the hospital. Driving through the crowded streets of Los Angeles was hard enough, checking into the hospital was almost more than she could take. For twelve hours she screamed and yelled in pain. Then in the early morning hours with Ema, her best friend, and a room filled with nurses and one doctor, Dani gave birth to her best gift ever—baby boy Vaduva. From the first moment they put him into her arms, Dani's world had exploded with love. She kissed his perfect hands and then his feet. Then she handed him to her mother. Ema held him tight to her chest as she began to well up. Ema handed him back and stood there with pride as Dani touched his little head topped with black hair, and promised, "I will take care of you forever!"

Dani watched her mother as tears spilled over. Life had spun around in a full circle and Dani felt what her mother had felt, but could never truly articulate through words. It didn't matter that Ema had been alone and in a foreign country—nothing mattered except for that small baby girl that she held in her arms that day twenty-eight years ago. Nothing!

Dani held her baby close and knew that feeling. Nothing would every take that feeling or that moment away. Nothing!

Dani took a deep breath and looked into the beautiful blue sky. The breeze was ruffling her bangs and all her thoughts seemed to fade. Carefully, she took her flowers and divided them in half and laid them on each plaque. It was difficult enough to have to live with the harsh reality of the death of her young son the year before. Then six months later, she was forced to bury her mother. One tear began to slide down her cheek—as always. From the day her mother unexpectedly died, nothing in her life had any meaning left at all. Nothing made any sense to her anymore. Life had ceased to exist;

and death had taken over this once vibrant young woman who desperately grieved. She was now completely alone in the world, and no one knew or cared—no one really, except Anton.

Dani didn't want to exist. She just wanted to let go and drift off into oblivion like Levi and Ema—that place where nothing could hurt you and all your pain just stopped. She was done with struggling and dealing with responsibilities that were now meaningless.

Dani laid her head on Levi's cold plaque and tried once again, like she had for the past year, to make sense of why God had taken her family. It always turned into a bitter battleground when Dani came to the cemetery, but it didn't stop her. Dani's constant unanswered questions were spit out like rounds of bullets, as though someone could give her answers—but none ever came. Dani laid there ranting as she looked into the sky. 'Why couldn't you leave my son alone? Why did you have to take him? Why me—what did I ever do to make you hate me?' As if she didn't suffer enough. 'Why did you take my mother? Why her? She was the only one I had left in my life. Why? Why? Why?' Her pain was so piercing she could feel her heart breaking apart in her chest. Tears flowed as the deep ache continued to consume her thoughts. *Would it ever stop...? Oh dear God, would the pain never end?*

Ema and Dani had tried so hard to save Levi's life. They relentlessly took turns taking him to the hospital as he rotated in and out of remission. For a year, they had continuously revolved their schedules to fit into his flailing health. They did everything that was asked by his doctors. They even believed the doctors when they said 'we might be able to save him'—but they hadn't. Levi was barely four years old and had so much to live for—why him? *Is this my fault?* she often wondered. *Is God punishing me for my irresponsible and naïve actions of a one-night stand?*

Dani and Ema both knew, from the first diagnosis, that Levi was dying. Dr. Cal had sat down with both of them, showing no emotional restraint as he choked out the prognosis and everything that went with it. Levi was playing in the corner with some interesting toys, oblivious to the death sentence that was being placed on his head.

Dani whispered to Dr. Cal, "Where did this come from; how—how did he get it?"

Dr. Cal shrugged his shoulders. Unable to accept the silence, Dani stubbornly persisted, "Is it something in my chromosomes? Was it something I fed him? Something from the environment of our old apartment?" Dani wanted an answer—any answer. She wanted to blame anyone, anything, including herself.

But the doctors had no answers. Leukemia just came from damaged chromosomes and most occurred in children under five. Blaming everyone was useless— blaming herself was pointless. Dani was angry and needed to point that finger and unfortunately she had no family history to look at—it was just Ema and her—no one else.

What they did know was that Levi had leukemia and he needed a matching bone marrow donor. Ema and Dani weren't a match, so they had to look elsewhere. With limited time and no matches on the hospital's donor lists, Dani reluctantly tried to find Levi's father. But it was hopeless. What very little she knew about him and what little she could remember left her desperate. The stranger who had left his seed planted in her belly had slipped into obscurity. He had traveled in and out of her life one lonely winter night. Without any link or way of finding him—she felt this tremendous guilt weighing heavy on her shoulders.

Dani had never done anything like that before. She never dated or considered having a relationship. Her life was too busy working and finishing college. But then one night it all changed with just a smile. He had come into the restaurant and was so handsome and sophisticated. She had never met anyone like him. She was smitten from his first kind words, and was unwisely naïve in the romance department—but not Christopher Martinez. He knew the game from start to finish and executed it well. Inevitably, he had done this more than once. He set his sights on Dani, and by his second night in town, she had shared his bed and conceived her son. As quickly as he appeared in the restaurant, he disappeared the next morning. Feeling stupid and insignificant was just the beginning of her biggest lesson in life. Never would she let herself to be used and discarded like a dirty rag again. Never would she allow herself to be as vulnerable as she was that night.

It wasn't until two months later that she realized her whole life was about to change. Not only did she make a huge mistake—now she had to explain how it happened to the one person in the world who worshipped her—Ema.

Dani was laying on the plaque sobbing as she remembered that evening. It was as though it had happened yesterday. Dani recalled crying all that day. She didn't know if it was her changing hormones, or if it was from the fear that was lodged in her throat because she had to tell her mother. She knew in her heart and felt it in her belly—she was pregnant. But it wasn't until that afternoon, when she got the plus sign on the pregnancy test that reality had stuck her in the gut. She didn't want to believe in her heart that one lousy mistake could change the course of her life forever—but it had. There was no fight; no anger; no disappointment; or any kind of negativity that came from Ema's mouth that evening when she told her. There was just a big hug and a tear that slid down her mother's cheek, as her words flowed from her mouth, "It is what it is—so be it." Dani thought at the time that her mother would be disappointed, and harbor resentment when she found out, but instead she smiled and patted Dani's flat belly. It would not be until years later that Dani would learn of the hidden secrets that her mother had almost taken to her grave.

Dani's sobs did not go without notice as her finger outlined the name on her mother's plaque. After a few minutes a raspy, strong, familiar voice broke into Dani's fog of grief. "You need to stop this incessant sobbing, sweetheart. It doesn't bring them back and it will only make you sick. I haven't seen you for a few weeks, but I can see that you're having a harder time than you usually do. Why? Do you think that your mother or your son would want to see you falling apart like this?" Estelle said, from ten feet away.

Estelle was sitting in an old vinyl beach chair that had a very colorful umbrella attached to the arm and opened up above her head. Her small frame barely fit in the chair and her short legs dangled just above the trimmed grass. The umbrella shaded her from the strong California sun, and her big floppy hat protected her old blue eyes from the glare. Her ruby red lipstick stood out against her chalky white skin, and wisps of white hair peeked out along the edge of the hat. With eyes opened wide, she was staring at Dani waiting for an answer—clicking her tongue and wagging a wizened finger from side to side.

Dani stopped her sobbing and was reduced to small hiccups. She turned her head slightly, and looked at the little old lady who had been her cemetery companion for the past year. "I haven't been here for two weeks because I had to work extra hours. I'm just feeling really lonely today; and I guess I look a little silly. After all, it's been a year now." Dani lifted her head and sat up. She began to wipe the tears that had stained her face. "I just miss them terribly. And I feel guilty...." she whispered.

This rigid old voice piped up a few octaves. "Well, of course you miss them! Just like I miss my old Harold! But what is this blistering 'guilt' that you're crying about? I've planted my ass here almost every day for the past twelve years pining over my dear dead husband Harold! Did it bring him back? Do you think he or anyone else gives a rat's ass?" She twisted a little in her chair and winced in pain, just so she could meet Dani's eyes. Her harsh voice continued, "Hell, we were married for forty-seven years, young lady, and there isn't a day that goes by I don't miss him or think about the great times we had together. But you are too damn young to waste your life away carrying on over something that wasn't fair and didn't deserve to happen! You...are...just...too damn young!"

Dani blew her nose into a kleenex. "I know, Estelle...."

Estelle grabbed ahold of each arm of the chair, and pushed herself up into a straighter sitting position, then her voice rose louder with each word. "Now what...? You want me to pitch a fit right here? If I drop dead...then you have a real reason to feel this 'guilty crap' you are trying to fling at me!"

Dani picked up her backpack and moved closer to the old lady. When she got close enough, she bent over, and bent down under her floppy hat, kissing her cheek. "I don't want to upset you. I'm just still trying to figure it all out. Why it all happened and why to me."

Estelle grabbed her hand. "Shit happens sometimes and there is no rhyme or reason...it just happens. Sit down, young lady!"

Dani sat down on the grass next to Estelle and a small smile turned up her lips.

"Life is not fair sometimes. It hurts, and the only thing we can do is pick ourselves up by our bootstraps and push forward. I know all about that at my age. I'm eighty-eight and I've lived through plenty of crap in those years. But look at me…it just made me stronger. This wallowing is a waste of your precious time in life."

Dani looked down and whispered, "Then why do you come here almost every day?"

Estelle leaned down and put one small crooked finger under Dani's chin and lifted up her face to look directly in her squinting eyes. "I'm too old to do anything else. I have buried my only two children and my husband, and at my age, I could go any minute." There was a pause. "What do you want me to do? Sit in the hallway or lay in bed at an old peoples' home with a bunch of old stick-in-the-muds who have stopped living and are just waiting to die? I can't do that! I'd rather be here looking out over the city, sitting in the sun, with fresh air, and enjoying my years of memories. I'm not sad that Harold died. I'm just sad I'm not young like you…so I can start over."

Dani look at her with questioning eyes.

Estelle leaned forward and continued in her stern voice, "Don't you get it, child? At my age, coming down here is a lot of work, but it keeps me moving forward." Estelle took a deep breath. "You coming down here all the time only sucks the life out of you. You are beautiful—and you have a whole lifetime ahead of you. You have so much to experience other than crying over death. Keep them close to your heart, but don't let them steal your youth. Go out and find the things that make you happy. You might even one day find that young man who will steal your heart and give you more babies. Don't stop living…your mother wouldn't want you to do that."

Dani's eyes filled with tears and one spilled over. Estelle leaned over and wiped it with her little embroidered handkerchief. "As hard as it is to hear, it is spoken from my heart." Estelle looked at her watch. "Shoo, get out of here or you will be late for work. I'll keep them company for you! Besides, your mother and I talk all the time!"

Dani opened up her backpack and took out the paper bag Anton left her, as she always did on Sunday mornings, and handed it to Estelle. "I brought you lunch."

Estelle took the bag and smiled. "You sweet, dear girl. What did you bring me today?"

Dani didn't know, so she smiled and said, "It's a surprise, enjoy it!" She turned around and walked down the hill feeling much better than she did when she walked up.

chapter three

DANI SAT AT THE BUS STOP. SHE WAS STARTING TO GET hungry, so she pulled out her apple. Within minutes, the bus pulled up and she was on her way for the forty-minute ride to work. Working in the heart of Los Angeles was not exactly where she wanted to be, but it had a stronger and wealthier clientele than in most areas, and the tips were enough to support her humble and quiet lifestyle.

Los Angeles was one of the largest cities in the United States, and it was split up into different and diverse areas. She worked in West Los Angeles, right on the outskirts of Beverly Hills. If you were able to find a job in that area, then you considered yourself lucky. Dani had been lucky for the past six years. After graduating college with a degree in business, she was unable to find a job. Using what resources life had given her, she decided to become a waitress in a high-end restaurant with affluent clientele. Not only was it lucrative, but it also gave her flexible hours when she had her son.

When the bus finally reached her destination, she got off and walked down the street. She usually worked the brunch shift on Sunday at the seafood restaurant. It had an expensive but popular buffet. It was known throughout the area for its great food, fabulous service, and celebrity sightings. Dani was unimpressed with most of the patrons. Most of the time she considered them privileged and extremely pompous individuals. Some went out of their way to be nice and were very generous.

Others flinched at the slightest neglect and went screaming to the manager like a stuck pig. Dani did her best to give great service and she had her own little clientele of regulars that requested her tables on a regular basis. The management liked Dani and appreciated her ability to please the customers.

Dani mostly kept to herself. She never fraternized with any of the customers. She was also very careful not to hang around with the staff—except for Stephenee Orman. Most of the staff were struggling actors waiting to catch their lucky break, while others were there simply for the large tips. Dani needed the money. Now that she had to survive on her own, she found it much harder to make it on fewer hours. Splitting a lot of the household bills with her mother was so much easier. But she never complained. There was no one left to complain to. She was just another sad story mixed into the group of waiters, and each one carried their own private burdens.

Dani walked to the back entrance of the restaurant, in the alley. She opened the door and walked in. Immediately, she slipped into the employee's bathroom. She released a deep sigh and opened her backpack. Inside her backpack was the simple and characteristic uniform of the waiters. Black straight-legged pants, a crisp white shirt with a ruffled-bib, and a ribbon that slipped under her stiff collar. It was very clean looking and carried a very classic look. It fit her body to perfection and enhanced her delicate curves. She wasn't considered very tall, but her long legs made up for that. Her petite build was more from the stress of the past few years than struggling with a diet or anorexia. Her tiny perky breasts could barely be noticed through the ruffle bib and many of the waitresses constantly teased her. Of course, many of them had augmentations and flaunted them without a second's thought. Dani would only laugh.

She took out her makeup bag and dusted some blush onto her alabaster white skin to give her some color. Then, with a steady hand, she rolled on some black mascara to emphasize her extraordinarily long lashes and finished it off with a very pale lip gloss. Dani was a natural beauty and never overindulged in heavy cosmetics. Most men would stop at nothing to stare at her. Her big blue eyes, tiny nose, full lips, and long dark hair were enticing to the eyes. She could have been competition in any fashion magazine.

She combed her hair and pulled it back off her face, into a ponytail. Once she was finished getting ready, she leaned toward the mirror to make sure she didn't have any smudges on her face. Then she smacked her lips together. She was just about to turn around when the door flung open.

A shrill, whiny voice bounced off the walls. "That son-of-a-bitch! Who the hell does he think he is? Why the hell doesn't somebody just put him out of his misery and run him over!"

Dani grabbed the sink to keep from being knocked over as this little whirlwind flew past her. Dani thought Nicole was finished swearing like a sailor, but the actual storm had just begun.

"That fucking little twerp! How dare he?" Nicole shouted, kicking the stall door. The crashing noise had surely attracted attention outside.

Dani knew that the staff and all of the chefs were probably standing outside the door laughing their heads off.

"What are you talking about? What happened?" Dani whispered.

With a stunned look on her face, and eyes opened wide like saucers, Nicole turned around to see who that voice belonged to. When she saw Dani, she closed her eyes and sighed. "Oh brother. How can you stand to work for that jack-off?" Nicole asked.

When Nicole was in one of her moods, Dani always hated to say anything or do anything that would really kick her into full-gear. So she played it as cool as she could. "I just ignore him. When he gets in one of his moods, or he's fighting with his girlfriend, he gets very foul and nasty." Dani frowned.

"Nasty...foul.... Lawrence is a fucking idiot! He's pushing me to my limits. One day, he's going to get his balls chopped off by Jace. He's not going to let his waitresses take that crap from his manager!" Nicole started to pace the small bathroom.

Dani picked up her backpack and got out of her way. "Jace is too busy cooking and running the back kitchen. He doesn't have the time to mess with the front staff. You know that, I know that. Why don't you calm down? What could he have done to get you in such a snit?"

Nicole's mouth opened and then a slow smile crossed her face. "Snit? What would you do if he made you feel like the town idiot in front of a whole room filled with customers?"

Dani shifted her legs and was careful with what she said—trying the diplomatic approach. "I'd just let him do his thing. Then I would walk away and go back to the customers later and apologize. Then maybe tell the customers what a jack-off he is." Dani looked at her and added, "What did you do?"

Nicole started to undress and slip into her street clothes. "I yelled at him like any moron would do and then I walked away thinking, 'why did I do that?'"

Dani patted her back. "You're not quitting, are you?" she asked, wondering why she was changing when her shift wasn't over yet.

Nicole looked up and muttered, her eyes squinted, "He told me to leave for the day. He said I was a fucking mess and he wanted me out of here."

Dani looked at her with questioning eyes. "What was the big deal that set him off?"

Nicole started to laugh. "The chef gave me the wrong sauce on the pasta I was serving. I didn't notice it had calamari in it. So the customer complained like a little baby. I got in a huff and sat down and started to eat it myself. I turned to both of them and said, 'this shit is really good, and I think I'll go tell Jace.'"

Dani backed up to the wall with a mortified look on her face. "Are you kidding me? You really did that?"

Nicole started to laugh hysterically. "Of course not, I'm just messing with you! I need this job, so I'm not that stupid." She started to shove her clothes in her backpack. "I was so busy with eight tables today, I was a little slow getting the customer his fourth coke. So, Lawrence served him the coke and told the customer not to tip me if my service was poor!"

Dani looked horrified. "He really told the customer to clip your tip?"

Nicole nodded with anger written all over her frowning face.

"Why did you have so many tables? Who the hell can give great service with eight tables?"

Nicole reached into her backpack and said, "Tommy didn't show up for work today, so Steph and I doubled up on his tables!" She started to finger her stylish shaggy blonde hair with gel. "I was on my way to the table with a coke when he grabs my arm and told me, 'if you can't keep up with the customers, I'll hire someone who can!'"

Dani smiled. "He always says that to us. He's just a jerk with an ego the size of Mount Everest! I just ignore him when he gets into one of those moods. Personally, I can't afford to get fired either. So, I just do the best I can and tomorrow he'll forget all about it."

Nicole stopped applying her makeup and looked at Dani. "One of these days, I'm really going to walk out.

But not today, I need this paycheck. Besides, the tips in this joint are a lot better than most."

Dani opened the door to leave, and the chefs and a few of the waiters began to scatter. They must have been listening to Nicole's tirade. Nicole was right behind Dani and she patted her on the back. "Hope you have a better day. Maybe we will get lucky and someone will run him over when he crosses the street tonight!" Both the girls laughed.

"Thank goodness I only have a short shift today. Especially if he is in one of his moods. I work at the hospital tonight."

Nicole looked at Dani with curious eyes. "Don't you ever get tired of being around sick kids? That would be so depressing for me."

Dani bent her head over to look at her fingernail. With restraint, Dani said politely, "No...I love each and every one of those amazing children! And Nicole...just for your information—even if they didn't pay me for being there—I would go!"

"Yeah, well, they really aren't paying you. They are just making you work off what you owe them! That's like being an indentured servant!"

Dani stared hard at Nicole, taken aback. Nicole started shifting her legs back and forth uncomfortably. Dani said in a tight whisper, "I go there because Dr. Cal and the hospital staff were constantly there with nothing but kindness and love for Levi. They never asked for a dime. Never asked for repayment, and never made Levi feel insignificant, like you have just made me feel. I chose to work there! It was all I could do to thank them for the wonderful care my son got. Now, if you will excuse me, I have tables to tend to." Dani turned away with tears in her eyes. It wasn't very often she spoke her mind. Usually, she held it all in and when she had taken enough, she exploded. That subject was too near and dear to her heart. Especially coming from someone who had never experienced any kind of loss. Since everything around her had changed, she had become intolerant to those who were oblivious to other's feelings and pain.

Dani walked through the back of the restaurant and into the kitchen. She placed her backpack into the small lockers set up in the corner for all of the staff members. After one of the waitress's backpack was stolen, Lawrence had this unit of lockers built in. Dani didn't have any valuables, and never carried any money, especially because she traveled around the city by bus—sometimes late into the night. The only things she always carried were her bus passes. She didn't have a car, it was too great of an expense. Dani's mother made sure they were centrally located near the bus system in Los Angeles. Apartment complexes required a high monthly fee just to be able to have an assigned parking spot. Parking was limited in most areas. The high cost of gasoline and insurance left her no other option than to use the inadequate bus system the city had to offer and the limited routes to which they served. At times, it left Dani scrambling to use an expensive cab or asking for a ride.

With her small order book tucked tightly into the pocket of her pants, she started to walk toward the front of the restaurant. Dani was walking on the same path as another waitress. Stephenee was short like Dani, but her shoulder-length, auburn hair was always free flowing, and her big blue eyes complemented her warm smile. She wasn't thin or considered overweight, by any means. Dani thought Steph was a perfect size eight.

Stephenee did a little dance step in front of Dani and smiled. Steph, as Dani would call her, was the only person that Dani ever really socialized with outside of work. They were good friends and had shared a boatload of grief lately. They could understand how hard it was to live through the pain. Steph's older brother had been killed in an auto accident—the loss had devastated her family—leaving their world spinning. Her parents couldn't afford a proper funeral, so Steph took on double shifts to help pay back the enormous financial debt that her family had incurred.

Dani knew what that was like. Her mountain of debt made her feel like there would never be an end in sight. Not only were there the medical bills, but bottomless burial fees along with student loans loomed over her every day.

Steph and Dani could relate to each other and shared a great deal of empathy not many young people could comprehend.

Dani stopped in front of Steph and smiled. "Hey, girl, how's it going?"

Steph smiled back. "Not bad today. Well, except for Nic. Sometimes I just wish she would save all that drama for her own time—not ours."

Dani scrunched up her face. "I was changing in the bathroom when she threw the biggest fit, again! Was it really that bad or is Nicole into her 'theatrics' today?"

Steph laughed, almost dropping her tray filled with a pitcher of ice water. "It was drama, baby! That is all she is about—heavy, high school-like drama!"

Dani sighed and pretended to shoot herself in the head. "Okay then, it is safe for me to go out on the floor? I'm not going to get spiked to death by Lawrence?"

"Nah! Although, I don't know how much more he and the staff are going to take from Nic!"

Dani leaned closer and whispered, "He'll have to take it, if he doesn't want to get hit with a sexual harassment lawsuit! I mean, after all, they got pretty drunk that night months ago, and she claims she woke up next to him—the next morning. She was smart enough to say, 'she didn't know what happened' without making any accusations! So, he's pretty much locked into her constant fits of anger since he doesn't want his girlfriend to find out or Jace to fire him."

Steph whispered, "I bet she set the whole thing up and knew what she was doing. The killer is—everyone takes her drama in stride and thinks she's pretty stupid. You and I both know differently. That girl knows exactly how to play her cards and when to lay them on the table. I heard through the grapevine a while back that she did it to her last boss, too."

Dani looked surprised. "Really? Wow…I didn't know that!"

Steph nodded her head. "Yeah, only he played her bluff and threw her the hell out of the restaurant. He was the smart cookie. He had his office bugged with video cameras, and when she set him up, he pulled out the film and told her he was going to go to the police and tell them he was being blackmailed. It shut her up real quick!"

Both girls quietly giggled like school kids, holding their hands over their mouths.

Steph reached across and patted Dani on the shoulder. "How are you doing? I worry about you going home every night to the empty apartment. You okay?" Steph's eyes showed her concern.

"Just like you, Steph. We make it through each day and hope that it gets a little easier. How's your mother and father?"

"They're having a tough time. You know he was their baby!"

Dani nodded. "I cry sometimes because I know how terrible it is to outlive your child. I know parents are not supposed to bury their babies." Tears started to well in her eyes.

"No, neither is a sister supposed to lose her only sibling. We need to go to dinner on a night that you are free. Or better yet, I would love to go and see Levi one day."

Dani leaned over and kissed Steph's rosy cheek. "That's very kind of you, but let's go do something different. We both need a break."

Steph whizzed by Dani, and said as she departed, "You're on, kiddo!"

Dani turned and walked out into the restaurant. It was nearly lunch hour and the place was beginning to fill up with customers. The Sea Turtle, the restaurant, was written up in a lot of big-name magazines for its interesting and unique cuisine. The chef, Jace—or JJ as most called him, was world-renowned and had once been the host of a popular cooking show. His competitions and throwdowns with Bobby Flay, Mario Batali, Emeril Lagasse, and others had skyrocketed his popularity.

Customers often made reservations a year in advance and celebrities had their own tables reserved so frequently that made it almost impossible to get in. The constant flow was good for the restaurant, but it never gave any of the waiters a break.

Dani liked working there. The hours were consistent, and the tips were more than she could have ever imagined. Never had she thought she could make this kind of money working such a short period of time each day. Work ethics were not the same as the generations before, when sweat and long hours were a valued commodity. Dani was one of the few that appreciated just having a job. Most of her peer group only worshiped the mighty dollar and not the backbone that went into earning it.

Nothing had been more important in Dani's life than her family. Hers was all gone now. The final blow of her mother's sudden death had completely knocked the wind out of her. She had no one; and her mother had left her with no names or birthrights to research. Her mother's lips had been sealed tight concerning the details of her childhood history in Romania. Even Dani's biological father's name went to Ema's grave.

chapter four

DANI WAS EXHAUSTED, BUT HER SECOND JOB WAS STILL waiting for her. She changed clothes in the small bathroom and stuffed her work clothes into her backpack. Wearing her jeans and red sweater, she took a deep breath and looked in the mirror. She put on some lip gloss and smacked her lips together. As she was just about to turn around toward the door to leave, it swung open. Steph walked in with another waitress.

Betina was one of the most beautiful black women Dani had ever seen—besides Halle Barry. At thirty-five, Betina was tall, thin, firm, and very statuesque. Her light brown skin was flawless and her piercing green eyes showed she had a mixture of heritage. Her facial features were defined and perfectly proportioned. Her small nose, high cheekbones, and plump lips were a photographer's dream. Besides of this, Betina had a very fascinating story. Growing up, Betina lived in the heart of Los Angeles with her father and Grandma. In those days, tensions ran deep and bigotry was showing its ugly face everywhere. Everything came to a head in Los Angeles one evening. The riots that had ensued due to the verdict of the Rodney King trial destroyed the city. Suddenly, Betina's community was filled with unbridled racial tension. Hatred was flowing on both sides. The officers were put on trial. When the verdict was read and the officers were acquitted, riots broke out. For the next two days, houses, buildings, and storefronts were burned; and the rioting and looting was out of control. By the time the riots had ended, a week later, fifty-two people had died. One of those was Betina's father. Betina was barely fourteen. Her pain was ugly and deep. It was a horrible time in the country. With the loss of her father, a mother in jail, all she had left was her grandmother.

When Betina turned nineteen, she was spotted on a street in Los Angeles by an owner of a top modeling agency. For a year she built up her reputation doing numerous magazine covers and photo layouts. Then she went off to Europe, where all models go to become famous. She was on a shoot in England, for a famous magazine, when she met Thomas Gaitland. It was a whirlwind romance, and one his family was extremely unhappy with. They never accepted her color difference. In spite of their racial slurs, Thomas continued to see Betina. When they got back from Europe, Betina was pregnant. A courthouse marriage was arranged and he moved to Los Angeles. His parents cut him off from any inheritance, and by the time the baby was born, Thomas had become a violent drunkard. A year later, she had another baby. By then, the police were called to their house on a regular basis because of his abusive behavior. Betina threw him out. Like a dog with his tail between his legs, he went home to his parents. The annulment was quickly arranged, and their two sons became her sole responsibility. Thomas's family had bought him out of all the obligations to his marriage, including the two small children. The paltry settlement Betina was forced to accept was a mockery. Betina accepted her responsibility and became the sole support of her children—and the damn best mother Dani had ever met.

Steph walked toward Dani. She dropped her backpack on the ground, and leaned up against the wall. Then as though some weight had been lifted off her shoulders, she let out a big sigh. "It was crazy tonight! Being short one server part of the evening and taking half of Nicole's tables near killed me. I didn't have a chance to breathe or even say 'hello' to you or anyone else."

Dani said, "It was long. But good for tips. I just wish I could go home and relax. Sometimes I feel like all I ever do is work."

"You do—" Steph yawned and stretched her arms over her head.

"I'm used to it, I guess." Dani took down her ponytail, combed out her long hair, and braided it down one side.

Betina was relaxing against the wall. "I'm exhausted. I don't know how you do it, Dani."

Dani smiled. "The same way you do it, Betina. Your second job is those two terrific sons of yours."

Steph stood up and bent down to get her backpack. "I'm headed home. It's been a long week. Mom was sick, so I had to help them out with a lot of their chores."

Dani turned her head to the side with a questioning look. "What's wrong with your mom? And why didn't you call and let me know, I would have been happy to help."

Steph patted Dani on the shoulder. "She's fine. Just a miserable cold. Don't look so scared. What happened to your mother was a fluke." Steph bent over and gave Dani a hug.

Betina stepped forward and said, "Hey, I have to go pick up the boys at the sitter, I go right past the hospital, Dani, why don't you let me drop you off."

"I don't want you to go out of the way. I know the sitter is in the other direction." Dani smiled.

"No, I have a new one for a few weeks; besides what's a few blocks out of the way?"

Dani knew the girls were sometimes concerned about her on the street waiting for the bus or walking at night by herself. "You know me, I hate to impose on anyone." Dani lifted her backpack and strapped it on her shoulders. She closed her eyes and let out a deep sigh. "I think I may take you up on that ride, Betina!"

Betina started to laugh. "Holy Mother of Jesus! The girl finally will let me drop her off without a fight!"

Steph opened the door to the bathroom and all three girls started forward. "She must be either really tired or maybe she is finally realizing that it is okay to say 'yes.'"

They all hugged each other outside the bathroom and walked out into the alley to the parking lot adjacent to the back of the building. Dani followed Betina to her car. It was an older model double-cab truck that always made Dani smile. It was not the kind of car she pictured Betina in a few years back when she first met her. Dani figured her for a Mercedes or a Lexus.

"I'm just curious. I guess it's silly to ask if Thomas has ever contacted you at all in regards to the boys," Dani asked.

Betina turned and gave Dani a sarcastic grin. "Hell no! I heard from someone a few years back that he had married the Tennessee beauty pageant queen. She was a friend of the family. And his parents bought them a big, beautiful Southern mansion."

"I'm sorry," Dani said, her voice sad.

Betina shook her head. "Don't be. The boys and I have done just fine. After Grammy passed away, she left me the house. At least I know I have a permanent roof over our heads."

"I haven't seen the boys in a while. Maybe one day we can meet for lunch or go bowling or something. Don't kids like those type of activities?"

"Absolutely! Our favorite family outing on a Sunday afternoon is going down to the Santa Monica pier and fishing. I know it sounds crazy, but it's a lot of fun!" She giggled.

Dani looked sad. "I used to take Levi to the pet store to watch all the fish swim around. That was one of his favorite things to do. He loved to touch the cold glass of the aquariums and watch the fish scatter."

"It's hard, isn't it, Dani?" Betina pulled up to the front of Barouch Memorial Hospital and stopped.

Dani shook her head. "It hurts more than I could say. Thank you for the ride, I really appreciate it."

Betina leaned over and kissed Dani on the cheek. "Anytime, Dani."

Dani climbed out of the truck and grabbed her backpack from the floorboard. She watched the truck drive off, then she sat down on the curb for a moment to gather herself—a horrible reoccurring feeling flowed through her veins every time she entered the hospital.

Even though it had been a year, it always seemed like it was still yesterday when her mother had called her to come down. Without hesitation, she gathered her things at work and ran out the front door. Waiting for the bus was like a countdown on a time bomb. Each second pounded in her head—one by one. Once she got off, she ran the two blocks towards the hospital. Her heart was beating out of her chest. She was trying to remember what she had said to him hours before. Did I tell him how much I loved him? Did I tell him what a wonderful son he was? Or what a strong soldier he had been?

When she finally made it to the front of the hospital, Dani straightened up her back. She knew that she was going to have to be strong. Her mother never called her unless it was an emergency; she knew what was coming. And it came…the worst day of her life.

Dani wiped the tears sliding down her face with the sleeve of her sweater. She had done so many times sitting on this same curb—remembering that day. It was like a recurring nightmare. Will this pain ever stop?

She got up and walked toward the big doors. The glass doors automatically swung open, giving her a full view of the entire lobby. The hospital wasn't as daunting as it was the first time she walked inside years ago. This prodigious hospital had become more like an old friend—who held out its arms to welcome her.

Barouch Memorial would always be affluent, stylish, and more than her eyes could absorb. With floors that were highly polished, the gray-veined marble looked like shimmering water. Dark marble walls rose over two stories, making a person feel small and insignificant. In the middle of the lobby, a large bronze water fountain was a mountain of slivered bronze, eight-feet high, with two small children perched on top. The little boy was standing with a balloon in his hand while the little girl was sitting with a puppy nestled in her lap. Water dribbled down the metal, falling into a pond around the base of the sculpture.

Seeing the fountain was always an emotional and mesmerizing moment for Dani each time she walked through the lobby. No matter the time of day or her reason for being there—she always took a minute to stop and watch the hypnotic ribbons of water as they cascaded down the metal and rippled into the surrounding pool.

Sparkling mosaic tiles glistened in the water of the pond and spelled out the words: "Miracles Do Happen."

Only—Dani knew that not everyone experienced a miracle. Levi wasn't that lucky. Over the past year, she had gradually learned that there were many children who this hospital and its amazing doctors had saved. There were children who got better and better, able to walk out of here to lead productive lives.

Dani smiled when she gazed at all the sparkly coins that were piled in the bottom of the pond. Each coin represented a person who was hoping for a miracle. Levi loved to put his hands in the water and throw his pennies in. His childish antics always made Dani laugh. He would jump up and down begging for coins to toss into the water. Dr. Cal always made sure he had a pile of coins to place in his swollen little fingers to throw in. Sometimes, Dr. Cal would put him on his shoulders or in a wheelchair just so he could see the water flowing down the metal. Levi loved the bronze sculpture and all the water surrounding it. What four-year-old boy wouldn't?

Dani stood by the sculpture and pulled out a penny from her pocket, looked for a good spot, and tossed it in. That shiny penny flew high in the air and dropped into the water. "Please let one lucky child experience that miracle today!" she whispered to herself.

Barouch Memorial was located in the heart and pulse of Los Angeles, just blocks from the restaurant, and a short bus ride from Dani's apartment. The hospital was considered the best on the west coast. Its reputation was one of the most prominent in the country, well known for its advanced technology. Barouch continually housed a handpicked medical staff of the best doctors in the States. Unfortunately, some of the most influential doctors were unable to participate in staffing, because of the impressive waiting list to get in. In a lot of ways, Barouch catered to the rich and famous, accommodating a large clientele from the entertainment industry. Celebrities donated large sums of money to support the hospital; some even built wings and named them after their families. Megastars, musicians, and world-famous dignitaries were just a few who were associated and sat on the Board of Directors.

The hospital was normally out of the affordability range of most people, but on a very rare occasion, the hospital would take on a charity case referred to them— especially when the patient needed lifesaving attention and a certain expertise in the cancer field. Dani knew that first day she tossed in her shiny penny that she had gotten lucky.

Dr. Susan Goldman was Levi's pediatrician and an excellent doctor. When she had received Levi's blood tests back from the lab she immediately contacted a few specialists in the field of pediatric oncology. She knew a few with outstanding reputations, but each one she talked to would point their finger at the one who would be the best—Dr. Caleb Cohen—who specialized in childhood oncology. He was following in the footsteps of his famous mother, Dr. Sarah Orsini. His mother was now retired and her son had chosen to pick up the baton.

Dr. Susan Goldman had gone to school with Caleb Cohen. He was the brightest, funniest, and silliest young man she had ever met. His zest for life and living on the edge was perfect for working with children, especially those who had cancer. He had also started out at a young age becoming one of the leading activists in the country. He wasn't one to sit around and watch. He was more of a motivator in the field of clinical studies. For years he had pushed the pharmaceuticals to initiate new and successful drugs. But he was not always successful. Most of the time this would lead to major confrontations with insurance companies who refused to pay for the expensive drugs—pharmaceuticals refused to produce them, and the government closed its eyes. Many times Caleb had sat in front of Congress getting grilled for his outspoken voice for the patients that were dying, while waiting for the pharmaceuticals as they dragged their feet. Angry and disillusioned, he recruited as many organizations, as well as anyone with a strong voice, that was willing to help pursue his cause.

It had been years since Susan had talked to him or seen him. After talking to the few oncologists she had contacted, Dr. Goldman realized that Dr. Cal would be the right fit for four-year-old Levi, who was unknowingly struggling with leukemia.

Dani did not really know what was going on when Dr. Goldman sent her to see Dr. Cal at Barouch Memorial. She suspected something had been found in his blood, and immediately the appointment was made. Dani had never been in a big hospital before. She had always used the neighborhood Urgent Care or a doctor in a private practice in her area. Dani and her mother had always been healthy, so there was never a need to set foot in a hospital.

This sudden need to see a specialist was not only frightening to Dani and her mother, but it was also alarming to think that something could be seriously wrong with Levi. Both Dani and Ema had taken the day off from work to go see this new doctor with Levi.

Levi was a typical, feisty little boy who was filled with curiosity and wonder of all the things that surrounded him. He was loving and caring, and he never complained or stepped out of his comfort zone. Dani was always so proud of his accomplishments, whether they were big or small. And she always made a huge deal of those that marked a new triumph in his tiny world of growing up. It had been the highlight of Dani's life to watch him grow and experience all that life had to offer. Not one moment went by that Dani or her mother regretted her decision to have Levi and raise him by herself. When he had showed signs of lethargic physical mobility, she became very concerned and watchful. That was when she decided to take him in to see Dr. Goldman. From there, it was just a downward spiral into a world Dani knew nothing about—and refused to accept.

When they walked through those big glass doors that opened to the lobby of Barouch Memorial, Dani felt this heavy weight lay across her shoulders. Why were they here and how much was this going to cost? Was Levi really this sick or was this precautionary? Why now—and why Levi?

Ema had looked at her daughter's terrified face and commented in her broken English, "Whatever it is— we will deal with it. No matter how much it will cost, we will find a way. Levi needs the best right now. Nothing...and I mean nothing...will get in our way of getting him better! Even if it means I break my solemn promise...."

"Thank you, Mom, for being here with us. What is this promise? You're not making any sense. You must be as scared as I am!"

Ema pulled her daughter tight against her chest and whispered in her ear, "You are my child and of my blood. I had made a promise to God that I would take care of you forever."

Dani looked at this woman whose actions spoke louder than her words. "I know, Mamma...."

Ema watched Dani as one tear rolled down her cheek. Levi was already running towards the water sculpture in the middle of the lobby as the two women held hands and slowly walked over to see it.

Within minutes, they found themselves upstairs in the pediatric oncology department, waiting to meet this new doctor. The staff was very accommodating and made them feel very comfortable. They settled in a childlike room that had toys stacked in the corner. Within five minutes, the door opened and a nice looking young man came into the room in a wheelchair, popping wheelies and spinning around. Levi turned around, and within seconds, he started to giggle.

Dani thought it was odd to see this young man making noise and having fun playing around in the wheelchair. After all, it was an impressive and overwhelming hospital. The man was wearing blue jeans, a collared cotton shirt, a pair of brown leather Doc Martin shoes, and a long white lab coat. His hair was light brown, short, and spiked. The blond highlights appeared natural, and not generated by a bottle. The smile lighting up face gave him a boyish appearance; he definitely didn't look old enough to be the doctor. A lab tech or assistant, maybe.

The young man bent forward in his wheelchair in front of Levi, who was laughing excitedly. The man peered at Levi and grinned. "Are you laughing at my wheelies?"

Levi shook his head and giggled. His shiny, dark hair fell across his eyes, which were opened wide like saucers. Levi's small, slim body just stood there watching the antics of this adult.

The man pointed at Levi. "What's your name, kiddo?"

Levi stood their staring, but did not utter a word.

Dani leaned over and tapped the man on the shoulder, and said, "His name is Levi."

The man never glanced back to see who had spoken to him. Instead, he looked directly at Levi. "Come on, Levi! Jump onto my lap and I'll take you for a spin around the ward! Let's go have some fun!"

Levi got so excited that his legs were shaking and it looked like he was dancing. He took one little step at a time, watching his mother's reaction. Everyone watched as he slipped his hands over his mouth to keep from giggling. Slowly, he climbed onto his lap and nestled in. That was the most animated and the happiest Dani had seen him in weeks. It was as though his energy level had jumped up to where he used to be months before.

Levi got really enthusiastic and started squirming around. "Mommy, look at me. I'm going for a ride on this big toy!"

Dani laughed and said, "Yes, I can see that, sweetheart." Then she looked at the young man and said, "Maybe he should wait here for the doctor. I don't want anyone to be mad at us because you whisked him off to Neverland!" Dani smiled, thinking of Peter Pan and how he sprinkled fairy dust on the kids to make them fly.

The man was spinning in a circle on the two back wheels and Levi was holding on tight around his neck. "Oh, I don't think the doctor will mind. I know him pretty well!"

Levi was screaming with laughter.

Ema looked a little nervous. "But we don't know him! We do know that he has been very generous to put himself out for Levi, so we want to make a good impression. Please, get down, Levi."

Dani looked at her mother as Levi's laughter filled the room. Then suddenly it stopped and the silence was deafening. Feeling a little remorseful, Dani said, "Okay...take him for a ride. But who can I say has kidnapped my son?" she politely asked.

The wheelchair was already out the door, when the young man yelled over his shoulder, laughing, "Dr. Cal."

Dani opened her mouth to say something, but instead just stared. When the realization of what Dr. Cal was doing sunk in, she realized that Levi was in good hands. It was Dr. Cal's way of doing his own evaluation with Levi. And at the same time, he was gaining Levi's trust and lowering his fear of why they were there. Dani liked Dr. Cal's style; she liked his discretion, and she knew she was placing her son's life into caring hands.

Ema and Dani held hands and watched her son with Dr. Cal. He had taken him into each room and introduced him to the other patients. Eventually, he had all the children laughing, and the nurses were chasing them everywhere. To hear Levi's laughter one more time like this had been a blessing Dani would hold onto forever. It was a wonderful beginning to a tragic ending. That afternoon, the bottom had dropped out of Dani's world. Even her mother, who was the strongest woman, had a difficult time holding herself together.

After the ride was over, Dr. Cal gave Levi to the nurses and they took him into the playroom, then he sat down and explained what was going on to Dani and Ema. He tried to explain it as simply as he could but with the intensity it deserved. "Leukemia is a hematological malignancy or a cancer of the blood. It develops in the bone marrow, the soft inner part of bones where new blood cells are made. When a child has leukemia, the bone marrow produces white blood cells that do not mature correctly. Normal, healthy cells only reproduce when there is enough space for them. The body will regulate the production of cells by sending signals to stop production. With leukemia, the cells do not respond to the signals telling them when to stop and when to produce cells, regardless of the available space."

Dani's world was spinning in circles. She had no clue as to what was going on or how Levi was going to survive this. All Dani wanted to do was lay down on the floor and cry until there were no more tears left. But…she knew she couldn't. The ache in her heart was beyond any pain she could have ever imagined. It was the beginning of the grieving process. When a mother's child is given a death sentence, when no one is looking, mothers purge their fears by curling up into a little ball and begging God to take them—instead of their child. They start each sentence with 'If I could….'

If I could switch places….

If I could stop the clock….

If I could make him better….

If I could have one wish….

If I could…just pretend…this was a bad dream….

chapter five

PINNED ON EVERY SQUARE INCH OF DR. CAL'S WALLS were pictures of small girls and boys with big smiles on their faces. Dani was having a hard time focusing on their beautiful faces. She was wondering which ones had made it and which ones hadn't. She finally turned to her mother who had not spoken one word. Her ashen face was all that Dani needed to see. She knew her mother was dying inside. Together, they had listened to the doctor tell them what needed to be done, and how they were going to do it. He didn't sugarcoat anything and wanted them to know exactly what hard road was needed to get Levi into remission. He also wanted to give them solid, sound advice as to the best way to keep Levi from being terrified.

"No crying…unless he is out of the room or sleeping. Children just don't understand at his age why parents cry. They think it is something they did to make them unhappy. Keep everything as normal as possible. This is not going to be easy and sometimes you're going to hate everything and everyone around you. That's okay. Hate me…don't hate what we can't change or what isn't working. This is going to be a living hell, but we are going to try to make it like Disneyland or as much fun as we can, to lessen his burden."

Dani and her mother nodded. Dani didn't know if she could ever laugh again, or if looking at Levi would bust her into tears.

"It's going to get pretty intense. The form of leukemia he has is very destructive, so we are going to fight it aggressively. I'm going to give it my all, to try to get him out of this mess...."

Dani's hands were folded in her lap and she was afraid to meet Dr. Cal's eyes. Her world began to spin; there was no way to climb out of that deep, dark abyss she was slowly sinking into.

"Promise me you will try to do what we discussed. I will also find a group of mothers going through the same thing that you can join in for discussions and support. Many of them have been through it more than once, and they have rock-solid advice that will help you out."

"Thank you, Dr. Cal. I appreciate anything you can give me to hold onto. At least that will give me hope."

"I want you to come to me if you have any questions. I'm always available. I don't care how small or silly the question, just let my staff know and they will contact me. I imagine you will have lots of questions."

With a quiver in her voice, Dani said, "I do have one question." Her hands were shaking in her lap. "How long does he have…?"

Dr. Cal looked at Dani and said, "Let's not worry about that now. Let's walk down that yellow brick road together, and see what happens."

Dani, her mother, and Levi went home that night and had huge ice cream sundaes. If Dr. Cal wanted them to have fun, then that's what they were going to do. The party had just began. The ice cream stuck in Dani's throat as she watched Levi dig into his gleefully.

Dani was exhausted from just thinking about the past and what an extraordinary doctor Dr. Cal had been for Levi. He tried everything to save him and refused to give up, even at the end. Days, nights, never stopping, she watched his devotion to all the sick children in his ward as her respect for him grew into a mountain of admiration. It really wasn't as much about repayment of her medical bills that brought her back to the hospital to work. She knew they were going to absorb them on a gratuitous account. It was about Dani herself. For once, she felt she had found a place that she truly belonged—a place where she could help other little ones as they faced the same possible fate as Levi. She loved the nurses and the staff who endlessly forfeited so much to make this a better place for the kids. She felt comfortable and everyone liked Dani and her perky personality, but most of all, they respected her for stepping up to her obligations. It wasn't about a financial payback—it was about giving back.

As she walked toward the information desk in the lobby, the young woman looked up and smiled at her. "Hello, Becky. What a beautiful evening it is outside," Dani said. "Not too hot and just cool enough to feel your skin begin to tingle. It looks like we are about done with summer. I so love the Fall when the cooler weather comes back."

Becky turned to look at the darkened windows. The sky was filled with twinkling stars and the full moon lit up the outside. "I haven't seen it outside tonight. Today has been crazy. I came in this afternoon and I'm headed out of here in a few minutes! How are you doing, Dani? You look really tired."

Dani laughed. "I think that is my new look nowadays. The tired look! I'm starting a new fad. Can you see my dark circles? They are smudge proof!"

Becky started to laugh. Dani leaned over the tall counter and said, "You must like the new look, because you look tired, too! Here, let me give you some dark circles and we can become twins!"

Becky was really laughing now. "Stop it...go on upstairs! I'm too tired to laugh! I'm meeting the girls at the club tonight, shoo, shoo!"

"One day, I'm going to have to go with you just so I can see what a young woman like me is missing!" Dani threw her backpack over her shoulder and started to walk over to the bank of elevators.

In a loud whisper, Becky said, "Pick an evening, Dani. The girls and I would love you to come out and have a little fun! You deserve it!"

Dani pushed the elevator button. She turned toward Becky. "Fun? What's that?" The elevator door opened and Dani walked inside. She waved her hand to Becky and it nearly got stuck in the closing doors.

Dani pushed the button to the third floor. Then she looked at her watch and was happy her shift was over in four hours. She enjoyed coming to the hospital and she loved the children in the pediatric ward. They were all so sweet, and most of them very sick. Levi had spent his last three months there. Dani and her mother couldn't be at the hospital every moment. They had to work to pay their bills. So there were times that Dani relied on the nurses and aides to help Levi. The nurses all became surrogate parents—in a wonderful kind of way. Basically, that was what Dani did every night when she came to the hospital. She was a nurse's aide who sat with the children, fed those who needed help, laid with the ones who were having a hard time getting to sleep or staying asleep, and she would calm them down when they were frightened.

This job had taken up a big space in her life that had been left empty when her mother died. It gave her back some meaning as to why she was still here. It also bought her some time as she tried to figure out what she was going to do with the rest of her life. She had no family, no one at home. When she finally walked into the hospital again, after those few months, it gave her a sense of belonging and the security that someone actually still needed her. At least four hours a day, three days a week.

When the elevator doors opened she looked toward the nurse's station. The three night nurses were sitting at the desk going over the patients' charts and inputting notes into the computer. Dani smiled. That was something she was not very proficient at, nor did they ask her to do it. Anything that had to do with computers was far out of her league. She had made it through college with as little use of technology as possible.

Dani walked up to the wall-to-wall desk that cut off the nurses from the patients. She leaned against it and laughed as the nurses concentrated on their projects and didn't notice her. "Is anyone home…or am I on the wrong floor?"

Lola, Alva, and Malaya looked up and began to laugh at the same time. Lola, in her gruff voice, said, "It's about time you got here! I'm tired of hearing Dr. Cal ask where you are. And for all the tea in China…I am damn worn out from telling Jacob that you are on your way! You just spoil these babies too much! Then all we hear from them is moaning and groaning, while asking, 'where is Dani?'" Lola rolled her eyes and everyone began to laugh.

"It's nice to feel so wanted!" Dani replied.

"Well, I hope you enjoy that feeling, because you have a lot of little faces who waited up this late just to see you and say goodnight," Alva said.

Dani leaned on the counter and smiled.

Lola's eyes squinted as she took another look at Dani's smile. "Holy mother of Satan, who the hell gave you two black eyes?"

Dani laughed. "It's either my cheap mascara, or it's because I haven't been getting enough sleep. Don't you like my new raccoon look?" Dani teased.

"Darlin'…if I wanted to see a raccoon, I'd go to the zoo!" She looked closer and said, "I'm sending you home early to get some sleep. A beautiful face like yours should not be maimed with black circles and bags the size of suitcases!"

"I'm fine, I'll do my four."

Lola stood up and leaned against the counter as though she was ready to stand her ground. "To hell you will." She gave Dani a big frown.

"Okay. I will leave a little early."

These three night nurses worked most of the time with Dani. Lola was an older Hispanic lady, whose temper would peek out occasionally with aggressive parents or a doctor with an attitude. Everyone thought her bark was worse than the bite, but no one dared to mess with her—including Dr. Cal. Her large body and short height was a deterrent to butt heads with her, along with her threatening reputation.

The other two nurses, Malaya and Alva, swayed in the opposite direction. They were quiet Filipino women whose kind hearts and soft hands balanced out the night shift. These three nurses were a close tight-knit family that had worked together for over ten years. Dani was the baby and they adored her.

Malaya stood up and reached her arm out toward Dani. "Here, give me your backpack and I'll put it away." She grunted as Dani passed the heavy bag to her. "This feels like a bag of bricks. You're going to break your back carrying this around. Hummmpf…" Malaya muttered as she nearly dragged the bag across the floor.

Dani started to giggle. "My whole life is in there; be careful, Malaya."

Lola laughed and yelled toward Malaya, "Maybe we should get you a gym membership so you can lift a lousy little backpack!"

Alva wiggled her finger back and forth and said, "Play nice, Lola! Don't want to be ruffling any feathers tonight. We've been busy this evening."

Dani's eyes looked sad. "New ones?" she whispered. She always hated to see new little patients. It always meant that two parents were now going through a very traumatic time in their lives.

Alva clapped her hands together and said, "Ali is going home tomorrow morning."

Dani looked a little forlorn. "Oh brother. I'm really going to miss that little one. I prayed every night that she'd go into a full remission. So, she must be doing well enough to go home?"

Lola leaned over the counter and handed Dani a chart. "Her remission is perfect! She needs to get the hell out of here to spend some time alone with her family! Here, this is our new 'inductee.'"

Dani opened the chart and read some of the notes. "Oh, he's the same age as Levi." She sighed. "At least he is in early stages and has a better chance."

Lola took the chart back. "He's coming in tomorrow just to spend the night. Dr. Cal wants to get some extra tests on him."

A loud voice boomed across the floor. "Did I hear my name? I hope it wasn't being used in vain?" He laughed as he walked up to the desk.

Lola clicked her tongue and shook her head from side to side. "First of all, Dr. Cal...YOU...are not God! Although, sometimes you may pretend to be—you're just a mere mortal like the rest of us! Second, using God's name in vain is considered blasphemy to most religious fanatics. I wouldn't dare do that. Hell, my Mother would be turning in her dear, sweet grave!" Lola moved one step closer, and pointed a finger inches from his nose as she held up a chart. "Now, using YOUR name in vain is completely appropriate sometimes, especially when you don't fill out your charts correctly or forget to do it altogether!"

Alva and Malaya were quietly giggling at the banter. Dani just stood there with her eyes wide, watching to see who was going to strike next and how deep the wound would be.

The silence was broken by Dr. Cal. "Ouch. I feel like I've been in ten rounds with Muhammad Ali!" He reached for the chart Lola was dangling in front of his face.

"Floats like a butterfly, stings like a bee! That happens to be one of my favorite quotes!" Lola laughed out loud.

"Ouch, again!" he said. "How is the evening going? Anything I need to know or do, ladies?"

Alva handed him another chart and said, "The little Mendoza boy can't keep his food down. His parents are still here, because they are very worried."

"Thanks. I'll go in and see what's going on and talk with the parents. Poor kid is just having the most difficult time with the chemotherapy. The other night I feel asleep with him on the bed, trying to keep him calm."

Malaya spoke up. "What kind of fluids can the little princess have in room three?"

"Single ice chips for right now. She loves to drink anything, but her body is completely retaining fluids right now."

Dr. Cal looked directly at Dani and smiled. "Cat's got your tongue. Or did you have it surgically removed tonight? Don't you want to take a swing at this exhausted doctor, too?" All three nurses began to laugh.

Dani stood up a little taller and lifted her head up higher. "Nope. I'll let you know if I need you or have a question. But thanks for asking." Dani walked off to go get the room prepared for the patient coming in.

Dr. Cal and the nurses just sat there and stared for a second. Lola burst out laughing. "Looks like you were put in your place just now. That must have been a big 'ouch' in your book!"

Dr. Cal had a confused look on his face. "What's wrong with her?"

Malaya spoke, "I think she is just working too much. She's exhausted; and if you look at her eyes, you can see it."

Dr. Cal looked concerned. "Send her home, Lola."

Lola hissed, "You send her home. She don't listen to me. I have no idea why this unforgiving, driving force is pushing her to total exhaustion. I know if she doesn't take a break, she'll wind up in the ER. I told her to leave early tonight."

"I want you to push her out the door in two hours. No ands, ifs, or buts!"

chapter six

HOURS PASSED, AND DANI WAS MORE EXHAUSTED THAN she could ever remember. She could barely hold her head up. She shuffled through the ward for the last time. She knew if she didn't get out in the next few minutes, the buses stopped running and she'd have to walk twelve blocks to get home. At this hour in the night, she usually carried her Mace and a small knife tucked in her pocket. The streets of Los Angeles weren't the safest place to be. Along with the homeless, drunks from the bars, and creepy characters, she always seemed to run across some raving lunatic. Only once had she been accosted on the street. And that once was enough. Over the years she had become wiser and more street savvy.

That night, long ago, had been a heads-up awakening.

She had left the hospital and was walking down the well-lit street, when out of nowhere a young Hispanic man approached her. He said something in Spanish, and then leaped in her direction, aiming for her backpack. Not one to let someone take something that belonged to her, she snapped into action and began to scream at the top her lungs. At the same time, she began to pound his body with her heavy backpack and kick him so hard in his thigh that he dropped to the ground. Suddenly, a small crowd began to build around her, and with amazing force, her hands scratched his eyes.

The young man looked around with embarrassment and took off in a run. At the same time, a squad car pulled up and barely came to a stop before two officers lunged from the car. One went in pursuit of the attacker and the other stopped in front of Dani.

"Wow, remind me not to tangle with a small might like you, great left hook! Seriously, young lady…are you okay? These are pretty dangerous streets at this time of night. And the predators out there are not usually that weak."

Dani looked visibly shaken. "I had no choice. I don't have a car, and I had to get home. I only live twelve blocks from the hospital where I work. The buses stopped; so I guess next time I have to carry a gun!"

The officer's eyes opened wide. "I don't think a gun is the answer. It would take too long to get it out of your backpack. My suggestion is a bottle of Mace in your pocket and a small knife that he won't see. Something to protect yourself."

Dani shook her head as she bent down to pick up her backpack. "Officer, I—"

Dani was cut off by another male voice. "I will take her home from here. She works with me, and she refused a ride home." He held out his hand to the officer and said, "I'm Dr. Cal from Barouch Memorial."

The officer, for the second time in just a few minutes, opened his eyes wide and was nearly speechless. "The same Dr. Cal who is treating Simon Blanche?"

Dr. Cal nodded his head. "He's a great kid and I'm so glad he's getting better."

The officer nearly choked on his next words. "Our station had a big fundraiser a few months back for the Blanche family. That little tyke is the son of one of our young officers, Jarrod Blanche. We can't thank you enough."

Dr. Cal said very graciously, "This young woman is responsible for a lot of his care and getting him into remission."

The officer took off his hat and bowed his head at Dani. 'Thank you, madam. I'm just glad this evening worked out as it did. I'd sure hate to see something happen to an angel of mercy."

Dani smiled and touched his hand. "He's a great little boy, and I adored the family too. Now, if you don't mind, I'd like to start walking home so I can get some rest."

Dr. Cal took her elbow and started steering her toward his car. "I'll take her home, Officer. And if you catch that kid, let me know, and I will come down. Or you can come to the hospital tomorrow and we can take care of this," he yelled over his shoulder.

Dani didn't know what to say or what to do. She just wanted to go home. As she climbed into his sports car, she said awkwardly, "Thank you."

Nothing else was said in the car, except instructions on how to get to her apartment. When he got there, she got out of the car and thanked him again and walked up the stairs while he watched her get into the lobby. Next to her front door was a note taped to a large brown bag filled with groceries. The note read: Knock on the wall when you get home.

Dani had smiled as she walked through the door.

Dani had learned a big lesson that night. She started to walk down the street toward the bus stop. She didn't know if she had missed the last bus, but it really didn't matter one way or the other—she had to get home. She was almost to the bus stop when she heard someone call her name. As sleepy as she was, she thought she was imaging the sound of her name.

"Damn it! Dani, look over to the curb," a male voice yelled.

Dani looked up, and was shocked to see Dr. Cal slowly following her in his fancy sport car. His window was open and he had just yelled something at her.

Slightly perturbed, she stopped short and bent down to look in the window. "Did I forget something at work, Dr. Cal?"

He stopped his car from moving, but the engine continued to rumble. "I thought I would take you home. I think the last bus left here ten minutes ago. Open the door and get in."

Dani's face turned red. "Thank you." She looked up at the stars in the sky, and said, "It's a nice evening for a walk."

Dr. Cal rolled his eyes. "Okay, let's just see if another pervert attacks you! Damn...you are so fucking stubborn!" He bent over the front seat. "Humphfff," came flying out of his mouth as he pushed open the door.

Looking at his red, angry face, she realized he was right. She took her backpack off her shoulder, and bent down to slide into the front seat. "Okay, so I'm a little stubborn, not a lot...just a little. It's just hard for me to take when I can't repay it back. That's just who I am! Get used to it!"

"I get that. God knows I've watched that for the last two years. It's just sometimes you have to weigh out the benefits. In this case, I've just saved a pervert from committing an assault and going to jail! And...you can get home sooner where you will be safe and sound."

His eyes were glued to the traffic. Out of the corner on his eye he glanced at Dani, and she had a slight smirk on her face.

Feeling uncomfortable with the silence that was consuming the confined small two-seater sports car, Dr. Cal asked, "Have you thought about maybe buying a car to get around town in, so you don't have to take a bus or walk at these hours of the night?"

Dani turned slightly toward him and adjusted her seatbelt. "I can't afford one, and I really don't go anywhere except to work and the hospital. My mother and I have lived in the same area for over twenty-five years and we never had a car."

In a gruff voice, Dr. Cal said, "Well, that was then, and this is now. The crime in the city has quadrupled and the streets aren't as safe as they used to be."

Flippantly, Dani said, "Well, I guess I just have to take my chances. I don't have family anymore, and my friends are into themselves, so I only have to worry about me. And...if I'm not worried...then why should you be?"

"Maybe because I'm a doctor who happens to see crime victims all the time." He had just pulled up to her apartment building.

Dani's hand grabbed her backpack. She plastered a sweet smile on her face and said, "The perverts and I thank you very much." She slipped her hand on the door handle and opened the door. As she was ready to slide out of the low-slung seat, she felt his hand hold her back.

"Look, I'm just concerned." He stared at her with his big green eyes.

She looked down at his hand, and he immediately released her. "Thank you very much for the ride. I will see you Tuesday." She slid out of the car and shut the door. When he didn't drive off, she realized he was waiting for her to get safely into the lobby of the apartment building. She typed in the combination to the lock and pulled the door open. Then she turned with a big smile and waved. As the door slowly closed, she watched him drive off.

Feeling the fatigue of the long day, she slowly sauntered to her apartment door. At the bottom of the door was a package with a note: Went to the deli today and thought you might like some bagels. Knock when you get home.

Dani picked up the note and took a pen out of her purse and wrote on it—thank you. She slipped it into the doorjamb and then walked into her apartment.

It always felt so empty now when she came home. There was no childish laughter coming from the rooms or cartoons blaring on the television. Just darkness and silence. The same way she had left it earlier this morning.

With what little oomph she had left, she took off her clothes, slipped into a T-shirt, and laid down on her bed. With visions of a pair of angry green eyes, she drifted off to sleep with a smile on her face.

chapter seven

DANI WAS LYING ON HER STOMACH IN BED, PONDERING over what she was going to do with a whole day off. The week had flown by, like every other week. Today was Saturday, and living in the heart of the city, she could find just about everything or anything that would keep her busy. She thought about it for a few minutes while lying in the dark. She came up with some interesting ideas. "Maybe I should go down to the museum and see the new dinosaur exhibit like I've been wanting to do for months." Smiling in the dark, she continued, "Or maybe I should go down to Grauman's Chinese Theater in Hollywood to catch a good movie or see if my footprints fit into Judy Garland's?"

It had been so long since she really had an entire free day to herself. The last time she had been to the movies was over a year ago. Her mother had nearly dragged her out of the house to see a special showing of *Gone with the Wind*. Her mother was a pushover for really old sappy movies that made her cry. She was not one to cry often, but for some reason a solid love story always did that to her. On special occasions, they would go to the Geffen Playhouse or Kirk Douglas Theater to catch an off-Broadway play. Dani loved those days that they spent together just enjoying time together.

She flipped onto her back and indulged in a slow stretch. When she finally relaxed, she started again with her list of places to go. "I could take two buses down to Santa Monica Pier, where I could get lost in the enormous crowds. Or maybe I could go to Griffith Observatory? No…that is much better at night when the stars are out and I could look through the large telescopes and see the craters on the moon." Things like that always seemed to fascinate her. When she was young she used to go down to Hollywood and hang around at the Walk of Fame, or the House of Wax, and even Ripley's Believe It or Not. She loved to browse the Hollywood Odditorium and look through all the bizarre and preposterous memorabilia that had been accumulated over the years. The eclectic collection of nearly 500 different exhibits always entertained Ema and her. It was a day filled with wonder and awe and was always topped off with a casual dinner at the other end of town in the farmer's market. Those were the kind of days she now valued and kept stored away deep in her heart.

Dani appreciated living in the city. The bus system could get her everywhere without the need of a car. As she thought more and more of the lecture Dr. Cal had given her, she hated to admit it, but Dr. Cal was right. But, she would never tell him that. The city had definitely changed over the past ten years. The streets were riddled with crimes of all kinds. The transients and homeless were constantly lurking around, looking for handouts. Random shootings and robberies were taking place in broad daylight. Brazen thieves were snatching purses from old ladies who couldn't defend themselves.

Dani sighed, and then sat up in bed. As she was stretching her arms over her head, trying to limber up, she heard a knock on the wall. Dani smiled and leaned back onto the bed, and then she knocked back.

"Oh, I forgot to tell you, Anton, that I had the day off!" she said to the wall, and giggled.

She stood up and put on the robe that always rested at the bottom corner of her bed. She tucked her feet into furry slippers she bought herself for Christmas, and walked toward the door. She gripped the doorknob, swung the door open, and looked down both sides of the hallway. She stepped into the hall and moved toward Anton's door. Lightly she tapped. She didn't want to tap too hard and attract the attention of her busybody neighbor across the hall. Mrs. Brodsky was as meddlesome as they came. There wasn't one thing in that apartment building she didn't know about or blab to anyone who would listen. Most of the time Dani knew she was harmless, it was just the point that the older woman constantly meddled into other tenants' business without a thought about their privacy. Sometimes she spun major drama into such a high intensity, that complaints poured into the manager's office. Dani even had a few run-ins with Mrs. Brodsky over the years when she tried to compromise Ema's integrity.

Mrs. Busybody didn't care about anyone but herself. She thrived on gossip. As long as she was stirring up the pot, creating drama, she was as happy as a pig in a pool full of mud. But one day Mrs. Brodsky stepped over the line. She was spreading gossip about Ema, telling anyone who would listen that Ema was having a secret affair with Anton. Ema just laughed—but not Dani. When Dani caught wind of the rumor, she marched over to Mrs. Brodsky's apartment and pounded on the door. The old lady answered, a big smile spread across her face. "What can I do for you, young lady?" she asked, her voice dripping with a hint of sarcasm.

With a face as red as a fire truck, Dani said with a lot of control, "I would be pleased if you did not spread gossip about my mother or me anymore."

The older woman stood there with a smug expression and said defiantly, "I don't spread gossip, young lady. I tell people the truth!"

As mad as a raging bull, Dani took a step forward and whispered, "Are you out of your damn mind?! I swear, Mrs. Brodsky, if you keep spreading rumors about my mother and me, I will make sure that the wrath of Zeus strikes upon your head!"

Mrs. Brodsky crossed her arms over her chest and started to cackle. "I'm not scared of you, young lady! I know what I see." She uncrossed her arms and started to shut the door.

Dani's hand stopped the door, and she stared defiantly into Mrs. Brodsky's beady little eyes. "Say anything more and I will make sure the government knows that you are still getting your husband's social security checks, even though he died nearly two years ago! How do you think you will look in those charming black and white stripped pajamas in jail?"

Mrs. Brodsky sucked in her breath and turned a slight shade of blue. "You don't know that!" she muttered in panic.

Dani smiled, backed off, and turned around to leave. She could still hear the old lady choking on her breath. Then with calculated drama, Dani slowly turned around and said very sweetly, "Oh, did I tell you the other day that Jimmy the mailman was holding a check in his hand when he asked me how Mr. Brodsky was doing? And that he hopes he gets better soon. He also said, 'I haven't seen him lately!'"

Mrs. Brodsky could barely catch her breath. "I…I…."

"You…will keep your mouth shut when it comes to us. Got it?"

The old lady slammed her door.

This morning, with her robe tied tight and her slippers sliding along the tile hallway, Dani said to herself, "I really don't give a rat's ass about her gossip anymore. Let her think and talk all she wants. I'm wearing my robe and slippers, and if people think I'm have a morning rendezvous with Anton—good for them."

Dani knocked on his door again.

The door swung open and Anton's eyes opened wide with pleasure. "And, young lady, what do I owe this morning's visit?"

Dani smiled and said, "I never mentioned that I had the day off and I didn't want you to get anxious that I had slept in and would be late to work." She looked down as though embarrassed and started to shuffle her feet. "And…because I owe you a debt of gratitude for watching out for me with those wonderful paper bag lunches and your morning knocks. I don't think I say thank you enough, or what it means to me, since my mother is gone."

Anton leaned over and put a hand on her shoulder. "Thank you, Dani. I know how hard the past two years have been, and I thought I would help as much as I could. Just so you know—I miss Ema immensely, too! She was a very admirable woman who did an amazing job raising you all alone."

Dani was still looking down at the floor; her pain from mentioning her mother was very evident.

Suddenly, a tear hit the ground and Anton noticed it. "So, you have the day off? That's wonderful! Care to come in and join me for a bagel and coffee?"

Dani looked up. "That's very…."

He leaned over and took her hand. "Come on, young lady. I make the best coffee and I even have lox and tomato to go with that bagel."

Dani followed him into the apartment that was just like hers, except his was a little sparser, but as clean as could be. She sat down at the small table in the kitchen area while he busied himself with making a plate filled with cream cheese, sliced onions, tomatoes, and toasted bagels. Dani watched as he meticulously cut, sliced, and plated, as he got things ready.

He turned around and asked, "I remember correctly—you like your coffee black, and your mother liked one lump of sugar."

Dani smiled as she remember her mother rummaging through all the neighborhood stores, trying to find a box of sugar cubes. It was something the stores had ceased to stock for years. It was an old, European habit, amongst the country-dwellers and laborers, to use sugar cubes in place of granular sugar. And although it was something from the past generations, it was something her mother had adamantly continued and refused to give up. Ema took the bus around town for days until she found a small tea shop that had imported boxes from England. She bought a carton of those boxes, just to insure she would never run out.

"Yes, I like mine black."

Anton walked over with the cup and saucer and placed it in front of Dani. Then he put the plate filled with breakfast on the table and went back for his coffee. He reached up, got two plates, and went to sit down at the table.

Dani noticed the sugar cube on his saucer next to his cup of coffee. "You're just like my mother."

He laughed. "I hope not! I'm not wearing a dress or have my hair braided down my back, do I?"

Dani laughed. "No. You just have the sugar cube like she did with her coffee."

He dropped the cube into the coffee and began to stir it. "I think it was an old Romanian custom we both picked up somewhere. It is one perfectly measured teaspoon of sugar with no mess and it makes the coffee taste the same all the time." He leaned over and took her plate, placed a bagel on it, and handed it to her. "There…if you have a full day of fun ahead of you, then you'll need to start off with a hearty breakfast."

Dani was putting her bagel together with the condiments. "I don't know what I'm doing today. I just know I have a full day off!"

"Well, then you have to find something exciting to do. Don't waste it sitting in your apartment."

"I don't know what to do. Mother used to push me and plan all our day excursions. I'm afraid I'm not very good at planning or finding things."

"You should do something pleasurable and entertaining—like a stroll down Venice beach where all the street venders go. I've been there a few times and it is highly entertaining." He laughed out loud.

"I was there once, years ago, with mother. She felt a bit uncomfortable with all the crazies." She took another bite of her bagel and groaned.

"Is that a good moan or bad one?" He smiled as he got up to get another cup of coffee.

Dani grinned, as her face reddened. "I rarely have breakfast or bagels…this is wonderful. Thank you, Anton!"

"How about going down to Melrose Blvd? I heard that was a woman's paradise with all the unique shops and clothing stores. A young girl like you should jump at the chance to do that!"

"Maybe if I had a girlfriend to share it with." She looked unhappy.

"Humm…."

She sat up straight, and her eyes opened wide. "I have an idea."

Anton bent his head and looked over the rim of his glasses. "What…?"

Dani stood up and walked her empty plate over to the sink, then she turned around. "I think I'd like to go to Venice Beach, but I don't know my way around. You sound like you do. Would you like to go down there with me for just a few hours?"

Anton sat in silence for a moment stirring his coffee and thought about what she was asking. Then he looked up and noticed her smile. "You don't want to hang around with an old man!"

Dani looked defiant. "Okay, then I will just go to my apartment and mope all day." She started to walk toward the door.

Anton stood up and put up his hand to stop her. "Okay, but I'll drive there! I never got the hang of the bus systems in the city like you and Ema."

Dani smiled. "Let's say...be ready in an hour."

He chuckled. "An hour it is, young lady!"

Dani was dressed in a pair of cuffed denim capris, a white tank top, and a pair of sandals. She tied her hair into a ponytail and put on a denim baseball cap. She assessed herself in the mirror, put on some mascara, blush, lips gloss, and walked out the door. She walked next door to Anton's apartment and knocked. Of course, she turned around and who was spying out her window—Mrs. Nosybody! Anton opened the door and walked out. He was wearing dark slacks and a cotton polo shirt. His leather shoes were the ones he always wore. He took his sunglasses out of his shirt pocket and put them on.

Suddenly, Dani cuddled up next to him, took his hand, and started to walk toward the building's parking lot. After just a few steps she turned around and waved to Mrs. Brodsky. "Have a nice day, Gladys!"

Anton started to chuckle. "So, you thought you would give her something to talk about, did you?"

Dani let go of his hand and started to giggle. "Damn right!"

It took them thirty minutes in traffic to get to Venice Beach. It is a definite highlight on California's list of tourist attractions and has a big reputation of being wild and crazy. Venice Beach is located next to Santa Monica Beach and near the pier with the big Ferris wheel that Dani loved as a little girl. The Venice Strand

(Ocean Front walk) is the place on the coast to see and be seen on any Saturday or Sunday afternoon. The beachfront sidewalk is lined with shops and restaurants, and all who use it are onstage. With street performers, bodybuilders, and beach bums, there's hardly a dull day on the Strand. Venice beach was a place for everyone and anyone; you never knew who might show up.

Anton was watching Dani and she walked down the strand mesmerized by all the street performers and freaks that were walking around. Sometimes she would walk closer to him as they passed some unsavory character. Other times, she pulled his hand, wanting to see some entertaining fire-eater or glass walker. It was all so enjoyable and harmless that she asked herself, 'why did I wait so long to come back?'

Anton was so pleased to finally see Dani laugh and have a good time. There was a time she did have friends and was carefree and loved to have fun and laugh. He had been around to witness it, and he loved the sound of her laughter.

Dani loved having the day off, enjoying the outdoors. She pulled Anton's hand and was dragging him over to see a street performer. It was a young black boy who was dancing like Michael Jackson. His movements were amazing and Dani tried to squirm her way into the crowd to get closer. "Come on, slowpoke! I need to get closer," she said to Anton.

Anton just smiled as she pulled him deeper and deeper into the crowd.

"Are you coming or do I have to leave you behind," she said over her shoulder without looking back.

Suddenly, a voice whispered her ear, "Hey, be careful as to whom you push out of the way!"

Dani jumped and swung around terrified to see who was daring enough to whisper in her ear. When she looked up into the face only inches from hers—her eyes narrowed. "Hey, I'm sorry. I didn't mean to push you out of the way. I just wanted to see the dancing!"

Dr. Cal laughed. "I saw that! You wheedled your way from the back to nearly the front!"

Dani started to laugh.

Dr. Cal looked at her and smiled. "It's great to hear you laugh again, Dani."

Dani's eyes darted to the side and noticed the young woman standing next to Dr. Cal. She had possessively put her hand on his shoulder and was leaning in to see what Dani and Dr. Cal were saying. Then she whispered into his ear. He turned around and gave the young woman a stinging look.

Then he turned around to Dani and said, "Dani, I'd like you to meet my friend, Dawn."

Dawn smiled sweetly and put her other arm around his waist.

Dani nodded. "It's nice to meet you." Then she looked at Dr. Cal and said, "I don't know if you remember Anton. He came to the hospital a few times to see Levi with my mother."

Anton held out his hand and said, "I believe we did meet. Nice to see you again."

The moment was really awkward, and all Dani wanted to do was hightail it out of the crowd that had pushed them all closer together. Dani took Anton's hand and then quickly looked at Dr. Cal. "Hope you have a wonderful day. See you at work."

Dani was surprised to hear Dawn say, "Oh…we definitely will!"

Dani felt a twinge of disbelief seeing Dr. Cal at Venice Beach. Dani was speechless as they headed back to Anton's car. Of all the places she could have spent a Saturday afternoon at in the city, how they both ended up at the same place was beyond belief.

In the car, Anton broke the silence. "Dr. Cal seems like a nice fellow. How is he to work for?"

Dani grinned. "He's wonderful with the children and he's a fierce opponent and activist when it comes to the medical rights of his patients. I've seen him shred an insurance company that refused to pay for a special drug for one of his children."

Anton kept his eyes on the road. After the last question, he chanced a quick look at her. He could see something in her eyes that made him believe it was more than his professionalism she was attracted to. But he didn't say a word.

To keep the conversation going, he said, "I just wish you didn't have to work at the hospital. It seems like that is all you do lately. Work and no play."

Dani touched his arm. "Oh...but I did play, today! Thank you so much for making me get out of the house; I had such a great time."

"It was my pleasure. I think you need to go out more often. You're young and these are the best years of your life to enjoy and maybe meet someone special."

Dani thought about it and then decided to ask him a question she had been holding in for years. "Why did you come to the United States twelve years ago?"

He glimpsed over and smiled. "Because I had a successful business in Romania that my brother was managing and I had been here a few times. I decided I needed a break and a change of scenery."

Dani moved forward with another question. "How come you never married or have children?"

A sad look crossed his face. "I loved once, but it was not meant to be. So, instead, I traveled around the world looking for a place where I belonged. Kind of like a nomad. My younger values circled around wealth and power; as I got older it became tiresome. At the same time, I had watched my brother's marriage fall apart and his children become so damaged from the opulence, that I decided I didn't want any part of it anymore. So, I ran away, so to speak...." his voice trailed off at the last sentence.

"What about your brother? You never have visitors and you have very few friends."

His face showed his sorrow. "My brother died years ago of a broken heart. My sister died when she was three and my mother and father are long gone. So, you see, I'm just as alone in the world as you!"

Dani looked at his sad face and said, "It sucks, doesn't it?"

Anton started to laugh at her choice of words. "Yes, Dani. It does suck!"

"Well, thanks for sharing Venice Beach with me today. Maybe we could do it again sometime."

"I'd like that."

chapter eight

THE NEXT DAY DANI TOOK THE BUS TO THE CEMETERY. She stopped at her favorite flower shop to see Paige and then walked through the gates with her backpack on her shoulder. As she was climbing up the hill, she noticed Estelle was sitting in her old vinyl chair—sound asleep. Soundlessly, Dani sat down and placed a flower on each grave. Then she took out an apple and decided to just sit and absorb the fresh air and beautiful sunny day. After an hour, she stood up and quietly walked over to Estelle and gently laid the brown paper bag next to her purse. Dani smiled at the loving loyalty this woman gave of herself every day.

She walked down the hill, and toward the bus stop. When she got to the bench she sat down. The bus came by, but it wasn't the bus to take her to work. It was Harry's bus; and when he pulled up to the curb Dani yelled out, "Hi, Harry. How's it going today?"

Harry smiled and waved, and then he yelled as the door was shutting, "I have a different route today, but I'm running on time, missy!"

Dani laughed. Harry was a creature of habit like most people. Certain things were very meaningful to him. Running on time was a big one.

The next bus pulled up and Dani walked up the two steps, handed the driver her ticket, and headed to the back. Once she was seated, she put her backpack next to her and started to hum her favorite song. There were about ten people in the bus and most of them were sitting in the front—all except one. It was an older Hispanic gentleman who was trying to stay awake. His head kept dropping down to his chin, and then it would wake him up and a minute later he repeated it. Dani watched, in lieu of nothing better to do. She always sat quietly and never took anything out of her backpack. Especially her cellphone. Those were considered 'liquid gold' on the streets and worth a lot of money. Dani could tell the old man had his phone in his shirt pocket. How silly to expose it to others, she thought. That's like setting yourself up for trouble.

Dani's hand slid into her pocket and felt the small canister of Mace. They made a few more stops and a few more people got on. Dani loved to sit on the bus and try to guess the age and occupation of each rider. She carefully watched the old man and thought maybe he worked on a graveyard shift in some all-night restaurant, gas station, or liquor store. He was having such a difficult time staying awake. Dani looked out the window and watched the tall buildings as they floated by. People were walking down the sidewalks and everything was moving so quickly. Just three more stops and she was at the restaurant. The bus came to a stop and two young men got on. They looked like they were friends when they sauntered onto the bus, but they didn't sit down next to each other. Dani was not normally a suspicious person; but years of experience riding on buses taught her to be cautious. She trusted everyone, and tried to find the positive in life around her. For some reason this struck a chord of being odd.

One of the boys sat next to the old man. It woke him up. He sat up and smiled. Then it happened, so quickly and spontaneously. Dani did not have time to stop or hesitate to react. The young boy took out a knife and started reaching for the phone in the man's pocket. His voice was angry and he couldn't get the phone out. Dani watched in horror as instinct made the old man fight the boy off. Rapidly, the knife came down and slashed the old Hispanic man in the face, and if that wasn't enough, the boy pulled his hand back, driving the sharp blade forward as he pushed it into his gut. Blood was everywhere. Fear and chaos consumed the bus. Dani stood up and started swinging her backpack at the young man who was starting to panic. "Leave him alone, you asshole!" she screamed.

He looked at her with crazy eyes. "Shut the fuck up!"

Dani swung the backpack again at the perpetrator. Her adrenalin was pumping.

The bus driver had locked the door and simultaneously pushed an alarm button. The bus briskly stopped in the middle of the road, throwing everyone off balance. Dani watched as the other boy slid out of one of the bus's large open windows. With his knife-wielding hand, the angry young boy left behind went after Dani. His blade slashed through the air. Dani pushed her backpack in front of her, but he knocked it out of her hand and stabbed her in the arm. Now fighting mad, she took out her Mace and sprayed the boy over and over again in the face. He started screaming in agony as the Mace burned his eyes, leaving him incapacitated.

The bus driver was trying to calm everyone down. Two men were holding down the angry young assailant as three police officers quickly stormed the bus and got him out of there. Dani heard the sirens, screeching from every direction, and she knew what was next. She looked at the older man who was lying across a seat holding his stomach and moaning as blood gushed out of his wound. An older woman was holding her sweater on his stomach and chest, trying to stem the flow of blood. Dani slowly pulled a t-shirt from her backpack and wrapped it around her arm to stop the bleeding. People were panicked, screaming and speaking so loud that Dani's head began to pound just before her anxiety and deferred fear caused her to pass out.

When she opened her eyes, people were all around her asking questions and trying to administer first aid. A young paramedic said in a kind voice, "We need to take you to the hospital. This cut on your arm is going to need stitches."

Dani looked up into his face. "Is the old man okay?" was the first thing she uttered.

The paramedic grinned and said, "Yes, he is going to make it."

"What about the assailant?" She closed her eyes and tried to recall the whole scene that had happened so quickly, it felt like a dream.

He put thick tape on her arm to keep the two edges of the cut taped together until they got her to the hospital for some stitches. "The police have him cuffed and he's on his way to be booked. I might say you did a very brave thing and drew his attention away from the old man. Usually, those nut cases go ballistic and will just keep attacking."

Dani took a good look at the paramedic who was busy working on her arm. At the same time, another was taking her blood pressure and checking her vital signs. He was a handsome young man, about her age, with big dimples on each side of his cheeks. When he smiled his whole face lit up.

When he was done taping her up, he yelled to the guys outside to bring in the gurney. "Ever taken a ride in an ambulance before?'

"No."

"Well, you're about to feel like you're on Disneyland ride. Not to worry...I will be right there with you." He dipped his head to look into her eyes, then he winked.

Dani inhaled a large breath and exhaled slowly. "Can I call someone to take me there instead of the ambulance?" she asked. If her mother was here, she would know what to do and take care of everything. Now all her decisions in life were only hers to make. Dani turned her head to the side and stared at the spot on the floor—willing herself not to cry.

"Can I have my backpack so I can get my phone?" She was trying her best not to lose it.

"Sure." He leaned down and handed it to her.

"I'll just call my work. Looks like I won't be making it in today." She lifted the arm with the cut and winced in pain.

She hit the contact number of the restaurant and listened to it ring. Finally, Lawrence answered.

"Lawrence, this is Dani. I can't come in tonight," she whispered.

Before she could get out the reason why, Lawrence started to throw one of his tantrums. "What the hell do you mean you won't be in today? Where the hell are you and why? You know I can fire you for leaving me in a lurch today."

Dani closed her eyes. She could tell the paramedic was listening to her insensitive boss. "There was an attempted robbery on the bus. This jerk slashed me with a knife. I'm in the ambulance on the way to the hospital. Sorry, Lawrence."

There was silence. Then she heard his lower voice say, "Sorry to hear that. I hope you're okay. Let me know about tomorrow in case I need to bring someone in."

With her eyes still closed, she said, "Thanks, Lawrence, I will." Her finger hit the disconnect button and she remained quiet.

She heard the ambulance siren blare as it took off with the old man. She prayed he was okay. Then she felt herself being lifted onto a gurney, and all she could think about was how fortunate she was to be alive...or was she?

She heard the paramedic whisper in her ear, "You ready to go, princess?'

A tear slid down the side of her face and she nodded.

Dani was really sedated. She assumed she was still lying in her bed at home and somewhere between sleep and reality.

She heard a voice whisper in her ear, "Are you okay?"

Dani felt woozy and thought she might still be asleep and that this horrible dream had frightened her awake. She asked herself again, *What is a man's voice doing in my bedroom?*

Suddenly, her eyes flew open and she looked straight ahead at a familiar emergency room. The sterile white room jarred her memory of so many things, but what finally came to surface was that she was not dreaming, and she was not at home. She had been knifed on the bus by a young punk, who nearly killed two people over a lousy phone.

She heard the male voice whisper again and she turned her head to the side. "How are you feeling?" Dr. Cal asked her.

Dani looked confused and faint. "I'm okay. It's just a little cut. No biggie! What are you doing here?"

Dr. Cal smiled. "I work here, remember!"

Dani sighed. "How did you know I was here?"

He pulled the chair over and sat down. Then he stretched his legs and rested them on the bed. "Becky heard from the emergency room that you were admitted. She called Lola, and the rest is history! That 'little cut' is not so little. I had a plastic surgeon come in and stitch it so it wouldn't leave a scar. Thank God it missed your tendon—by a fraction of an inch. I had them give you a shot to relax you. When you came in, you were so anxious and nuts, we needed to calm you down. Then they numbed your arm up. You should be pretty woozy for awhile. I don't know if you even remember being stitched up or very much after you got out of the ambulance."

"Actually, I thought it was a dream. I do feel lightheaded...."

"Tell me, what the hell happened?"

Dani closed her eyes and she quietly told him the whole ugly incident. He listened intently, without saying a word, and when she was done, she asked, "Do you know if that old man is going to be okay?"

"They rushed him into surgery. He's doing fine." He took a sip of his coffee he was holding and said, "Nice job with the Mace. That creep had no chance going up against you!"

"I saw his friend climb out the window. Did they catch him?" Dani questioned.

"Yup. They are two petty offenders who have rap sheets a mile long."

Dani tried to sit up in bed, but a shooting pain traveled up her arm and she yelped. Dr. Cal threw his legs onto the floor and stood up next to her with concern all over his face. "What's going on? Let me call the emergency room doc." He took one step toward the door.

Dani shook her head. "No, I'm fine, I just twisted it a little." She sighed. "When can I go home? I'm beginning to feel a lot better. Anton can pick me up."

He came back and sat down. "They want to keep you overnight for observation."

She pushed herself up and started to get out of bed. Her eyes darted all around the room looking for her clothes and backpack. "I want to go home!"

Dr. Cal did not looked pleased, but he could see the stubborn look on Dani's face. "Let me see what I can do. But only if I take you home and make sure you're okay. Do you have anyone who can stay with you for the night?"

"No. I'm fine alone. My mother and I have been alone all our lives. I can handle it!"

He stepped closer. "Your mother is not here. They gave you a Xanax and some hefty shots to numb your arm. When it wears off, you will be in pain. Someone should be there to make sure you're okay."

Just to get his prying eyes off her and give him a decent answer, she replied, "My next-door neighbor, Anton, will make sure I'm okay." She wasn't going to tell Anton, but Dr. Call didn't have to know that.

An hour later, he was wheeling Dani through the hospital in a wheelchair. When he got down to the front doors, he told her to wait as he went into the hospital garage and got his car.

On the ride to her house, Dani put her head back against the seat and closed her eyes. She had developed a bad headache and just wanted to get home and into her bed. When he parked the car against the curb, he was very careful to help her out. She wasn't very steady on her feet and walking a straight line was nearly impossible. When she went to open the door, Dr. Cal bent down and picked up a brown bag and handed it to her. She grasped the bag and said, "Thank you, I can handle it from here."

Once she opened the door, she walked in and began to close it. He put his hand up to stop the door from closing and followed her inside the apartment. He noticed her anger but still continued to follow her into the kitchen. He looked around her place. He had never been there and it intrigued him how simple and sparse it was. Everything was clean and in its place. It was a typical apartment with two small bedrooms, a living room, one full bathroom, and a small kitchen. The living room had a nice tan leather couch with an end and coffee table. The large bay window had wood blinds, so the sidewalk traffic was blocked from looking in. The overhead recessed lighting was evenly placed around the undersized room. The kitchen had one window that lit up the space with the warm afternoon sun. The kitchen table was barely big enough to seat two people.

Dani felt slightly lightheaded so she walked over to the couch and sat down. Rubbing her temples where her headache was beginning, she finally said, "I'm okay, Dr. Cal, you can leave now."

He stood there with his arms folded across his chest. "Not until you call Anton."

Dani sighed. "I will, once I rest for a few minutes."

He walked toward the door and Dani felt a sudden twinge of relief. Then he turned around and said, "Is he on the right or left side of your apartment?"

At first she didn't get the question, but then the light went on and immediately the pounding in her head intensified. He continued to stare at her without moving an inch further. Knowing this could be a serious standoff between them, she relented and said, "Left."

Ten minutes later, Anton and Dr. Cal walked through the door. Dr. Cal shook Anton's hand and said to Dani, "Now I feel better. If you need anything, I gave my private phone number to Anton and he gave me his as well."

Feeling miffed, she replied, "Why don't you leave it with Mrs. Nosybody, too! She probably watched this whole circus of musical doors with men going in and out today!"

Dr. Cal tried not to smile, he knew who she was talking about. He had seen her standing outside her door across the hall watching what was going on. "Which apartment does she live in…I'd be glad to leave her my number too."

"Hummpff," was her only response.

He walked out the door. She could not see the big smile on his face.

Hours later, Anton laid the tray on the table and quietly walked out of Dani's apartment. When Dr. Cal had left earlier, Dani had told Anton the whole wretched fiasco that had left her arm with fourteen stitches. He had lectured her on her mode of transportation and offered to take her and pick her up from work. Dani was stubborn and refused to acknowledge his offer. "Come on, Anton. That was probably a once in a lifetime occurrence. I mean, what are the chances of it happening again? You're beginning to sound like Dr. Cal. Look, I'm a big girl and I can take care of myself."

Anton looked at Dani as a father would look at his daughter who was being obstinate. "You're not being rational right now. At least let me do it for a few weeks until you heal." Then he smiled and said, "Why won't you let me loan you some money and you can get a car."

"Because I don't want a car. Besides, I don't know how to drive; and it seems very scary to me in this big city congested with traffic."

"It's not that hard. It's like riding a bike, once you learn—"

She cut off his new lecture that was beginning to take shape. "Okay. Just for a few weeks while I heal."

Dani laid down on the couch and turned on the television. She was exhausted from the ordeal and all she wanted to do was go to sleep. Anton went into the kitchen. He knew she would be hungry when she woke up.

So he made her a quick dinner, covered it, and put it in the refrigerator. Then he took another plate out, wrote a note telling her where she could find her dinner, and left it on the coffee table in front of her sleeping form. Anton looked down at her and shook his head.

chapter nine

HER ARM LOOKED ALMOST BACK TO NORMAL. IT HAD healed perfectly; and thanks to the quick thinking of Dr. Cal, you could hardly see a scar. She had stayed home for two days just to sleep and release herself of the trauma of going through such an ugly experience. For those first few days, Anton brought over meals he had either cooked or bought from nearby restaurants. He was compassionate and thoughtful, and many times Dani had expressed her gratitude. Dr. Cal stopped by on the third day, throwing her off with his bag filled with groceries. "Thought you might need something in the fridge, so I went to Whole Foods and bought a few things."

Dani looked into the bag, and one by one she picked out the items. "Humm. Ice cream, apples, chips, crackers, dip, beef jerky, and...what's this?" She held up a container with something in it.

"My favorite—stuffed cabbage!" He smiled shyly and shrugged his shoulders.

"Everything I could ever want!" she smiled pleasantly.

He smiled back.

Dani went to the kitchen drawer and came back with a fork and a spoon. She handed him the fork along with the box. "You have the stuffed cabbage—and I'll have the ice cream."

Dr. Cal smiled as he took the fork and opened the box. "Thanks. I didn't have lunch today." He followed

Dani into the living room and they both sat down on the couch.

Dr. Cal settled in and got comfortable, and then he broke the silence. "The girls sent you their healing vibes."

Dani smiled and continued to enjoy her ice cream. It had been a long time since she enjoyed the creamy treat. She didn't know why, other than she never picked it up when she was in the store. She was just like her mother, focused on the bare minimum without extras.

"I'm really sorry you had to go through what you did. Our streets are getting almost impossible to navigate without crime." He broke the silence again.

"Thank you," she said as she spooned a dollop of ice cream into her mouth and moaned.

Dr. Cal laughed. "How come my box doesn't come with a moan? Did I choose the wrong one?"

Dani nodded her head and laughed. "Would you like a taste? But you have to promise not to moan!" She handed him the spoon with a large scoop of ice cream.

He slowly placed it in his mouth. Suddenly, he laid down on the couch and began to moan. Then just as quickly, he sat back up and snatched the carton out of her hand and looked at it and started to laugh.

Dani asked. "What are you laughing at?"

He looked at the carton again. "I didn't realize I bought 'moan and groan chocolate!' No wonder we are moaning! I thought it just said plain old chocolate."

Dani grabbed her spoon and container back. "Sorry, doc, you wanted that delicious stuffed cabbage so I get the 'moan and groan' chocolate ice cream."

He looked at his cabbage, and said, "It's not that good now I've tried your ice cream!"

Dani shrugged her shoulders and tightened her grip on the ice cream carton.

The following day she went to the restaurant to do a shorter shift. She needed the money and couldn't afford to lose much work. Lawrence was extremely sympathetic and went out of his way to be nice. He also gave her the earlier afternoon hours and made sure she could leave work early. When Dani saw the girls, they were beyond horrified that she was stuck in the middle of a robbery and that she had to appear in court for the trial of the criminals. Steph had talked to her the day it happened; and she wanted Dani to stay at her home for a few weeks, but Dani wouldn't hear of it. They were all so grateful that she had survived the attack and her injuries were not life threatening.

After work, Dani walked out the door and got into the car that was waiting for her at the curb. Anton had made good on his promise to take her and pick her up the first week. By the end of the week, Dani had felt a little uncomfortable. Not necessarily with Anton. He was very kind and always so cheerful. She was feeling more like a child; and she knew it was time for her to start depending on herself again.

So, politely on the sixth day, she announced to Anton, "I'm going to take the bus tomorrow. I'm a big girl and I will be fine. Besides, I've changed my hours in the restaurant, to leave an hour earlier, so that I can get to the hospital earlier and make it onto the last bus no problem."

Anton didn't look happy. There was never any stopping her where her mind was made up.

Dani had taken off a week from the hospital. Tonight was her first night back. She couldn't wait to see all the little faces and how they were doing. She missed them and their overwhelming excitement when she walked into a room. She loved their innocence and resilience to dealing with their illnesses. It was always hard for most of the little ones to stay in the hospital without their family around. Dani had learned many lessons in life about patience, because of all those spirited young children. On those days she missed Levi, it was a reprieve for her to go into their rooms to watch their childish exuberance.

Walking through the front doors of Barouch Memorial had sent this feeling of renewal through her. She had missed everyone and the comfort of belonging. Dani walked up to information desk and whispered 'boo' into Becky's ear. Becky jumped up in fright and turned around. Then she leaned over the counter and gave Dani a big hug. "It's so good to see you! Welcome back, we missed you!"

Dani smiled as she walked toward the elevators. "Thanks, Becky. I missed you too!"

When she stepped off the elevator she only saw one nurse behind the desk. Lola looked up and excitement lit up her face. She stood up and did a happy dance, her wild hips moving in all directions. Dani started to laugh as she walked toward the desk, almost afraid Lola might wrestle her to the floor in excitement. Lola frantically screamed to the other nurses. They all came running down the hall to see what all the uproar was about. Watching the spirited burst of enthusiasm upon her return, Dani thought she wasn't as alone in the world as she had thought.

Lola calmed down and carefully took Dani's arm to get a better look at the injury. "Let me see what that bastard did!"

Alva carefully ran a finger down the thin scar that ran parallel to her arm. "I'm glad you're okay. Thank god it wasn't worse," Alva said. "What an awful thing to happen. When we heard the news you were in the emergency room, we all went crazy with worry. Then, just as quickly, we heard Dr. Cal was taking you home."

Dani watched as a tear spilled over onto Alva's cheek. With one finger she wiped it away. "I'm okay, Alva. I actually sprayed so much Mace into his eyes I heard from the police that he was cursing my name and crying for days!" The girls laughed. Lola gave Dani a knuckle bump.

"It's nice to have you back. All our babies missed you," Malaya announced.

Dani blushed as she swiftly walked towards the rooms of all her little patients. "Well, I'm going to make sure I see each and every one of them tonight before I leave. Even if I have to break the rules and wake them up!"

The evening went great; and at nine o'clock she was ready to go home, as the fatigue from telling her story over and over took over. She was so thankful she had tomorrow off to do whatever she wanted. She needed some sleep. It had been a few days of tossing and turning with nightmares. Her dreams kept reflecting the horrible experience that could have taken her life.

Sleep was the first thing on her list. Then she needed to clean out her mother's closet, something that she had been putting off for months. It had taken her a while before she could gather the emotional strength to go through Ema's things and dredge up a lot of memories. Personal belongings of loved ones who died were tough to go through. Each article of clothing usually came attached with wonderful memories of the past. It was hard to think about letting go. She had done that once already.

Anton was waiting outside in his car alongside of the curb of the hospital. When Dani saw him, she was relieved to have a ride home. Sometimes her stubbornness got her into so much trouble with unnecessary obstacles. She didn't know how to accept help graciously. Instead, she pushed it away, creating a tougher existence for herself. Dani smiled as she opened the door and slid into the front seat of the expensive car. "Thank you, Anton. I really appreciated your help this week."

Anton tipped his head and grinned. "You're welcome. I don't mind at all. In fact, it gives me comfort to know that you are not on that bus late at night."

"Oh, Anton. I've been doing it for so long, it doesn't bother me."

Once they were almost home Dani got up the courage to say, "I really do think I can manage on my own next week, Anton."

Anton was just about to argue with her when she quickly added, "Would you like to go to a movie tomorrow? If I get some of the things done I need to do around the house, I'd love to see a movie. Your choice. I'm afraid, I'm not a very good movie picker!"

Anton smiled and replied, "Sure...I'll see if there is anything decent playing. Or maybe there might be a good play in the local little playhouses we have in Hollywood."

Dani's eyes opened wide. "I'd love that! Mom and I used to go all the time. It always seemed like a special occasion."

Anton pulled the car into his designated parking spot in the back of the apartment. "Then we'll call this a special occasion. It's my treat."

"You've done so much for me already."

"No argument, young lady, I insist."

Dani turned on her side and slowly came out of her deep sleep. She had been dreaming about something, but she couldn't remember what about. She laid there trying to recall, but for some reason, she could only remember a horse that changed colors every ten seconds.

She rolled onto her back and closed her eyes. It felt good to sleep in.

She twisted her head and looked at the digital clock. "Wow…I can't believe I slept in this late," she mumbled to herself. Feeling a little guilty, she slowly slid to the side of the bed and sat up. She planted her feet on the ground and walked into the kitchen to make coffee.

Once she had a hot cup of coffee in her hands, she sat down on the couch. She finally decided today she was definitely going to clean out her mother's closet. She had made the attempt a few times. She gripped the doorknob, but she just didn't have the heart to go through with it. Dani knew it had to be done, and she was determined that today, there was no backing out.

Ema had left all of Levi's stuff exactly where it was the night he died. Then Ema watched as it was slowly becoming a shrine to Dani. One morning they had gotten into a terrible fight. They had said some pretty mean things to each other. Dani closed her eyes, leaned her head back on the couch, took a sip of coffee, and remembered that awful day.

Dani and her mother were having coffee in the kitchen, like they did every morning. Dani was holding the little teddy bear that Levi had slept with every night. Dani's mother gently took the bear out of her daughter's hand and put it on the counter.

Ema turned to her sad daughter and said, "Dani, we need to go through Levi's things and give the toys and clothes to an orphanage for those children who could make use of it," she said softly.

Dani looked at her mother in horror and vehemently shook her head. "No! You're not touching a thing! I'm leaving it right where it all belongs. Those are Levi's toys and nobody is going to ever have them!"

Ema frowned at the distraught and panicked expression on Dani's face. "It's not doing either of us any good looking at it day after day and grieving twice as hard. The memories are what count, not all his things scattered everywhere like he is still living here. This is not right! I refuse to have you hold everything in the same place like it's a memorial to him. It's not healthy."

Tears were streaming down Dani's face. "I'm not moving a thing, Mother!"

Ema grabbed her daughter's shoulders and looked into her eyes. "He died, Dani. He died a happy little boy who had four wonderful years with us. There was nothing we could do. Please don't keep pushing yourself deeper and deeper into this depression. It's going to kill you and it is going to kill me watching you."

Dani shrugged away. "If I could—"

Her mother screamed, "YOU couldn't do more than you did. I couldn't do more…Dr. Cal couldn't do more…it was an awful thing that happened. You just have to let go of the material things that keep you tied to this ugly guilt you keep carrying around."

Dani fell to the floor and curled into a ball. "I can't…I miss him so much," she cried.

Ema laid down on the floor next to her daughter and hugged her tight. "So do I. Deep inside, my heart breaks every time I walk into the room and see the things that made him so happy. Deep inside, I remember him holding his little bear the night he died. But deep inside, I think of all the little boys at the orphanage that would be really happy with his superman pajamas, his toys, his plastic bug collection and all those things that brought his wonderful laughter into our home. There is no reason to keep it here. We could even give a few things to the hospital, to the kids that are still there fighting for their lives."

"I don't think I can...." Dani whispered, choking on her words.

"We don't think we can do a lot of things—yet we do. I didn't think I could leave Romania and find a better life for my daughter—but I did."

"But I didn't die."

"No, you didn't die, but the only country that I had ever known had ceased to exist the moment I got on the train. I died deep in my heart that day I left." Then she said in a whisper, "Death is never easy, nor is it ever wanted. Living with the memories becomes our only absolution. Let's think of him as our brave little angel who fought with all his heart."

Ema held her daughter for hours until the tears would not come anymore.

Dani finally lifted her hand and touched her mother's wet face. "Okay, but there are a few things I need to keep close to me. I need his bear, so I can still smell him at night when I sleep with it. I need his silly pictures he painted of me. I need...."

Ema slowly stood and helped Dani up. "Come show me the things you need to keep. And let's put everything else into a box. Okay?"

Dani's hands began to shake. Although she didn't want to, she knew this is what you had to do when death had knocked at your door. And now, she knew her mother would want her to do the same thing. She'd want Dani to keep those special things, and give the rest to those that needed it. She remembered the softness of her mother that day and how she handled her grieving daughter. She remembered so many things; but then there was a whole life that came before Dani that nobody knew about. Not even Dani....

chapter ten

DANI WALKED INTO HER MOTHER'S ROOM. IT WAS NEAT, comfortable, and exactly the way she had left it that morning. It was filled with all those things that told you what kind of a person she was. The bed was perfectly made, stacked with decorative pillows. On the end table, next to her bed, was a picture of Dani when she was four, and one of Levi at the same age. They were the last things her mother would look at every night when she would reach over to shut off her light. Her mother's favorite reading glasses were sitting on the table as well as a small bible she had brought from Romania. The big lamp was the only light in the room, and her mother used it to read late into the night. Her mother loved to read. Sitting on the other bedside table was her latest book, still opened on the last page she had finished.

Dani always loved to come into her room and sit or lay down on the bed. There they would talk about life. It was a place of solace that kept them as close as a mother and daughter could be. Those special nights that they talked into the early morning hours were what kept Dani grounded as she made it through her tumultuous high school years.

Dani looked at the closet door and realized that she had never opened it or looked inside. It was the only thing that Ema had set off limits to Dani at a young age. Dani had always respected her mother's wishes. She took a deep breath, and with shaking hands, she opened it. Immediately, the floral scent of her mother permeated the space around her. Dani closed her eyes and took a deep breath. Her heart was beating a mile a minute. This was her mother's sanctuary, and for some reason, Dani felt she was invading her space. Dani instantly reprimanded herself for being so silly. There was nothing in there that Dani wanted or even cared about. Ema's style of dress was extremely conservative and rode the fine line of matronly. Her shoes were old-fashioned, made for comfort, nothing Dani would ever consider wearing. They had shared everything else in life, but this was where mother and daughter were different. Dani was trendy and loved high fashion. Although she could never afford most of the clothes she worshipped in magazines and storefront windows, she respected her mother's choices.

Dani turned on the overhead light and suddenly she could see everything. Years and years of things of importance that her mother had saved, boxes stacked high in the corner and each covered. Dani was becoming overwhelmed with everything she had never seen before. Her mother was not a hoarder, but her closet seemed to be filled with a lifetime of things, and hardly anything looked familiar to Dani. She only recognized a few of her dresses, and most of her shoes looked like they had never been worn. Dani turned and touched the shoe rack that hung from the inside of the door. There were so many pairs of shoes. Not any more or any less, just the exact amount of pairs to fill the rack. That is how her mother was—very precise. Dani could see that her clothes were hung according to spring, summer, and winter. Dresses were together, slacks, and skirts—nothing out of place. Dani knew that the dresser held all her underclothes, nightwear, and sweaters. After touching a few familiar garments on the hangers, Dani took a step back and was about to close the door.

Instead she said out loud to herself, "You have to get through this. She would have wanted you to. Don't stop now, or you may never have the nerve to attempt it again. Do it for her, Dani. Do it for your mother!"

Dani listened to her own voice and stepped forward again. This time she knew she would get through it. Dani lovingly took each garment off its hanger and folded it neatly and placed it into a box. Each box was labeled with the destination she planned on taking it to. In big black letters she had written: women's shelter; homeless shelter; thrift shop for handicapped children. Ema and she had always donated to those charitable organizations; and many times they had gone down to help with fundraising. Her mother was always one to give back to her community. A community she had always been so thankful to have.

Once she had packed the clothes and shoes, Dani knew she had to start rummaging through the boxes. Then she would tackle the top shelf that had boxes stacked to the ceiling. She couldn't imagine what would be in all the stacked boxes.

Dani lifted her arms up and grabbed the first box. So overwhelmed, she sat down on the floor. When she took off the lid, her eyes opened wide with surprise. It was a box filled with most of Dani's favorite stuffed toys she had neatly arranged on her bed as a young child. Dani had loved her stuffed animal and doll collection. She refused to let Ema put them away until one day when her girlfriends had made fun of her. She was thirteen, and they all thought she was silly to have them in her room. That night Ema and Dani packed them up and they were never to be seen again—until just now. Dani picked up the little sock monkey she had loved so much.

Dani hugged FiFi and held her close to her heart as wonderful memories of the past resurfaced. "Mother must have been saving them for me," Dani softly said, as she put FiFi into a box labeled 'Dani.' She kept one or two of her other favorites and knew the children in the orphanage would love the rest, just as she had when she was little. The next box had her two favorite dolls. Looking and touching the dolls made Dani's heart heavy recalling those years of childhood tea parties and hours playing house in her room. She kept those too.

The next box was not surprising at all. It was all of her report cards, special projects, and class pictures through her high school years. Pictures of her friends, locks of her hair, her first loose tooth; all those things mothers save and are unwilling to let go of. Dani went through this box laughing, misty eyed, as she remembered those days so long ago. Dani put that box next to the others that she was going to keep. Then she opened the next box. By now, she could almost guess what it was going to be. And she was right. It was all those pictures her mother had taken on that cheap little drugstore camera she always carried around whenever they went somewhere of importance, hundreds of pictures that Dani hadn't seen in so many years. So many fun and exciting things they did together as mother and daughter—it was a history of their past right there on paper. Not like now, with technology and the newer generations. Nobody used cameras or had real pictures anymore.

Each picture had a written note on the back with the date and description. Dani's first day at school; her two front teeth missing; birthdays; graduations; happy days; sad days; and she had them almost until the end. Dani was overwhelmed as she started to go through them.

"Okay, you have a lifetime to look at these. Put them away for a rainy day," Dani said to herself.

With expectations of finding some more nostalgic remembrances tucked away in yet another box, she grabbed the next one with great anticipation of finding something special. Anticipating what surprise Ema had next, Dani flipped up the lid and immediately was puzzled. Lying on top was an old, discolored newspaper—folded in half. She picked it up and looked at it. It was dated twenty-eight years earlier and was printed in Romania.

Dani felt a chill run down her spine. Her fears were surfacing as she realized that this box just might hold some answers to her mother's past, hidden secrets and memories that she had never shared with anyone—not even her own daughter. Dani picked up the box and walked into the living room and placed it on the coffee table. She felt this strange self-consciousness about sitting in her mother's room as she was about to delve into her dark secret. It made her feel vulnerable.

She went into the kitchen and poured a cup of coffee and heated it in the microwave. Then, with all the eeriness, she sat down in front of the box and waited for all the ghosts to step forward. As she picked up the newspaper again, she placed it on the table and continued to look inside. It was no use trying to read the paper, she had never been exposed to the Romanian language, nor did she ever hear her mother speak anything but English. The pictures were not of anything she would ever recognize. The only clue that could be learned from the newspaper was that her mother was still in Romania when she was four months pregnant with Dani.

She then opened a manila envelope with a paid ticket for a train from Romania, through Austria, and into France. It looked like a standard ticket with no name, just a stamp at each destination. The next receipt clipped to it was for a cargo boat to Ireland. Then the final destination, on the White Star Line, was a voucher for a boat from Ireland to the United States. When Dani figured out the days she spent traveling, it meant that she was in her sixth month of pregnancy when she finally flew from New York to California. The first two didn't have any information about who paid for the tickets. The voucher that brought her from Europe to the United States had her mother's name stamped on it.

Dani sat there staring in shock. It was almost more than she could handle, because her mother's last name on the voucher was not Ema Vaduva—it was Emila Silivasi. Dani was shaken, confused, and angry. Most of all, lots of questions were starting to surface and there was no one to answer them. Her eyes never moved from the tickets as she kept asking herself the same questions over and over. Was that her last name on the ticket? Was it her family name? Was it an alias that she was traveling under? Was she married before she came here and left him? Then her questions starting spinning in another direction. Is my mother really my mother? Was she hiding from some awful past or from the law and had that forced her to leave her country and abandon her family? Who is my father and why didn't he come with Ema? Dani was beginning to panic and her heart was racing like a jackhammer. Thump-thump-thump— she pulled out the next envelope and was afraid to open it. What more could it hold? Years of trust were now turning into doubt about all that her mother had ever told her.

The next envelope was just as disturbing as the last. Inside there were five very old black and white photographs taken years and years ago. They were so old that the paper was beginning to disintegrate in her fingers, so she had to hold them very gently. One picture had a man and a woman. The woman was dressed very honorably and the man was wearing a suit and tie. The man was much taller and looked to be in his thirties, and the woman was younger—small and petite. The pictures were so old and faded it was really hard for Dani to see any distinguishable clarity. She gently put it down, and quickly got up off the couch, ran into the kitchen, and started digging through the drawer. When she found what she was looking for, she ran back into the room and sat down. Now, using the magnifying glass her mother always used, she lifted the picture for a better look. She turned on the little light on its handle and drew the photo up as close to her eyes as she could.

"Who are these two people? Am I related to them? Why does my mother have these pictures?" Dani was nervous as she took the pictures out and counted them. There were only five, and no one was recognizable. Not that she could ever recognize anyone from Romania from over thirty years ago. She had never seen a picture of her mother taken in her homeland or before she came to the United States. No childhood picture of her as a baby, in school, or a family portrait. This was the first time a picture from Ema's past had surfaced. It was like Dani was handed a huge puzzle piece.

The second picture was a woman and three small children. It looked like one boy and two small girls. In those days, children under three usually wore bloomers—whether they were male or female. So it was hard for Dani to figure out the gender of each child. Dani stared at the picture and she finally realized the woman in the photo was Ema. She was young, thin, and had beautiful hair flowing over her shoulders and down her back. Her nose was straight and symmetrical with high cheekbones, but it was her smile that finally convinced Dani the young woman was her mother. She couldn't have been much older than eighteen. It must have been taken just before she came to America.

The young children in the picture must have belonged to that wealthy family she worked for. She never talked about the family. Dani was strictly going by intuition and the few things she did say. The background was a large home. Dani could only compare it to some of the enormous mansions in Beverly Hills. The circular driveway was cobblestone. In the middle was a large fountain that was at least ten feet tall, water cascading into a surrounding pool. There were many expensive cars parked to the side of the home, and a young man dressed in a uniform was polishing one. Ema and the three children were in front of the fountain. She was holding a baby in her arms, and the two smaller children were clutched tightly to her side.

Dani turned her attention to the next picture. Two young boys who looked to be brothers—or friends—were standing next to a building with part of a Romanian name on it. The building looked like a school surrounded by manicured lawns and beautiful brick buildings. She could also see the shadows of other young men walking in the distance. The two young boys were exactly the same height, same light build, same clothes and hair, but with distinguishing features in each of their faces. Dani thought they looked young, maybe in their early teens. They both had big smiles on their faces and looked like perhaps they got into more than their fair share of mischief. Their long woolen slacks and white, ironed shirts and ties bespoke of a higher class. Their suspenders were over their shoulders and more for looks than anything else. The boys' long hair hit the edge of their collars, and their leather shoes looked highly polished. Dani liked this picture, although, part of it was disintegrated. She made a mental note to get some special plastic sheets to maintain these old and priceless photographs.

Dani laid that one down very carefully, and picked up another. This one was very old and faded. It was a wedding photo. The bride was wearing a simple long dress and she was carrying a bouquet of tightly compressed flowers. The man was standing next to her with his arm resting on her shoulder. Dani wondered who this could be. Was it Ema's mother and father? Who were these newlyweds, and how did they fit into Ema's life? The past few minutes were spinning Dani around in so many directions that she felt like a spinning top. Why were these pictures here and how come my mother never showed them to me? Did she lead a secret life in Romania? Or were these unrelated to her life and she had forgotten about them?

Dani knew she would be lying to herself if she thought they were unrelated to her mother's life in Romania, but she had no way to find out. They were just old pictures of people. Her mother had written nothing on the back to describe or inform anyone of the faces. That was so unlike her mother. Ema always documented their pictures.

The final one was a man. Dani stared at the picture and knew he was the same tall young man who was in the first photograph with the younger woman. He was handsome and debonair. His pose showed his arrogance. It was taken in front of the mansion and he stood next to massive entry doors. One hand was leaning on the doorknob, and a cocky smile consumed his face. Dani didn't like him. She could tell he was egotistical, just by the way he stood and looked into the camera. She had seen many men like him at the restaurant. They all acted like everyone was beneath them, some even became more vocal and let her know of their societal positions. Dani scrutinized his face. Something looked vaguely familiar about him. His features were handsomely chiseled and his full head of hair was black and wavy. But it was his eyes that Dani kept looking at. Without any closure, she finally put them back into the envelope. She reached over and pulled out the next envelope.

When she opened it—her eyes opened wide. It was many savings passbooks bundled together with an old rubber band. The bank's name was embossed on the covers; and they came from a local bank in the area. Not sure if this was another big surprise or not, she slowly opened the first one. Her mouth opened wide and she gasped. She shut the book immediately and held it to her chest. Then like a child trying to sneak another peek, she quickly opened it again. This time she saw her mother's name in dark bold print—Ema Vaduva. It had pages and pages of deposits that were all the same amount—one deposit on the first day of every month for three thousand dollars. She took the first book and flipped through it. Frantically she shook her head. "What is this? What's going on here? Where did all this fucking money come from?"

Dani sat there trying to make sense of all this stuff in the box. "Oh my god!" she screamed out loud when she got to the back page of the final passbook. "Thirty-six thousand a year, and for how many years?" Wildly she grabbed one book and flipped through the pages looking for the first posting. When she finally found it, she realized the date was in the same month and the same year she was born.

Dani felt a tremendous weight on her shoulders. She laid her head down on the couch and she began to rock back and forth—holding the book tightly to her chest. Whimpers rose from deep inside her chest as she felt her heart splintering into a thousand small pieces. Questions that blended into her sobs were coming out of her mouth quicker than a bolt of lightning. "Why...why was she hiding this? Why didn't...she use it? Who is it from? Was my whole life a lie...or was she protecting me from something...or somebody? Please, Mother...where did this come from?" There were no answers to any of her questions. All she had was a few pictures and a passbook filled with so many deposits. So much money...and no answers.

"Maybe this was not Ema's." Dani began to think. Maybe it was just a joke. Maybe she was just holding or keeping it for a friend? But...she didn't have any friends. She was a loner who just had me! Or did she...? Was I was just too busy...to notice? Dani laid there for a moment and then she knew she had to go next door to see Anton. Maybe he knew more. He lived next door to them for twelve years. He was from Romania. Maybe he saw something she didn't. Dani knew that Anton and her mother occasionally talked. Could she have told him something?

Energy stormed through her body. She picked up the pictures and the passbooks and ran out her front door. Without caring about her snoopy neighbor she began to pound on his door. Her hair was in disarray and her face reddened from tears. She continued to pound on the door. "Answer the door, damn it!" she silently screamed.

Suddenly, Mrs. Brodsky opened her door and stood there gawking. Dani looked at the old lady's smug face and continued to pound on Anton's door. Anton wasn't answering. Dani turned around, losing her patience, and yelled, "Go back in your damn house, Mrs. Brodsky. This is none of your business!"

"He's not home," she said self-righteously. "He's taking his daily walk down to the deli for lunch." She slammed her door and Dani could still hear the echo of her laugh.

Dani slumped down on the ground near his door hugging the envelopes to her chest and she began to rock back and forth. However long it was going to be, she didn't care. She closed her eyes and waited, hoping he would know something—anything! It was thirty minutes later when Dani felt a hand tap her shoulder.

"Dani, what's wrong? Why are you sitting at my front door with your eyes closed? Are you still playing those childish games with Mrs. Brodsky?" Anton smiled, shaking his head.

Dani slowly stood up and looked directly at Anton. In a serious whisper, she slowly said, "I need to talk to you."

Anton looked at Dani's red face and the envelopes she was carrying in her arms. Without another word he opened the door and guided her into the apartment.

"Come on in. No need for the neighbors to start their tongue wagging. What's happened?"

Dani followed him in. She went into his kitchen and sat at the table. "I have some questions for you, Anton."

Anton took a deep breath and exhaled slowly. "What kind of questions, Dani?"

He was standing there observing her disheveled look. He calmly took off his tailored sport coat, hung it on a hanger, and slipped it into the coat closet. Then he slowly walked back and started to make a pot of coffee. "I'm making some coffee? I love my coffee in the afternoon. But at my age, I have to be careful not to drink it too late, or I'm up all night," he said with a gentle composure that was unnerving to Dani.

Dani didn't want small talk today. She placed her hands on the envelopes and waited for Anton to have a seat. He poured one cup and handed it to Dani, then one for himself and took a seat.

She opened the first envelope and placed the pictures on the table. Anton just sat and stared. Carefully he picked them up and looked at them. He looked at Dani and asked, "Where did you get these from? Who are they? Do you know anything about them?"

Tears welled in Dani's eyes. "They were in my mother's closet. There was not a notation, not a note, not anything in the box—just these five pictures and these...." She placed the passbooks on the table. With shaky fingers, Anton picked them up. He opened the top one and said, "That's a lot of money. Where did it come from? Do you know?"

"My mother's closet...."

Anton asked cautiously, "No...I mean, where did she get it from? Do you know?"

She was glaring at him. "I thought maybe you could tell me. I mean, there has been a deposit in this account every month for twenty-five years and an exorbitant amount of interest it has been accumulating. They stopped a few years ago when I turned twenty-five. I'm thinking it might be payoff money or something."

"How would I know, Dani?" He slowly placed the books on the table.

"I thought someone must have dropped it off when I wasn't home and you may have seen them. Or maybe my mother had a friend I didn't know about. She had to get this money from someone—somehow. And living next door, I thought maybe you saw something that would be suspicious."

Anton saw that all of Dani's emotions were beginning to spin out of control. "You need to calm down, Dani. This is not the end of the world. You don't even know whose account this is or if it is still open."

Dani picked up the books. She pointed to first post and raised her voice, "It was posted the same month and year that I was born! This means I had a father, or someone who was raging with guilt and was paying my mother to shut up."

Anton remained calm and unperturbed. He crossed his legs and sat back. "You don't know that. You don't know anything of that sort. Maybe it was family money that was being deposited—maybe her mother's or father's?"

Dani sat forward and her voice got low and gruff, "Ema's mother died giving birth to her, and her putrid father gave her to his disgusting sister to be raised. She had six children in a two-bedroom home and an alcoholic husband. Now which one of those beauties do you think could have possibly left her that much money?"

Anton casually dropped a sugar cube into his coffee and began to stir it slowly. Dani watched as one of his eyes twitched. "Okay, you made a point. I had no idea she came from such clasa de jos."

"What...? What is clasa de whatever...?" Dani tried to pronounce the Romanian word.

Anton smiled. "It means lower-class in Romanian."

Dani was silent as her hand opened and closed the passbook over and over again. "I'm going to the bank Monday morning before work. I want to find out who was depositing the money into this account. They must have records."

"Why all the fuss, Dani? Why not just take the money and silently thank your mother for putting it away for you. I bet that was her plan. She probably felt that when she was gone...at least you would have something to fall back on."

Dani picked up the envelope. "And who do you think is in the pictures? Five strangers who must have had some meaning in my mother's life...."

Anton nodded his head.

Dani stood up. The coffee along with all the crazy revelations had her emotionally wired. "I think one of those pictures is of the wealthy family she worked for just before she came to the United States."

Anton picked up the picture of her mother and the children and stared at it. "How much of her life in Romania did she tell you about?" he asked.

She sat down again. "That's all I know. My mother was not one to spill her guts about her past. I don't even have a clue as to who my father is. I'm pretty sure that she came here pregnant and alone. She never mentioned a boyfriend, a lover—nobody. I must have been an 'immaculate conception!'"

Anton almost choked on his coffee. "That's an interesting concept!"

Dani stood up again; she was having a hard time controlling herself. "I have to go. I have so much to think about. My life completely changed with these damn envelopes."

Anton walked her to the door. He took her elbow and turned her around. "Don't let it, Dani. You can't change the past. Leave it alone."

Dani looked at Anton and walked out the door. When she glanced across the hall, she saw Mrs. Brodsky quietly close her door.

"Go to hell, Mrs. Brodsky!" Dani yelled, and she turned around and flipped her off, just in case she was looking through her peephole.

chapter eleven

DANI HEARD HER ALARM GO OFF AND SHE OPENED HER eyes. She looked at the hole in the blackout shade and smiled for the first time in twenty-four hours. She didn't know how much sleep she got, but she knew it was very little. She was up most of the night trying to figure out what had just happened in her life. Here she was opening her eyes to a new day and she knew the reality of that box was not a dream. With pictures that left her no answers to her mother's past, a passbook filled with more money than she had ever expected to see in her lifetime, there was not one answer in sight. "What was she going to do and how could her mother possibly do this to her?" she asked herself the whole night as she slipped in and out of sleep. "Where do I even begin to search for answers?"

It was Monday and her routine was about to begin. Dani closed her eyes and almost drifted back to sleep. Then she heard the loud knock on the wall. She leaned over and knocked back. In spite of her exhaustion, she got out of bed and walked toward the bathroom to take a shower. "Well, at least Anton isn't mad at me for throwing a fit last night. He must think I'm going crazy!" she said. She drew the shower curtain back and turned on the water. Or did he really know something and didn't tell me? I wonder if Ema confided in him. Questions were floating everywhere and with limited time she had to push herself harder to get ready. This morning, she was on a mission to interrogate the manager of the bank.

Dani wanted to check out the authenticity of the passbook or find out if it was just a bad joke.

Over an hour later, Dani was sitting on the bus as it headed up the street to the cemetery. She stopped off to see Paige at the flower shop, and walked up the grassy knoll. The weather was starting to cool down a little. From the distance she could see that Estelle was sitting with a heavy blanket wrapped around her slumped shoulders. Dani sat down and dusted off the plaques with her hand. She placed three beautiful daisies on each marker. Tucked in her backpack were the passbooks and a small brown bag Anton had left at her front door. She took everything out and placed them next to her mother's flowers. Then she stared at her mother's name on her stone and started spitting out questions. She knew she wasn't going to get any answers, but she just needed to hear herself verbalize her anger. "Is your name really Vaduva or is it Silivasi? Should I search by the passport or the voucher name? I went to the bank this morning and they confirmed that all the money was still there, plus more in interest that accumulated over the years. Why didn't you tell me about this trust account? What were you hiding? If this money was yours, why did we constantly struggle for pennies just to survive? I don't get it. I really love you, but I feel like I don't know you anymore," she said loudly and with resentment.

Dani exhaled a deep breath and sighed. Listening to the breeze sweep through the trees, she removed the peach from the bag and took a bite. The juice started to run down her chin. Without thinking, she wiped it with the sleeve of her sweater to keep it from dripping all over her shirt. She smiled when she saw a turkey and Swiss cheese sandwich and a cup of potato salad in the brown bag. That was her favorite kind of sandwich, and she would order potato salad over coleslaw any day of the week. How did Anton know so much about her, and why did he even care? Recently, Dani's life seemed to do nothing but hinge on a thousand unanswered questions—some so meaningless and others life changing. So many that she would probably never have answers to. Would she continue going through life without even knowing if her mother—was really her mother? That was the big one.

The bank couldn't answer any of her questions. They confirmed that she was definitely the beneficiary of the account that was controlled in a solid trust. The way her mother had set it up, she would not owe any taxes, and she could use as much or as little she wanted by just using a withdrawal slip. This all seemed so insane—in the span of twenty-four hours she had gone from rags to riches. It was inconceivable for her to even think that, at her fingertips, she had access to so much money. Her finances had always barely stretched from paycheck to paycheck. Most of the time she couldn't even pay all of her bills. How quickly one's life could change.

She grilled the young man in the bank over and over. His answer was always the same. He could not legally give her any answer as to where the money came from, other than a large bank in the Cayman Islands. Then, he explained that the Cayman Islands was now one of the only places where anonymity resides over financial laws. In short, it meant that the donor of all the money was to forever remain nameless.

Dani raised her voice and pointed a shaking finger at the young man. "But where did my mother get this money from? Can't you help me at all?"

He casually shook his head. "Only she can tell you, ma'am."

Dani's voice raised another octave. "She's dead!" She wanted to grab both of his lapels on his suit jacket and shake him until his teeth rattled, but she didn't want to go to jail for assault, either.

He smiled very condescendingly. "I understand that. But we are not able—nor are we responsible—to tell you anything."

Dani had walked out of the bank more frustrated than she had ever felt in her entire life.

Now, she was sitting here in a quiet cemetery pounding her mother's headstone and yelling. "Why did you do this? What were you thinking? I really hate you right now. I hate you...I hate you...I hate you!" she screamed.

Suddenly, a strong, raspy voice said, "Come here, child. What seems to be the problem today? Lordy be! You look like you're having one hell of a crappy time, and throwing a big ol' hissy fit, for what? Dear Lord, what seems to be your problem? Look at the beautiful sky with all those billowy clouds." There was a slight pause and then Estelle said, "She ain't going to answer you and there ain't no way she can change anything! So why are you yelling at her?"

Estelle sat in the same old vinyl beach chair with a very colorful umbrella—attached to the arm of it, staring at Dani with wide, honest eyes.

Dani stood up, picked up her backpack, and walked over to Estelle. Her red face spoke a thousand words as she sat down on the grass.

Estelle shaded her eyes with her hand, trying not to look into the sun. "Come a little closer. These eyes are having a hard time seeing you today!"

Dani move over right next to the chair and put up her arm to block the sun from Estelle's squinting eyes.

"Thank you. Now, tell me why you're so damn mad at your poor mother! What the hell could she have possibly done? Why...I remember when your son was buried here. She was at your side every moment, trying to absorb your pain. She was your pillar of strength. Who the hell did she kill to make you this mad?" She shook her head slowly and laughed.

Dani looked away and whispered, "I was going through—"

"Speak up, child! These old ears are almost deaf!" Estelle roared.

Dani turned toward her, grinded her teeth together, and said loudly, "I went into my mother's closet to clean it out and I found a box. I found old pictures of her and a few other people, a passport, and some passbooks! Why didn't she ever share the pictures or the passbooks with me? Why did she make me wait until she was dead to find them? What was her point?"

Estelle leaned forward and touched Dani's head with her old, shaky fingers. "Because she had her reasons, child. Mothers always have their reasons. She knew what she was doing. She probably thought this might cause less pain for you. She didn't want to answer any of those questions you want to throw at her! Maybe those questions were too painful for her. Or…maybe they would be too painful for you. It might have been her method of protection. Besides, she wasn't exactly planning on dying, was she? She could've been fixing to tell you."

Dani looked up at Estelle. "I know nothing of her past. All those pictures really scare me. What if one of those men in the photos is my father?"

"Sometimes things are better left alone, without stirring up the old hornets' nest. What are a few pictures worth, anyway? And what if it was your father? Where the hell has he been? That was her lifetime of bad memories—not yours. Don't you think she had enough in her life and she didn't want to burden you with it?" Estelle clicked her tongue and shook her head. "Was she a good mother who was their protecting you from the minute you were born? Did she give you lots of love and take care of you the very best she could? Why are you so…angry?"

Dani pushed the passbooks at Estelle, and said, "We lived like paupers most of our lives, and the whole time she had all this money." She waited for Estelle's trembling fingers to finally get the one on top open. "Why didn't she use it? Why did she put it away? What the hell...was she thinking?"

Estelle looked at the amount in the passbook without flinching, and puckered her lips. Then she handed it back to Dani. "You don't look like a pauper. Did you always have food on the table? Did you always have clothes on your back? Did I hear you say you had a college education? Gawd, child, you have no idea what poor really is!"

Dani took a deep breath and exhaled. "But she could have used the money to make her life easier. She didn't have to work two jobs just to make ends meet. She killed herself doing that. She had a fucking heart attack at work and I wasn't even there to say goodbye." Dani's head hung down, and she began weeping in pain.

Estelle's fingers lifted her chin up. "Your mother died because sometimes God has a plan for us. The only pain she constantly endured was watching you come to the cemetery every day to see your son. Maybe it was God's way of giving your son company. Or maybe she didn't want him to be alone."

Dani looked at Estelle with her tearstained cheeks. "Where did she get all this money? Why didn't she use it, or at least tell me?"

When Estelle smiled, you could see her years of wrinkles line her face. "Maybe she knew that the two of you worked well as a team, and the only person you had in life was her. Maybe she feared you would not make it alone, or make enough money to support yourself when she was gone. Maybe this was her gift to you when she died. After all, she knew you were going to find it eventually. Don't you think?"

Dani looked surprised at the analogy this wise old woman had been preaching to her. "I guess that is one way of looking at it."

Estelle patted Dani's hand. "It's the only way to look at it. You will never know why or how, so look at it as her parting gift to you. This nest egg was to help you make it through those tough times when she isn't here."

Dani looked at Estelle, appreciation in her eyes. "You are so wise, Estelle. I was so blinded by anger that I never considered of any of that. Thank you for giving me a different perspective."

Estelle smiled. "God has me here for a reason. Don't you think?" She sat back in the chair and closed her eyes, then she mumbled, "You need to scoot. You will be late for your bus to take you to work."

Dani reached into her backpack and took out the paper bag. She placed it in Estelle's lap. Estelle had fallen asleep and Dani bent over and kissed her forehead. "Thank you, dear lady, for taking the edge off of my anger. A lot of what you said made a lot of crazy sense. I was too angry to see any other side. Maybe my mother wanted me to have it after, because she knew I would be struggling. Maybe my mother didn't want me to know who was in those pictures because it was not important, and neither was her past. Maybe she was a wise old owl like you. Maybe…."

Dani stood up and walked down the knoll. Her steps were not as weighty as they were when she left the house in the morning. For some she was meant to have this conversation with Estelle. And for that same reason, Estelle's viewpoint seemed to calm Dani down. As Dani stepped onto the pavement, and was ready to walk through the gates that protected the cemetery, she turned around and took a final look at the sweet lady sleeping in her vinyl chair. With a sense of liberation, she brought her hand to her lips, and blew Estelle a kiss.

Steph was in the bathroom, having just got finished changing into her work clothes when Dani opened the door. Steph walked over and hugged her friend, then she pulled back and looked into Dani's sad face. "Gosh, you've been so quiet and on edge lately, and I've been so worried about you. Especially when I called and called this weekend. How come you never picked up the phone?" Dani could see tears gathering in Steph's eyes.

"Come here." Dani took her friend's hand and starting pulling her out of the bathroom. They walked down the hall. Then she surprised Steph and dragged her out the back door and into the alley. "I need to talk to you privately, and I don't want anyone else to overhear."

Dani walked towards another building and took a seat on a makeshift bench the staff constructed from cement cinderblocks and a large board. It was a peaceful place where the waiters could take a five-minute break. Dani nudged Steph to sit down, and then she said quietly, "This past weekend was very difficult in so many ways! I went through my mother's stuff this weekend. I found a box and inside were pictures, a passport, and passbooks...."

"Pictures and passbooks from where?" Steph looked confused.

Dani leaned over and took out one of the passbooks that she had stuffed into her bra after she left the cemetery. She handed it to Steph and watched her open it—then waited for her reaction.

Steph gasped so loudly the echo could be heard down the alleyway. "Oh my god! That is a hell of a lot of money! Where the fuck did all this come from?"

Dani slowly shook her head. "I don't have a clue. Here...look...." She took the passbook from Steph's hand and opened it to the first page. "For twenty-five years my mother put three thousand dollars a month away without me knowing."

Steph's eyes were like saucers. "Where did she get it from? Are you sure this isn't an old book or just a sick joke? That's—holy cow!"

"I went to the bank this morning and every penny was there, and they said the account has been accumulating interested ever since it was opened. It's well over a million dollars right now." Dani shrugged her shoulders.

"A million—" Steph cried out.

Dani frowned and interrupted. "I've been trying to figure it all out. I found some pictures and an old passport with a different last name. There were only five very old and faded pictures, and I don't have a clue as to who they were with the exception of one. I think one is my mother when she was eighteen and lived in Romania. The others look to be taken about the same time. The passport was for her trip to America."

Steph still looked like she was in shock. "Maybe we should try to research it."

Dani smiled and hugged her friend again. "Of my few friends, I knew you would be levelheaded and help me find what this is all about."

Steph laughed. "I love a good mystery, and I love puzzles! This is definitely both!"

Dani maintained the seriousness of her conversation. "I don't want anyone to know. And I'm not going to touch a dime until I find out if it really is mine and not from something my mother got herself tangled up in."

Steph looked confused. "What could your dear, sweet mother ever be tangled up in? She was as pure as newly fresh snow!"

Dani tittered. Then she asked, "What are you doing this weekend? Why don't we begin to search for some answers?"

"Okay…you sure you want to do this? What if you find something that will blow you away?"

Dani stood up and grabbed Steph's hand and pulled her up too. "I want to find the truth."

"It could be painful…."

Dani tucked the passbook back into her bra. "Not any more painful than not knowing."

chapter twelve

DANI WALKED DOWN THE HALL IN THE CHILDREN'S
ward and put her things away in her designated locker in
the nurse's room. No one was at the front desk, but that
wasn't unusual. It could sometimes get really busy in the
ward with the children, especially in the evenings. Dani
came back out and started to look around. The hairs on
her neck stood straight up when she heard a light
sobbing sound coming from one of the rooms. Slowly,
she walked toward Tessy's room and the weeping got
louder. Not sure what was going on, she stood at the
door and saw Malaya sitting on the bed comforting Alva
who was crying in her arms. Dani stood there for a
moment and then she quietly said, "What's going on?"

Both the night nurses looked up and Malaya
stated, "Our little princess died a few hours ago."

Dani gasped as she moved toward the two ladies.
With a look of disbelief she asked, "What do you mean
she died? I thought she was doing better. Dr. Cal was
waiting for the confirmation from the clinical study
program she was going to enter." Dani looked around
with panic in her eyes. "Where's Lola?"

Malaya said, "She's with the parents downstairs.
They wanted to sit with their daughter and Lola wanted
to make sure they were okay."

"I just don't get it. What happened to Tessy? Just
the other day, Tessy and I were jumping rope and
playing hide and seek. She was fine!"

Alva put her head down and began to cry harder. Malaya's next words were low and slow. "Her little heart gave out on her. Her mother called the front desk and said she was having a hard time breathing. I called Dr. Cal and he immediately came down. He tried everything to save her. This place was swarming with doctors and nurses from the ER and cardiology. She just couldn't hold on."

Dani tried not to stumble over her words. "Where's Dr. Cal? I know he's angry at the pharmaceutical company for prolonging that clinical study. And now, he must be really hurting. Tessy had a special bond with everyone on this floor. Just like Levi." Dani's eyes filled with tears. She knew Levi had held on for as long as he could, and in the end, she told him to let go.

Dani's heart was breaking again and the nurses were having a hard time too. They always did. Tessy was just one of all those special little ones that the nurses wanted to see survive. Her wonderful character and courageous personality were only a few of the endearing traits Tessy carried around the ward to the other children. She was always there to encourage them and keep them moving in a positive direction.

Dr. Cal spent most of his time shuffling between the pediatric oncology ward and fighting with Congress about greedy companies. The drug companies were refusing to produce the lifesaving drugs and the insurance companies would not pay for them. His anger had led to his second career in protesting. He wanted those medications for his young patients and half the time he had to fight hard for them. It took him five months of fighting with the pharmaceutical company to produce the drugs Tessy needed. The insurance company told her parents they would not pay for the infusion drug, so the pharmaceutical company finally agreed to have Tessy and two of his other young patients participate in a clinical study. He was hoping, and almost depending on it, to save her precious life.

"I'm going to look for Dr. Cal. Do you have any idea where he is?" Dani asked.

"He's taking this very hard. It's the first time I actually saw him lose it in front of everyone. He just ran down the hall pounding on the walls. I don't know where he went." Malaya sighed.

"He has to be somewhere in this hospital." Dani started walking around the ward, checking all the rooms and places he might hide. Then she hit the button on the elevator. She knew where she went when she needed some space. Dani was never a religious person and her mother never forced it on her. Ema didn't practice her religion, either. But on occasion, when things got tough, Dani would walk down to a neighborhood church and sit for a few hours and purge. Dani never realized why until she was faced with decisions and tribulations that led her into seeking comfort. There was a small room in this hospital for those who needed to feel closeness to God. The chapel was a glass-enclosed room with a table of lit candles, a simple statue of Christ, and a few rows of ornate wrought iron pews. The room was a sanctuary for those who needed to pray and make peace with their unbearable situations. It always gave Dani a place to hide. And Dr. Cal always knew where to find her.

The elevator door opened and she walked down the short hall to the door. She stood there for a moment and took a deep breath and then exhaled slowly as the lump in her throat began to grow. She didn't have any consoling words, yet she knew he needed comfort. Dani was too caught up in the moment—herself. As her hand gripped the door handle, her mind spun in circles. What was she going to say to him? How could she ease his pain? How deep did that cut into his soul?

With all her might, she wrenched the door open. Candles lit the room in a soft glow. Beautiful flower arrangements were sitting on pillars on each side of the table. In the middle of the table was a striking bronze statue of Christ on the cross. Dr. Cal was sitting on the first pew with his head hung in his hands. Dani watched for a moment as his shoulders slowly shook and the sound of his crying humbled her. She was suddenly afraid to break into his grief. Silently and slowly, she ambled over and gingerly took a seat next to him. Without thinking of what she was doing, she did what needed to be done. She placed her hand on his thigh. It startled him and without looking up to see who it was, he rested his hand over hers. They both sat silently for a few moments in the tranquility of the room, just listening to each other breathe.

Finally Dani whispered, "I'm so sorry, Cal."

He turned his head and looked into her sorrowful eyes. "I couldn't save her."

Dani wiped the tears off his cheeks and whispered, "You did all you could. It's not your fault. Life is not fair sometimes. You know that, and so do I. Sometimes there is no preventing the inevitable."

"Every time I lose a child I feel like I've failed. Tessy was so special. She was so loving and her acceptance of what was to come was so brave. I don't know if I could be as strong as her. Especially when I hinge on hope...."

Dani pushed his hair back off of his brow and said, "You're much stronger than all of us. You give it your best fight for each one of those little children. Most of the time, they go home to lead productive lives— thanks to you. Then once in a while, God has another plan for them. I know that now—I didn't know it then. And no one could have ever convinced me of that. I thought Levi was just being punished for my stupid mistake."

He took a deep breath to keep from crying. "Why did she leave? Why couldn't she hold on for a few weeks?

I had her enrolled in that study, and I really thought it would save her!"

Dani's mournful eyes opened wide. "How many times did you try to save her?" Dani paused but he remained silent. "I just talked to an old, wise friend today, and she said to me, 'we are all here for a special reason.' Tessy was here for a reason and so are you. I know her parents were thankful that she had you as her doctor and friend. Tessy always let us nurses know you were 'taken.' She always said she was going to marry you when she got older. Levi loved you. You were the only positive male role model in his young life. And I appreciated all the time you devoted to him, as you do with each and every patient."

Dr. Cal looked at Dani. "I don't know if I'm cut out for this job. Days like these make me think about going into research instead of treatment. The pain of losing patients takes a little piece of my heart each time. I remember my mother telling me that. For forty years, she was the best oncologist in her field and I wanted to be just like her. Now I'm questioning myself—all over again."

"You can't only think of the ones you lost. You have to think of all those amazing children you saved. Lots and lots of little ones are here because of you…." She lifted her hand off his thigh and took his hand. "Do you want to stay here or do you want to take a silent stroll around the park across the street? It's a beautiful evening and getting some fresh air would be good. I will show you my little trick to help me survive. We can name one of the stars in the sky after Tessy. Then you will always have her close to your heart. I'll show you which star is Levi's and which one is my mother's."

He looked at her with inquisitive eyes, and without saying a word, he stood up.

Just before they left the room, she said, "It's days like this that give us a true perspective of what life is really about. My mother taught me to focus on the positive...even after she had a longsuffering and sad childhood."

Becky watched as Dr. Cal and Dani walked out the front door, hand-in-hand. She smiled....

Saturday morning Dani was lying in bed thinking of the past week and how much had happened. Dr. Cal and she had peacefully walked around the park together in silence that night. Then she stopped and looked up into the sky and pointed to a bright star. "That's it," she whispered.

Dr. Cal looked up, and for the first time that evening, he grinned. "Why did you pick that one, out of the whole sky filled with stars?" he asked with curiosity.

Dani looked up and beamed. "It's the brightest one up there and it's surround by lots of other little ones. I think it reminds me of her big personality and the charming way she had with all the children in the ward that loved her."

"What a beautiful analogy, Dani." At that moment, Dr. Cal glanced down at Dani with contemplating eyes.

Dani knew she was no match for Dr. Cal, who was flirtatious and chased by all the eligible nurses in the hospital. He enjoyed the string of women who constantly threw attention his way. Dani knew nothing about men and she had this strange feeling he was playing with her—indirectly.

Not giving into his dreamy eyes, she immediately turned around and pointed to two bright stars right next to each other. "That is Levi and my mother. Those evenings when I get down, all I have to do is walk outside and look up into the sky. Then I remember how truly loved I was." She took his hand and tugged him to the doors of the hospital.

For the rest of the week, it was hard for her to go to the restaurant and put on a happy face—but she managed. She didn't let anyone know about her pain from the pediatric ward or Dr. Cal's sudden withdrawal—except for Steph. Each day they took their break out at the bench and talked about life and the ups and downs. Steph's mother was back in the hospital with complications from her diabetes. After work, Steph would take three buses to the hospital across town to visit her. It wasn't the fancy hospital that Dani now worked at, but it wasn't as costly either.

One night when Dani was getting ready to leave, Steph asked, "Would you like to go with me to visit my mother? I bet she would love to see you."

Dani was exhausted, but she replied, "I would love to see Rose."

Steph was happy beyond belief that her friend would take the time to do something so generous. On their way to the bus, Dani walked into a small liquor store. It didn't have much in the way of anything really special to bring to the hospital, but she managed to find a few things. With a brown bag filled with Rose's favorite snacks, and a few magazines thrown in, they took their hour journey to the county hospital.

Dani and Steph sat on Rose's bed talking about the restaurant and the drama queen—Nicole. They laughed so hard at times that tears rolled down their cheeks. Then Dani told Rose about Tessy. When she was just on the verge of tears, Rose called her over to lay down next to her. Dani, at first, felt a little awkward. She had never been that close to any woman except her mother. But rather than insult Rose's feelings, she cautiously laid down. Gently she felt Rose's arm encircle her. Dani closed her eyes, and she remembered how special it felt when her own mother had done that. Ema had always comforted Dani as though she was a baby. The relief of knowing that someone actually cared about how she felt and wanted to make her feel better was overwhelming. Dani wanted to stay wrapped up in her arms forever, but knew it was just a pipedream. Rose wasn't her mother, and no matter how good it felt, it was just one of those momentary things in life that makes you feel good—then disappears.

When they finally left, Dani and Steph quietly walked to the bus stop. The silence was deafening and they both were lost in their own thoughts.

Steph faintly said, "Thank you for coming to see my mother. She loved having you there. I could see it in her eyes."

Dani patted her hand. "Thank you for inviting me. She made me feel so comforted, and I appreciate that."

Steph asked, "Are we still on for tomorrow? I really want to see if we can find out any information."

Dani perked up. "Of course we are on! I want to find out anything we can too! We can go to the library and use their computers."

The next morning Dani's alarm went off. With great anticipation, she stepped down off her bed and into the kitchen to start a pot of coffee. With eyes still red, she decided today was only going to be spent finding out new information. She went into the bathroom and showered and put on some light makeup. Then she combed her shiny, dark hair into a ponytail. Once she was done in the bathroom, she went into her room, picked out some jeans, a fashionable blouse, and some sandals and headed back into the kitchen to have her coffee. On her second cup, there was a knock on the door. Dani smiled as she ran to the door to open it for Steph.

Dani swung it open, and her smile disappeared and became a look of surprise. "Morning, Anton. I'm surprised to see you this morning."

He smiled. "I can see that! I don't mean to disturb you, I just heard you knocking around in the apartment, and I was on my way down to the deli. I thought maybe you might want to join me."

At that moment, Steph walked down the hall and stood next to Anton. "Morning, Anton. You're up bright and early."

Anton turned to look at Steph and grinned. "Same here, Stephenee. I can see exactly why Dani was up early today. You ladies aren't working, so you must be doing something special on this beautiful day."

Dani quickly injected, "We are going to see if I can find anything out about what I found. There has to be someplace or somewhere I can get information on the Internet."

A slight frown crossed Anton's face. "Why create more grief for yourself, Dani. Haven't you had enough? Let it go…."

Dani looked surprised. "How can I just walk away from the clues my mother left me? Maybe her whole idea was to have me find the answers. And don't I deserve to find out about her past? Even if it means more pain. I am the only one left in my family of two. Wouldn't it be nice if I could discover distant relatives?"

Anton shuffled his feet, looking a little agitated. "Why open a can of worms? Why set yourself up for disappointment? Why not let it go?"

Steph touched Anton's arm. "I think, as a young woman, Dani needs to do what she feels right with. If we don't find anything then she knows she has tried. Our generation is not so quick to hide the past under the rug."

Anton was quick to announce, "What makes you think something is 'hidden?'"

Dani smiled at Anton. "Thanks for the offer of breakfast at the deli. It sounds so good...maybe next time."

Dani took Steph's hand and brought her into the apartment. Anton stood there with a disappointed look on his face.

Dani shut the door and turned toward Steph after they reached her living room. She said quietly, "Sometimes I feel like he tries to be my father! He's old, has very few friends, and these past few months he's been worried about me all of the time."

"Oh, Dani, don't be so hard on him. He really is a nice man, and he does care about you...you're very lucky he lives next door."

Dani sighed. "I know you're right. And I know he means well. I just feel like he is taking up where my mother left off. Sometimes I need to find more patience, especially this week. Right now, all I want to do is see if I can find anything about those items in my mother's box!"

Steph smiled at Dani, and said, "Okay...let's get this show on the road!"

chapter thirteen

"OKAY, SO WE TRIED LOOKING UP BOTH NAMES ON THE passports and came up with very little. The only thing we could find was your mother's father's name and his sister she lived with. But that didn't do us a lot of good, because he's dead; and we couldn't find anything on Maria," Steph said, sitting back on the couch and sipping her iced tea. They had spent the day researching everything they could. Then they walked to their favorite little hamburger dive with the best cheeseburgers in town. They carried the to-go order back to Dani's apartment and sat on the couch with their chocolate malts, fries, and greasy cheeseburgers. Dani licked her fingers for the last time and sat back on the couch.

Dani hugged her knees with both arms and laid her head in the crook of her arms. "My mother seldom mentioned her family. She only saw her father once in her eighteen years. He never wanted anything to do with her—it was just a fluke run-in one day. When her mother died giving birth to her, he must have really hated her. Isn't that pathetic? A father who abandons his newborn daughter," her voice shook.

Steph was quiet and looked very pensive for a moment before she asked, "Why didn't you ever tell Levi's father about him?"

Dani sat silently as she thought about what led to that difficult decision. "I met him on a whim at the restaurant. You remember that night? You thought he was handsome and charming, and Nicole hated the fact that he approached and pursued me." Steph nodded her head. "He plied me with charm and played me for a stupid fool, until he got what he wanted—a one-night stand. Only I was too smitten and naïve to see it then. I didn't know what I was doing. I was young and inexperienced and he saw that vulnerability. I was perfect prey and he probably did this to so many unsuspecting woman as he traveled all over the states with his job. God only knows how many children he has scattered around."

Steph sat back and asked, "But don't you think he deserved to know?"

Dani's eyes opened wide. "Do you think he would have believed me if I told him he was the first? Or do you think he would have laughed in my face, and called me a whore? Besides, I suspected he was probably already married with children." She paused. "And I didn't want to hear his excuses or have Levi go through any of that. It was one of those things that was best left alone. Levi was better off knowing, at the time, that his father was a war hero who lost his life protecting his country."

"What would you have done had Levi lived? How would you have dealt with that? He may have wanted to find out more about his father later in life. Eventually, he would have found out that you lied."

Dani looked at Steph with tears in her eyes. "That's a moot point now. He didn't know. At the time, I didn't want him to feel that pain of knowing he was unwanted. Did he die because I was being punished by God for lying...one never knows."

"You didn't have a father. How was it for you growing up?" Steph questioned.

"Painful...."

"What did your mother tell you about him?"

"Not much. She said she found out she was pregnant and he couldn't marry her, so she took the first boat to the United States to start a new life and to have me."

"Was that all she told you? Nothing else?"

Dani nodded

"How sad for her, to be nineteen and go through that alone."

"I watched my mother for years deal with the heartbreaking sadness that came from being abandoned. I heard her cry at night when she thought no one was listening. I felt that aching need whenever we went somewhere and there were fathers and daughters together. She never spoke a word or mentioned his name. And I will never know the reason why. It was something my mother hid from me my entire life. Was it right? But it was her decision. And I was okay with it until I opened the box the other day and found the photos and money. Inevitably, there is something more to my story. Someone took the responsibility by sending money. Maybe he did have a sense of right and wrong. Levi's father walked out that night, never to look back or give a damn about that naïve waitress he used and discarded. I had to give my son something more solid to hold on to. So, I gave him a hero."

Steph watched agony surface as Dani's tears spilled over. Then she asked, "Do you think one of those pictures is of your father?"

Dani considered it for a moment. "I don't know. But he could not have been much of a man to let my mother take his child across the world by herself—whatever the circumstances."

"What if the pictures have substantial meaning?"

Dani shrugged her shoulders.

Steph sighed. "Then why are we here spinning our wheels?"

Dani began to spit out questions a mile a minute, like bullets in a gun. "Because there could be another side of that coin. What if my mother took me without him knowing? What if he didn't even know I existed and she kept it a complete secret? What if I'm really not her daughter and she kidnapped me from that wealthy family she worked for? I could 'what if' it to death just thinking about a hundred different scenarios."

Steph laughed. "Yes, you could. All I know is that two and two does not add up together right now. Why was your mother given the money and by whom? Was it support for you? Was it 'shut-up' money to keep her quiet? Maybe he really cared and he was married? Or maybe it's something more sinister?" Steph made a scary sound after the word, 'sinister.'

Dani started to laugh. "Well, this is where we become the female sleuths that try to fit all the puzzle pieces together."

Steph shook her head and asked, "How? There are too many holes in this cheese!" She sighed and squared her shoulders. "We dig deeper…into the Romanian archives. I just love this new age of technology. We found a list of wealthy businessmen in the area. Now, during the next week, we have to research each one on the computer and see where that takes us." Steph paused for a moment. "I kind of like the investigation part. We may find out some interesting things in your past."

"Look, whatever we find or don't find, at least I know I tried." The two friends sat up on the couch and did a high-five. Dani had a long list in her hand and she was determined to find out if any of those families had pictures in the local newspapers or magazines at the time her mother's pictures were taken so they could compare them.

Steph sat forward and asked, "Do you want me to go with you to Tessy's funeral tomorrow?"

Dani looked pained. "No, I can handle it. I want to spend a few minutes with Levi, my mother, and my dear friend, Estelle. Then I will meet you at the restaurant. I sincerely appreciate you asking. Thanks, Steph!"

"I know you're a strong woman, but sometimes it helps to have a shoulder to lean on. And you know I am always here."

"I'm sure the nurses will be there and so will Dr. Cal. This was a hard blow to our ward and the hospital."

Unexpectedly, there was a knock on the door. Dani looked surprised as she jumped off the couch and ran to open it. Anton was standing there with a brown bag in his hand. "When I went to the deli I got a few extra chocolate chip cinnamon rolls this morning. I knew you girls would need a spike of sugar after a long day of investigating." He held out the bag.

"Come on in, Anton. And thanks for the rolls! Steph and I just downed the best damn gooey cheeseburger and malt, and I couldn't eat another damn thing! You want one, Steph?" She lifted the bag and shook it.

Steph shook her head, rubbed her tummy, and laughed.

Dani walked over and placed them on the coffee table and said, "Have a seat, Anton. How was your day?"

He started to laugh and replied, "Same old boring Friday. I came to see if you found out anything? Did you get any leads on the photos or the passbooks?" He lifted his brows with curiosity.

Dani pursed her lips and shook her head. "No, but we came home with a list of names and we are going to research them this week."

"What kind of names? Family or individuals?" he asked.

"Both. They were wealthy businessmen in the area my mother lived," Dani answered.

"Oh? Can I see the list? I might know one or two. I mean, I used to live in Romania. Not near your mother, but who knows, maybe I might recognize someone." He smiled.

"Sure. That would be helpful if you did." Dani got up and took the folder off the kitchen table and came back. She took out two sheets of paper and handed them to Anton.

As Anton slowly went down the list, his facial expression did not show any recognition. His eyes focused on each paper and he finally looked up. He handed back the papers and said, "I didn't recognize anyone I might have known. I guess my circles weren't that big."

"Oh, too bad. We're both going to spend some spare time looking each family up. Maybe there might be some photos in their archives. I hope we find something. We are very curious now."

"Maybe they are just your mother's family. Do you have their last names?"

"With the passport and travel voucher, I don't know what her last name is."

Anton looked at the girls and got up from the couch. "Well, I'm glad you had a productive day, including having that 'gooey' cheeseburger!" He laughed. "Would you like me to drive you to the cemetery tomorrow? I know you have the little one's funeral. I don't mind."

"Thanks for the offer, Anton. Steph offered too. I just want to do my routine and take the bus and stop off at the flower shop and try to stay as normal as I can. It's going to be a tough day."

Anton walked out the door, and Steph got her things and walked toward the door as well. Dani handed her one of the rolls and smiled. "Rose might like this! Thanks so much for the great day. It was crazy and fun. I will see you tomorrow at work."

Dani was walking down the street, toward the cemetery, with a big bouquet of flowers in her hand. In her backpack she had one of Levi's favorite stuffed animals she had saved from the box. That meant a lot to Dani. When Levi was buried she let everyone put something into the casket. Dani tucked in a picture of her mother, her, and Levi when they were at Disneyland. They were standing with Captain Hook and Peter Pan. He slept with that picture for months. Every night she read the story of Peter Pan; and once a week, she allowed him to watch the movie.

Today she was also carrying her fairy dust. It really wasn't fairy dust, but after watching Peter Pan sprinkle dust on children so they could fly, Levi had pleaded with Dani for some. One afternoon, she went to a nearby arts and crafts store and bought a few different colors of glitter and a small green bottle. She poured the glitter in the bottle and brought it home claiming she was given 'fairy dust' by Peter Pan himself. Levi loved his 'fairy dust.' The day he was buried she took out that little bottle and sprinkled him. With tears sliding down her mother's face, she smiled tremulously through her tears and said, "He can fly now!"

As Dani walked closer toward the gate of the cemetery for the funeral, she noticed a man standing alone on the bottom of the hill. He was dressed in a dark suit and his hands were in his pockets. She wondered if it was someone for the funeral or just a Saturday afternoon visitor. Dani was used to going on Sunday when the cemetery was empty. When she finally approached the bottom of the knoll, she recognized Dr. Cal. He was standing in front of a small fountain that allowed people to wash their hands. She tapped his back, and he turned around.

A smile lit up his face and he gave her a casual hug. "I thought I would wait for you here and we could walk up to the building together."

Estelle watched the exchange from the distance. She nodded her head in acknowledgement of the two young adults and waved. But they didn't notice her.

"That's very kind, Cal. But I would like to visit my mother and Levi while we have a few extra minutes. And say hello to Estelle." Dani pointed. This time Estelle waved even harder and Dani noticed and waved back.

"I'd like to join you, if I could? I'd like to say hi to Levi. He was my best friend." Dr. Cal winked.

Surprised and delighted, Dani nodded her head and they started to walk up the hill together. When she got to the top, she sat down where she always did, took out a cloth and wiped the plaques. She took out two beautiful flowers from the bouquet and placed one on each plaque. Dr. Cal sat down and watched as she meticulously did her routine. When she looked up she saw that Estelle's head was hanging on her chest. She was sleeping and taking deep, even breaths.

"I'm sorry, Cal, that you have to go through this with your patients. It's got to be so hard."

"It is. But I knew that going into this profession. My mother begged me not to go into this field. But, of course, who ever listens to their mother?" He laughed. "If I save just one, then I win!"

"And you do. I see lots of them walk out of the hospital." Dani turned and looked at Levi's plaque and touched it gently.

"His cancer was too aggressive, Dani. I tried everything. You know that, and so do I. But we gave him an extra year and he got to do some great things. The same as Tessy."

Dani turned her head away as a tear slid down her cheek. Dr. Cal touched her shoulder. "Don't cry, Dani."

Suddenly a hard, harsh voice yelled out, "Hey down there! Aren't you going to visit this lonely old lady on this mountaintop? You've been cuddling down there much too long. It's my turn!"

Dani turned back and started to laugh. "Did I ever tell you about Estelle? Wait until you meet her. What a damn interesting character straight out of the thirties!" She stood up and held out her hand to Dr. Cal.

Dr. Cal stood to the side of the brash-looking lady. Estelle was wearing bright red lipstick and a big brimmed hat with wisps of gray hair poking out. "Dear God, son! Don't stand off to the side where I can't see that young, handsome face. Step up and let me see who my little girl has with her."

Dr. Cal stepped directly in front of the old lady and squatted down to eye level. "So she's 'your' little girl?" He laughed.

"Damn right she is! Who else does she have in this world? She lost the only two people she had. So, I'll be here in life and death to protect her! Who else is going to take care of her?" She touched his shoulder and looked deep into his face. "Promise me you won't ever let her be alone…."

Dr. Cal chuckled out loud again, tapping the brim of her floppy hat. "I don't think you're going away anytime too soon. You seem just too ornery and pugnacious to leave!"

Dani sat down next to the arm of the chair where Estelle could touch her shoulder and stroke her hair. Estelle loved to show affection, only it was so hard for her to move around once she was in her chair. So Dani always tried to sit close enough for her to physically feel her presence.

In her raspy voice she continued, "Why are you here? Are you here to visit with Dani? Do I know you? I think I've seen you here before. You look familiar and this old head of mine never forgets a face!" His eyes didn't blink as she continued to scrutinize him. "How do you know my Dani? Are you her boyfriend?"

With the boldness of the questions, Dr. Cal lost his balance and fell backwards from his squatting position. Dani began to giggle. Once he righted himself, he said with great candor as he extended his hand, "I'm Dr. Cal. I was Levi's doctor while he was at Barouch Memorial. I don't think I have met you before. Dani works at the hospital with me and my children. We are here today for a funeral of another little one who lost her fight with cancer a few days ago."

Estelle clicked her tongue and waved a finger, then she extended her crippled arthritic hand for a handshake. "I remember where I have seen you now. You come to this cemetery often. I've seen you walking the hills and stopping occasionally to pay your respects. In fact, a few weeks ago you did stop at Levi's grave and tucked something under the plaque. Didn't you?" She shook her finger again, "I may be older than dirt, young man, but my memory rarely fails me...."

Dr. Cal looked away from her scrutiny. A moment later, when he turned back, he said, "Levi told me he loved the beach and watching the sailboats. I found a postcard with a beautiful picture and wanted him to have it. So, when I come up here occasionally to see my children, I like to bring something special."

Dani looked at Dr. Cal, her eyes wide in surprise.

Estelle's deep voice said, "Like I said, I may be old, but I can still remember a face, especially a handsome one like my Harold's! And I see a kind heart as well. I feel comfortable with you already, and that is a big plus in my world."

"Thank you. I can tell your Harold was a very lucky man to have you!"

Estelle ran her hand down Dani's beautiful long hair, and then rested it on her shoulder. "This child has been through hell. I wish I was twenty years younger to be here to make sure she's okay. I know my days are numbered and I just want to make sure she has someone who cares."

Dr. Cal patted Estelle's hand resting on the arm of the chair. "She has lots of friends who care. And as you know, she is a very strong young lady. You don't have to worry."

Estelle inhaled a deep breath, and exhaled. "Thank you, young man. That confirmation means the world to me."

Dani stood up and bent over and gave Estelle a big hug. Dani pushed aside the pieces of hair hanging in Estelle's eyes and tucked them under her hat. It was a gesture of love, and a thank you to a very unique and loving woman. "I will see you next week, Estelle." Then she opened her backpack and took out the brown bag. "It's a delicious chocolate and cinnamon sweet roll from a great deli on Fairfax. Enjoy it for a snack."

Estelle kissed Dani on the cheek, then she looked up at Dr. Cal and said, "She always brings me special treats…don't you be stealing her from me!" Estelle opened the bag and gave Dani a big smile. Then she placed it on her lap, snuggled into her chair, and rested her head back. Gradually her eyes began to close. Dani and Dr. Cal leisurely began to walk toward the building where the funeral was being held.

On his way, Dr. Cal made one quick stop at a small marker that didn't have a name. He took a coin out of his pocket and pushed it deep into the ground. Then he stood up and pointed to the blue sky.

Dani asked, "What did you do?"

"Little Joey loved to collect shiny coins. He was from Mexico and never had much in his life, not even his citizenship. The school raised enough money to pay for the burial, but not for a headstone. That's why it's unmarked. Lola and the girls are having a fundraiser in a few weeks to see what we can do about it. If you were to dig up the ground around that small marker you would find a king's ransom." Dr. Cal laughed. "I have pushed a zillion shiny pennies into the grass for him to enjoy. He was one of my toughest cases five years ago." He paused, and then continued after he cleared his throat. "Joey was a great kid. He never complained, never cried, and loved life with zeal until the end."

Dani looked at Dr. Cal. Then she opened her purse and took out a shiny penny and crouched down. With shaking fingers she pushed it into the soft grass as deep as it would go. "Say 'hi' to my Levi, Joey!"

Dr. Cal took her hand and they walked silently to the building.

Tessy's funeral service was touching and the turnout was more than expected. There was a cameraman with a newspaper journalist doing a small segment for the news. During the service, parents and children were telling stories of their experiences with Tessy, along with the nurses and doctors. There wasn't a dry eye in the room, but there was also a lot of laughter. Everyone had a humorous or outrageous story that they shared with the crowd.

Tessy's parents thought it was very touching when Dani told her story about the 'fairy dust.' She talked about Levi, and his excitement to fly with Peter Pan, and how much the little flakes of glitter would light up his eyes on some of his toughest days. She spoke about the children in the oncology ward. She explained how they loved helping each other, and how very protective they were over those who were having a difficult time as they got sicker and weaker. She brought praise to all the staff and doctors, who were now sitting in the audience. When she walked away from the pulpit, she took out her little green bottle and went to the small casket. Then and there, with her heart heavy with loss, she sprinkled Tessy with 'fairy dust' and said, "Fly with all your angels and enjoy your new life, my sweet Tess."

The silence was overwhelming as she went to take her seat between Dr. Cal and Lola. Dr. Cal took her hand and squeezed it, and Lola leaned over and hugged her. The theme music from Sesame Street began to fill the room. Everyone began to get up and pay their respects to the family as they began to file out of the little chapel. It had been a tough day, and now Dani was beginning to wonder if she should have taken the evening off from the restaurant.

"Can I drive you to work, Dani?" Dr. Cal leaned over and asked.

"Thanks for asking, I think I can manage."

He took ahold of her elbow and turned her toward him with a stern look. He was about to say something, when the look on his face softened. "I would really appreciate it if you let me drive you to work today." He said it more as a statement than a question this time.

Dani could see the pain of the day in his eyes, and how much he might need those few minutes in the car to compose himself before he went back to the hospital. "Okay, that would probably be better than me blubbering like a little baby on the bus."

They walked toward the hill to say goodbye to Estelle.

When they got close they noticed Estelle was sleeping and Dani didn't want to wake her.

Dr. Cal smiled and said, "I will have to make it a point to stop by when I come up this way. She's really a fun old lady with a perceptive knowledge of people."

When he pulled in front of the restaurant he stated, "Why don't you take a few days off—I know you've been having a tough time. I'll let the nurses know."

"I think you might be right. I will take off a few days from the restaurant and hospital. Tell them I will be in Wednesday. Thank you for the ride."

He jumped out of the car and came around, opened the door, and helped her out. It was the first time he had done that.

chapter fourteen

DANI WAS HAPPY SHE HAD TAKEN OFF WORK FOR A FEW days. It gave her a chance to focus on herself and the things she needed to do. Those days were filled with exploring Romania on her computer and trying to learn as much as she could about her mother's past. After searching through hundreds and hundreds of families with the surnames of Silivasi and Vaduva, Dani could only surmise that one of those names was Ema's maiden name—and one was fabricated to get her out of the communist country. Trying not to leave any stone unturned, she began with one and tried to collect as much information as she could. She poked through many different government records and different government agencies.

By the end of the second day, she became hopeful that she had found a major puzzle piece. She had to confirm and track down a little more information to verify her findings—but she was positive it was significant. She had come to the conclusion that she had finally found a family who lived in the same town her mother was born. Their last name had been Silivasi. She delved into the town's records, which in those days were limited. It revealed a man with Ema's father's first name with the last name of Silivasi. Shaking with anticipation, she pushed herself further and future into her research, stopping at nothing. She stayed up all hours of the early morning and briefly fell asleep as the sun began to rise.

The records showed that the head of the household was married to a woman who had died in her forties while giving birth to her fifth child. If this turned out to be her mother's family, the records indicated that her mother had two older brothers and two older sisters. Ema was a late-in-life baby born twelve years later than her youngest sister. The most important details that the records confirmed was that the head of household was now deceased too. He had died eight years earlier in an accident. Armed with that information, Dani went into the obituary pages of the local newspaper and searched for the last name around that date of death. Once she found that Romanian newspaper clipping, it was a difficult task of trying to figure out the translation into English. She printed it out and decided the only person who could help her interpret the article would be Anton. With her excitement barely contained, she walked out her front door.

Dani knocked on his door. Although it was past dinnertime, she knew Anton would still be up. With a desperate focus to find some truth, Dani was not going to give into her hunger until she had the one large tidbit of information she had been working on for the whole day confirmed.

Anton opened the door and smiled. "What a surprise. It's nice to see you this evening, Dani. What brings you to my door?"

Dani smiled like the Cheshire cat in Alice in Wonderland. "I think I found something today!"

"Oh...?" He observed her with narrowed eyes.

She was prancing around with excitement. "I think I might have found some information on my mother's father."

Anton's eyes opened wide. His smile slowly disappeared as he took a slow, even breath. "You've been a busy little bee today."

Dani smiled as she waved the paper back and forth like it was the first place prize in some contest. "I think I might be on to something. I just needed you to read the article I found in the paper to see if I hit gold!"

Anton looked down toward the ground, and shook his head slowly. When he looked up, his questioning eyes did not look so happy. "Dani, why are you doing this to yourself? Why would you want to open up this terrible past that your mother closed off years ago? Ema would be rolling in her grave if she knew you were going into places you don't belong."

With the wind knocked out of her sails, and her frown creasing her face, she said, "Why wouldn't I want to know about my past and my heritage? Besides, I would like to find out my family's history and their medical history. There has to be something that ran through our genes that killed my son. What if I get married and want more children? How do I know if it will happen again to another child?"

Anton shook his head again. "Because you will be more vigilant and have a more extensive DNA done to determine that now. They don't need all those absurd health records anymore."

"Why are you giving me such a hard time with this? What difference does it make to you?" Dani turned around and took a step toward her apartment. Immediately, Anton snatched her hand and pulled her inside his apartment. With a small grin, he pointed to the swinging curtains in Mrs. Brodsky's window. "Okay, I can see you are just as stubborn as your mother. What did you find today?" He closed the door and Dani followed him into the kitchen. "Would you like some coffee or tea? Maybe a piece of sponge cake? I got it at the deli today and it's just as good as Bercha's when I lived in Romania."

Dani gave Anton a curious look. "Who is Bercha? You never mentioned a Bercha before."

Anton's face lit up with a big grin. "She was my nanny. And she used to make the best sponge cake."

"You had a nanny?" Dani asked.

"Almost everyone had nannies in my town. My mother was not a very warm or loving person, so Bercha nurtured me through my childhood. Many Romanian women didn't raise their own children in our class structure. Come on, we'll discuss me later...after I see what trouble you got into today! I'll make some tea."

Dani sat down at his dining room table. She took out her notes and the copy of the newspaper article. She watched quietly as Anton prepared the tea and dished out the cake, and came back to the table.

When he sat down, Dani handed him the paper and said, "This was an article in the local paper about my grandfather, I think. Seeing as you read Romanian, I thought maybe you could interpret this for me."

Anton took the paper and his eyes opened wide with surprise. "This is an obituary!"

Dani started to laugh. "And your point is...?"

His eyes were open wide and he let out a deep breath. "I thought you found him!"

Dani nodded her head. "I did! He's just not alive."

Anton inhaled another deep breath and exhaled loudly. Then he pulled out his reading glasses from his pocket on his shirt and put them on. Silently he read it to himself, and then he turned toward Dani. "Yes. He was a local merchant who was in his seventies when he died eight years ago. He has three children and two grandchildren. It looks like he owned a small shop that sold mercantile to the local residents. This could possibly be your mother's father. However, Serghi Silivasi gave her up at birth to his sister, Maria. Didn't you say that?"

Dani nodded.

"These remaining siblings of your mother would probably not even know you existed. That's if they are still alive. The family records said, 'four siblings.' The article said, 'three.' Think long and hard, Dani, if this is a logical thing to do. What would the point be other than they could challenge any of your inheritance your mother left you, claiming it as theirs."

"I really don't care about them as much as want to see if I can find my father. If I need to go through these steps to get to him…and I won't stop."

Anton rubbed his hands together. "What if your father doesn't want you to know…or doesn't want you in his life? Maybe that money was 'shut-up' money?"

Dani started to get really frustrated at Anton's negativity. "Then he should have thought about that before he got my mother pregnant!"

"You sound hypocritical. You never told Levi's father." His face looked stern and his brows pinched together.

"I was stupid and I'll take all the responsibility for it."

"Maybe your mother was as stubborn as you." He took his final sip of tea.

Dani leaned forward on her elbows and looked directly at Anton. "Well…I'm going to continue until I run out of leads. My next relative is my mother's aunt Maria and her drunken husband who raised her in a different town."

"Just remember, you could be putting yourself in jeopardy."

"I could be doing a lot of things…but when you are completely alone in the world without one living relative, what does it matter and who really cares— except me." Dani stood up and brought her cup to the sink. She was having a difficult time trying to understand Anton's constant discouraging comments about this need to find her roots.

Anton stood up and walked her to the door. "Please keep me informed. I'll be happy to read or interpret for you, anytime."

Dani opened her door. Then she waved and blew a kiss to Mrs. Busybody!

Dani went up to the desk where Lola was distracted with the computer. "I'm off in an hour. Have you seen Dr. Cal at all today? I haven't seen him for days."

Lola looked up sadly. "He's been coming in the mornings and doing his rounds; seems he's had a lot of meetings and stuff going on and is out of here just before you get in. I've been pushing him out the door at times, knowing he needs some personal time to himself."

Dani leaned on the counter. "I get that. He was the one who told me to take some time off."

Lola laid her head on her two palms and said, "He's got a dozen nurses vying for his attention and he blatantly ignores them. He needs a social life! Not just his work."

"I saw him a while ago at Venice Beach with a woman. Is he still with her?"

"Dear lord, you mean that clingy little thing that called here ten times a day? She's long gone!"

Dani smiled.

"Did you by chance see Tessy's parents earlier?" Lola asked, picking up a chart.

"Yes. We went into the waiting room and had a lovely long talk. They want to start a fund that will help the children in this ward and their parents when financial stresses leave them devastated."

"That would be wonderful," Lola replied. "Did you notice the children are very quiet this week and seem terribly fearful?"

Dani stood straight up and reached into her pocket. "Yes, so I brought something special in." She pulled out her little green jar and waved it in the air. "I think I'm going to stir a little excitement tonight and sprinkle some fairy dust on those little sweethearts for Peter Pan!"

Lola smiled. "I think that's one hell of a terrific idea! Maybe we can get them out of their shells and can hear some laughter around here again."

With a lighter step and a smile on her face, Dani entered the room of Gia Sambora. She was one of Dani's favorites. She was seven years old, with a fast and quick wit, infectious laugh, and a positive attitude that amazed everyone. This past week she seemed more sedate and quiet. Her parents had left earlier in the afternoon with her three siblings, so Dani knew she would be alone.

Dani let her eyes adjust to the dimly lit room. She looked at the empty bed and gasped. At first her heart began to beat wildly in her chest, until she realized that Gia was sitting in the chair tucked in the corner of the room. A small light was on and Gia was looking through the pages of a book. Slowly, Dani walked over and sat down on the floor next to the chair.

"Whatcha reading?" Dani asked.

"Fairy tales. My mommy brought the book today. I can't read very well, but I like the pictures."

"Can I see the book for a minute?"

Gia handed Dani the book and watched as she quickly looked through the pages. Then Dani said, "Which story would you like me to read?"

Gia shrugged her shoulders.

"I know." Dani said with a big smile. "I'm going to read the story about the flying fairies. It's kind of like Peter Pan. And when I'm done, I have something really special just for you." Gia's eyes lit up and a smile spread across her face. "Before I do that, let's get into bed."

Dani picked Gia up and carried her to the hospital bed. Carefully she laid her down and crawled up next to her. "Are you ready for a great adventure?"

Gia nodded her head eagerly.

Dani began to read the story with great energy and animation. At times she would tickle Gia's tummy and sometimes she used voice simulations filled with unrestrained spirit. The smile never left Gia's face as she continuously asked questions about the fairies. Dani and Gia never noticed the man standing in the corner watching the two of them together. When Dani was finally done, she took out her little green jar and hid it in her hand.

"Remember the fairy dust in the book that let the fairies fly around the room?"

Gia nodded.

"You have to promise not to tell anybody…promise?" Gia silently nodded. "I was a fairy once, and I brought some of my fairy dust." Dani held up the jar and Gia gasped as her eyes lit up with excitement. "Once I sprinkle you with fairy dust, you have to go to sleep so you can fly with the fairies. Okay…?"

Gia's face lit up with excitement. "I want to fly with fairies…. I promise I'll go to sleep."

Dani hopped off the bed and tucked Gia in. She pulled her covers up and slowly opened the lid and said, "Are you ready…?" Gia nodded. Dani bent over and kissed her cheek, then she took out just a little glitter from the jar and sprinkled it over Gia. "Sweet Gia, go to sleep now so you can fly with the fairies."

Gia turned on her side and closed her eyes. The smile was still on her face when Dani turned around to leave and bumped into Dr. Cal. She nearly tripped over him, but he gripped her shoulder tightly against him and raised his finger over his mouth to keep her quiet. Silently he directed her out of the room.

Once they were outside Dani asked, "How long were you in the room? You nearly scared me witless!"

"I was being selfish. I enjoyed watching you with Gia. She's had a difficult week and it was nice to see her smile again. Thank you. It was beautiful to watch!"

"You don't have to thank me. I do it because these little ones need to feel freedom from their illness sometimes."

He opened up her hand and took the little green bottle. "Do you know where I can get some of this fairy dust? I haven't been sleeping much lately and I could use some." Dr. Cal smiled as he pushed his hair away from his face.

"Sorry, it is only for my little ones. You'll have to find your own wizard to get it from." Dani grabbed it back and tucked it into her hand. "Well, I better be going. I have a bus to catch." Dani took one step toward the door.

"I'm headed home. I had a long day and I had lots of reports that I had to get done. Can I offer you a ride? It's not out of my way and I know you must be tired too, after working your restaurant shift and this one."

Dani rolled the bottle of fairy dust in her hand before she made her decision. "Ok, you win this one. I'm exhausted."

As they were walking to the parking lot, Dani told Dr. Cal that she had been researching her mother's early years, in hopes of finding any information about her family tree in Romania

"I know you want to find some living descendants of your mother, and this is going to sound completely absurd, but maybe you should take a DNA test to see if she was really your mother. After all, didn't you say she left Romania when she was pregnant? Or was she? Or did you sail over with her as an infant? You really don't know anything except what she told you. The both of you have been alone all your lives and there is no story to back any of the things she told you. Anyway, it's something you can confirm, so that's a start."

Dani sat there silently as she thought about what he said. Dr. Cal turned the key and the engine hummed to life. Dani shook her head. "I'm sure she's my mom, but maybe a DNA test could be helpful, you know, to prove to any relative that I was her daughter and I am related to them...."

"It's really quite simple nowadays to do a test. It's just a little harder when the person is deceased. However, it is possible to establish paternity through biological remains or if you can obtain something from the familiar environment like toothbrush, hairs with root, clothes, cigarette butts, envelopes, stamps, or from hospital environments and records. I know your mother was ambulanced to the county hospital when she died. I wonder if they have any of her blood samples?"

Dani looked at him with curiosity lurking behind her eyes. "Do you think they would?"

"It's definitely a possibility."

His car came to a stop and Dani turned to look at him. "Thanks for the ride, and the advice. I appreciate your input."

"Well, if you need help finding the DNA, just let me know."

"Okay...."

"And thanks for the fairy dust. Gia has been really spooked lately. She needed to let it go, and what you did tonight—it helped."

Dani opened the door to the car and slid out. "Thanks again. I'll see you soon."

Dani slowly walked up the short set of stairs to the door into her apartment complex. She slipped her key in and once she opened the door, she turned around to wave. He always waited until she was safely inside the complex. Then she heard the loud roar of the engine and the tires squeal across the blacktop as it sped down the street.

Exhausted, she turned the corner, and sitting in front of her door was a brown bag. Dani grinned and picked it up, then she unlocked her door and walked into her   house.

chapter fifteen

SATURDAY MORNING STEPH CAME OVER AND THEY went down to the local coffee shop. It was a beautiful day, and Dani had dark circles under her eyes from staying up late the night before scanning through records. Now sitting here with Steph, she pulled out the folder and handed it to her.

Steph looked at the information so far and her eyes widened with surprise. "Holy cow! You think you may have found your mother's father. That's...huge! You are taking this really seriously. I can tell with those black circles under your eyes."

Steph closed the folder and handed it back to Dani. "You know Dani, this may sound a little bit crazy, but what if she wasn't really your mother? What if she was a kidnapper and stole you from someone? Oh my god...what if...."

"Stop the drama, Steph." Dani looked very unhappy at the thought. "I know she's my mother. I've never told anyone this, but we share a very similar birthmark in almost the same identical place. She used to tease me all the time. She would say we're fraternal twins twenty years apart and that she took the mark off her and put it on me. Only it came back to her." Dani grinned. "Besides, I look so much like her. I couldn't even imagine what my father looks like."

"Look, if anyone would know—it would be you! You lived with her your entire life. I think what we really should concentrate on is who your dad is."

"I know. Dr. Cal said in the car the other night that I should have my mother's DNA checked, so that if I find my father, it can all be matched up!"

"He's right!" Steph suddenly sat forward and opened her eyes wide. "When were you in his car, was it a d...a...t...e...?"

Dani pointed her finger and shook it back and forth. "No!" Then she sat back and said, "I was exhausted after work, and he was headed home, so he gave me a ride. That's all...nothing more, nothing less...period!"

Steph just looked at her friend. Then she said, "I think...thou dost protest too much!"

"Shut the hell up before I smack you!" Dani laughed.

"Okay, so what is on our agenda today?'

"I thought we would go down to the library. They have all sorts of files on their computers and links to different countries. At least I have a last name and the town that Serghei Silivasi lived in. If he's my mother's father, I know he pawned her off on his sister. I think my mother once called her Maria. She said, she was a poor excuse of a woman."

"Well, you found some great leads to your past. It's like reading an electrifying spy novel by Robert Ludlum! I haven't had this much adrenaline course through my body since that day I kissed little Bobby Tucker in the sixth grade!"

"Ewwww...."

The girls started to laugh.

Eight hours later, they were sitting at a small restaurant sipping a glass of wine and laughing out loud.

"I can't believe that the town's asshole is your grandfather!"

"He's not my grandfather...he was just a sperm donor to my mother's mother who died during her birth. Hell...he didn't even stick around long enough to see her. That was a horrible article in the town paper. Even a worse one when he died in a ditch after drinking all night with the town whores."

"Well, I can see why poor Ema left to start a new life. She had nothing to go back to!"

"But she did. She had three siblings who don't even know she existed! How sick is that? And she had my father who abandoned her."

Steph sat forward with her eyes opened wide. "You really aren't going to drag her siblings into this, are you? I mean, it's been nearly fifty years."

"No. My intentions are not to stir up the pot. I really don't care about them one way or another. I'm just curious about my father."

Dani's alarm went off and she laid in bed for a moment trying to remember her dream. It had something to do with a small town and all the people laughing at a drunk man. Dani turned over and was about to go back to sleep when she heard tapping on the wall. Tap…tap…tap…! She opened her eyes and rolled them as she slowly shook her head back and forth on her pillow. Was Anton taking the place of Ema? Was it a conspiracy or something? Did the two of them plan this? Did Mother ask Anton to look after me if something ever happened to her? The more Dani's mind began to spin, the more questions seemed to pop up from all over. When were these questions going to stop!

Sometimes Dani thought this need of Anton's, watching over her, seemed a little weird. Then again, she realized he probably was a lonely old man who had never allowed anyone to get close. He was like her mother. They both cut themselves off from any socialization or emotional attachments to others—marriage was never in their vocabulary. Once Ema had left Romania, she had made a conscious decision to avoid engaging in any personal connections. Superficial friends from work and around the apartment complex were the extent of her acquaintances—and even those were few.

For the past twelve years, Dani realized that Anton had indulged in similar habits that left him antisocial and alone and much more limited than Ema—he didn't have a job. His closed-off lifestyle was narrow and repetitive. Dani often wondered what had happened to him in Romania and what had created this separation from emotional attachments? What had let him allow Dani and Ema into his reclusive lifestyle? When she asked, he always managed to bypass the subject. After a while, she understood it was just who he was, and how he dealt with life.

Dani sat up and rolled her legs over the side of the bed. She pulled her arms over her head and took a long, solid stretch before she got up. She walked into the kitchen and put on a pot of coffee. She had one hour to get ready and head out the door.

Dani stopped at the flower shop and picked out a small bouquet of flowers. With wildflowers in her hand and her backpack nestled across her shoulders, she walked toward the entrance of the cemetery. She walked up the hill and stopped short when she did not see Estelle. This was the first time in nearly two years that the old woman had not been sitting at her husband's grave. Dani was concerned, but knew that either she needed a break or she wasn't feeling well. Without stopping at Levi's, she continued up the hill. When she stopped at the top, she gasped.

Next to Harold's grave was a newly dug and filled mound. There was no plaque or marker. There didn't have to be one. Dani laid down on the soft mound that had been recently planted with new grass. Her hand slid across the dampness from the early morning dew as it circled over and over the short-trimmed lawn. A tremendous pain buried deep in her heart began to surface and she cried...and cried...and cried. The past few years had taken a toll on her emotional stability. Life had been one painful loss after another without any reprieve. She was all alone and sitting on the edge. And one of her few remaining lifelines was gone now. Where was the fairness? How much more could she take?

As her mind spun out of control, her heart beat like a fast drum. Her hands began to shake as anger set in. Out of the blue, she began questioning her existence. One fist hit the ground and then the other. "Why God? Why me? Why when someone is close to me...you take them away? Why am I being punished? Why Estelle? I needed her...why now?"

Nothing seemed fair in her world. Not her losses...not the money...and definitely not the nameless faces in those pictures. Suddenly, with an anger that even surprised her, she stood up, slung her backpack over her shoulder, and headed over to the information desk in the building yards away. They knew everything. Dani had been there often enough to know she could find out what had happened to Estelle.

By some chance maybe it wasn't Estelle buried there. Maybe it was another family member. Rarely did Estelle ever mention anyone other than her Harold. Dani tried hard to think back through her conversations with Estelle, if she had ever mentioned family or friends. Once she talked about her son and something about her baby girl. Other than that, her chats were always centered on Dani and her advice to keep moving forward. For the past year, she had literally kept Dani from falling off that ledge. And Dani always looked forward to talking to the spunky, coarse, and brilliant old lady. Who was going to save her now?

Dani walked up the dramatic-looking stairs encircling the mortuary. It was a beautiful building where all the services were held. She knew exactly where she had to go. She pulled open the large, shiny mahogany door and walked into the lobby. It was filled with people who were just leaving a service, so quietly, Dani stepped off to the side. Once she gained some composure, she gradually walked over to the front desk. Mary was sitting behind the desk and talking on the phone. When she looked up, she noticed Dani. She smiled and held up one finger. Seconds later she hung up the phone, only to pick it up again. In a low whisper, she spoke into the receiver.

Mary inhaled and exhaled slowly. "Sorry, it's been a tough morning. It's nice to see you, Dani. You rarely come inside to see us anymore."

Dani's eyes were glassy and she didn't smile back. She could see that Mary was patronizing her and Dani did not want to deal with 'niceties' this morning. Abruptly she said, "Where is Estelle? I need to know if she's okay."

Mary's smile disappeared and a frown appeared. "I called Lena up front so she can answer your question."

Dani leaned closer to the counter. Her eyes narrowed as her face turned red. "Why can't you answer my question?"

"I'm not allowed to. Lena will be happy to answer all your questions."

At that moment, Lena Marsden walked up and immediately she saw the anger in Dani's eyes. "Come with me to my office so we can have some privacy."

"Privacy? I just have a few questions. Do you really think we need privacy?" Dani's voice rose a few octaves.

Lena grasped her elbow and steered her toward a closed door. She opened the door and said, "Have a seat, Dani." Then she closed the door behind her. Dani heard the click of the metal as the door locked into place.

Dani sat down in a chair, unclear as to why she was brought into the room. "Where is Estelle?" Dani stood up and turned toward Lena. "I noticed the new grave next to Harold. Is that her?"

Lena pulled some tissues out of a box and handed them to Dani. "Yes. She left us last Sunday."

Dani's eyes opened wide, realizing the magnitude of Lena's answer. In shock, she sat back down and in a low whisper she said, "But I spent part of Sunday afternoon with her after Tess's funeral. Did she go back home?"

Lena dabbed her eyes with a tissue. "No. She passed away moments after you left. She was sitting in her vinyl chair with a peaceful look on her face. She was right next to her Harold and her family."

"You mean right after Dr. Cal and I left?" Dani took a deep breath and let it out slowly.

Lena nodded. "When the home sent their car to get her, the driver came to us."

Dani looked confused. "Why didn't someone let me know? I would have liked to have paid my respects at her funeral. I'm really upset with her family and you for not letting me know."

It was Lena's turn to look confused. "What family, dear?"

"Doesn't she have a son? She talked about him once. She said she came to be with her family."

Lena looked down. "Estelle and Harold moved to California over thirty years ago to be here with her children. Unfortunately, that was after her son, daughter-in-law, and baby girl were killed in a car accident. They are all buried on the other side of Harold. Estelle has been alone for years and we will miss her sorely." Lena handed Dani a tissue and dabbed her own eyes again.

Dani looked stunned. "She never told me that. In the past few years she never told me she had no one. All her family died in an accident?" Dani walked toward the door almost incoherently. "She knew how I felt. She knew where I was coming from…."

Lena asked Dani as she was walking out the door, "Can I call someone to pick you up? I'm very worried about you, dear."

Dani whispered, "No thank you. I'm like Estelle—all alone now. I have no one."

Dani walked out the door, but she didn't know where she was going or what she was going to do. She couldn't go to work. Not today; definitely not when she was feeling more lost and alone than she had ever before. She wouldn't be able to do a good job for her customers, nor did she feel like being around people. She just wanted to crawl into a cocoon and hide forever. She wanted darkness to absorb her. Instead, she walked up to the hill and looked at the names of the markers on the other side of Harold Hinds. Gerald Hinds, Marsha Hinds, and baby Estela were all next to each other. There was a little bench that stretched across Estelle's children. Dani now knew why Estelle came every day to the cemetery. She felt at home amongst her family. She was surrounded by everyone she loved. All she was waiting for—was her turn to join them.

Dani sat down on the bench and began to sob. Eventually, she took out a small blanket from her backpack and covered herself, then she laid her head on the bench. Dani closed her eyes and pulled herself into a fetal position. All she wanted to do was be left alone to lick her deep bleeding wounds that had sucked the life out of her the past few years. Dani felt the warmth of the bench heat her cheek. It was pulling her towards sleep filled with a temporary peace.

Leave me alone, she was wordlessly screaming. Let me stay here in this darkness….

Dr. Cal gently shook her shoulder again. "Dani, I'm so sorry...."

Dani thought she was dreaming when she heard his soft voice repeat itself over and over again.

Dr. Cal sat down next to the bench. He looked around and noticed the new grave. He had seen so much death over the years. Young and old—it didn't discriminate. He thought about his mother and wondered how she would handle this. Would she let it work out on its own? What would she do with this young woman who was on the verge of giving up? How would she pull her back without breaking her fragile psyche?

He lifted his hand and touched her tearstained cheek. "Dani...you can't sleep on this bench all night. Let me take you home."

Dani opened one eye, stared at him for a moment, and then closed it. She remained silent and unmoving.

He whispered, "Don't do this to yourself, Dani. I've seen it too many times, when people lose someone and they fall into deep depressions—never letting go."

Dani did not move. She opened both eyes slowly and barely whispered, "How did you know I was here?"

"Steph called me to see why you didn't show up for work. She covered for you and told your boss you were having a tough time. Then she called me. I was panicking until Lena called and said you were asleep on the bench."

Dani closed her eyes and sighed. "God...why doesn't everyone just leave me alone?"

"Because we all care." He pushed her hair off her face. "Let me take you home. It's been a tough day."

Dani slowly sat up. Then she shielded her eyes from the setting sun. As though she was talking to herself, she mumbled, "I must have slept for a long time."

Dr. Cal nodded. "I'm sorry about Estelle. She was a kind and smart old lady, but she was very sick and she knew it. I'm surprised that she was still with us after I noticed the signs of her failing health."

Dani looked bewildered. "How do you know how sick she was? You weren't her doctor."

Dr. Cal grinned. "Isn't that the point? I'm a doctor. Diagnoses are often just visual. When we sat with her the other day, I shook her hand. It was very cold and clammy. That meant her heart was failing. And then I noticed that her breathing was extremely labored. Her skin was jaundiced, along with her eyes, so her liver wasn't functioning. Do I need to go on…?"

Dani looked away and quietly said, "No…it really doesn't matter, does it? Except that it was a shock when I came to visit her. She's just another person who touched my life and then died. Seems I have the 'Midas' touch of death.' Every time I come close to someone— they die."

Dr. Cal stood up and sat next to Dani on the bench and carefully put his arm around her shoulder. "That's a silly analogy. Life sometimes deals us a stacked deck of cards. Is it fair? No. Can we change the outcome? Not always…." Dr. Cal took her hand and picked up her backpack with the other. "Come on, I'm hungry; and I know this great little quiet restaurant with amazing cannolis! Your pity party is over." He stood and bowed like a knight of the round table. "Sir Lancelot has slayed the dragon and now has an appetite of a thousand men. Will this fair young maiden please come along to refresh her empty stomach?"

For the first time all day, Dani cracked a grin and stood up. Her heart was heavy, and before she left, she turned around and blew a kiss to Estelle and mouthed, "I will miss you, dear lady."

chapter sixteen

DANI AND DR. CAL WENT TO HIS FAVORITE SMALL restaurant with quiet little booths so they could talk. Dani didn't talk much. She was past the point. The pain of the day had settled around her heavy shoulders. But Dr. Cal had a lot to say. He was not one to readily open up his life to others. Privacy was important to him and he kept it that way, both publicly and in the hospital. Yet, there was something intriguing and trustworthy about Dani and the inner strength she possessed. He talked a little about his childhood and his two parents who constantly worked, leaving him with a nanny. Then, he laughed a lot about his college years spent partying and playing fraternity pranks that nearly left him expelled from Harvard.

Dani could relate to Dr. Cal losing his father at an early age. Cal and his dad had become best friends toward the end of high school and his dad visited Cal during college a lot. One day his father was here, and the next day, the newspapers had flaunted his pictures and tragic ending all over their front pages. No one had survived the plane crash and the newspapers and news stations were relentless in their coverage. The detailed images of the crash site were devastating to both his mother and himself. Yet there was nothing they could do to get them to stop. The coverage left them simmering in anger and overwhelmed with grief—the images haunted his dreams still.

His father had been the CEO of a major corporation and frequently on the go traveling all over the world. The crash happened on a stormy night and he was in his private jet headed home to spend Christmas vacation with his family. Cal was driving home from college when it happened. His mother was shattered, and he had to put aside his own grief to help her get through some really tough days. Their lives changed drastically and suddenly he became the head of the family.

Although his mother had a very resilient character, there were times he had to hold her up to keep her from self-destructing. Especially after her diagnosis of cancer a few years later. Being one of the leading cancer specialists herself, she knew what her odds were and what she was facing—and so did Dr. Cal.

He was barely out of his residency when he decided to enter into the same medical field as his mother. When he finally settled on pediatric oncology, his mother was quite stunned. Cancer was a heartbreaking medical field—specializing in children was emotionally challenging every day.

Dr. Cal took a sip of wine and the next words he said to Dani were filled with honesty and candor, "One day a few years ago, a young, beautiful woman with big blue eyes walked into my office. She was filled with an intensity as she demanded a straightforward diagnosis of her son's medical condition. Her mother, who spoke broken English, sat quietly and watched with unsheltered eyes as her daughter demanded answers to almost impossible questions. I did my best to diffuse her anxiety. How or why her son got cancer was not important. What mattered was the course of action that was needed to save his life. I had to explain all the facets that were needed to get him better and hopefully get him into remission. I remember she refused to accept the threat of death looming over him. Life wasn't fair, but she was determined to do whatever it took to save his life and she tried to convince me that the impossible could become possible—only it didn't. I hated myself the day her son died. With all my experience and wisdom, there was nothing I could do to give her son life."

She whispered, "I was so scared that first time I met you. Nothing you said made sense. I was naïve."

He sat back and said, "I get that; and I gave it my best fight. There were new and experimental medications out there that could help save the lives of these children, but the clinical studies were cut back."

"It's not fair," she murmured in a soft voice. "When will this stop? When will our healthcare system stand up for the patients?" she asked.

"It's been my never-ending fight...I don't know if they'll ever come around. But, I have to keep pushing forward so that all these kids can give a fair fight. Sometimes I think I failed them; but I've realized it's 'the system' who's failed them."

"There was nothing that you could do. I knew that."

"But just go back to the parents and try to explain this to them when they've buried their child." His anger showed on his face.

"Where do I go from here?" Dani asked in a whisper. She was fidgeting with her spoon and knife.

Dani had barely touched her meal. Despite his pushing her to eat something, she chose the glass of wine in hopes it would numb her horrible thoughts.

"Just don't use that knife on me!" He tapped his glass against hers.

Dani nodded her head. "I couldn't do that, I would have a lot of angry parents coming after me!"

He looked directly into her eyes when he said, "You are going to have to try to get yourself into a space where you can create some normalcy. That's all you can do right now."

"Normalcy? Normalcy? What the hell is that?" She placed the silverware down on the table and looked at him.

"Maybe I can suggest a good therapist? Or a group that will help you with some of this intense pain?"

"I don't have time for that. I'm too busy working two jobs and researching."

"Researching...? What are you up to now? I hope writing letters to the pharmaceuticals and Congressmen on the list I gave you a few weeks ago!"

Dani looked at the candle that was flickering in the glass on the table. "No...I promise I will get to those letters. I sort of mentioned it before...I found a box full of stuff tucked away in my mother's closet...."

"What kind of stuff?" He looked curious.

"I found five old pictures, a passport, and some bank passbooks."

"Really? I didn't realize that." He drew his brows together and looked curious.

"One picture is of my mother at eighteen. The passport is hers and has a different name. The passbooks...that's what really flipped my boat." She took one out of her purse and showed him.

"Holy smokes...will you marry me?" He teased her with a big grin on his face.

Dani grabbed the passbook away and slapped his hand. "No!" Then she settled back and slightly grinned. "All the nurses in the hospital would slice my throat if I took their favorite doctor off the most eligible bachelor list! Besides, I'm sure your bank account far exceeds this mere pittance!"

Dr. Cal chuckled. "Wow. That was quite an interesting surprise you found in her room. Any ideas as to what all of it means?"

"Nope. Steph and I have been trying to find some answers."

"If you need any help, let me know. I'm pretty good with research!"

They sat the next few minutes in silence; and then they got into his car and he took her home.

He was lucky and parked in a visitor parking spot in the back of the building and walked her to her door. "Do you think you will be okay? Do you want me to come in and keep you company?"

"I'll be fine."

He leaned his arm against the wall next to the door and leaned forward toward Dani's face. The other hand came up and his finger slid down her straight nose. "Sorry about Estelle. I think better days are ahead."

Dani looked down and started to nervously feel for her key. She lifted it out and shoved it into the door lock with tremendous force. Suddenly, Anton opened his front door and stepped out. As if that wasn't embarrassing enough, the curtains across the hall in Mrs. Busybody's front window opened slightly and showed one pair of beady eyes.

Dani sighed. "Evening, Anton. Are you holding down the fort?"

Anton walked over the few steps and reached out his hand to Dr. Cal for a handshake. Then he said, "I can see she is in reliable hands."

Dr. Cal was embarrassed, after a quick handshake, he put both hands in the air and turned them around. "I think they are more surgical than reliable!" He laughed as his face turned red.

Dani leaned forward and gave a big wave to Mrs. Busybody across the hall and suddenly the drapery snapped shut. Everyone smiled.

Dr. Cal nodded his head to Anton and then to Dani. "Well, you folks have a great evening. I will see you at work tomorrow night, Dani."

Dani nodded.

With that being said, Dr. Cal turned and walked toward the hall that took him to the back of the building towards his car.

Anton and Dani stood still for one awkward second until she turned and asked, "Would you like to come in for a cup of tea and I will tell you all about my upsetting day? Dr. Cal kind of rescued me."

"Sure…."

Steph and Dani were sitting on the floor of her living room with papers spread all around them. "Well, what do you think, Steph? Finding records and vital statistics for distant relatives is a big challenge."

Steph began to giggle. "Thank God we found a few websites that allowed us to search family records from different countries without a translator. It's one thing if your family is from the states…."

Dani laughed and threw a pillow at Steph. "What's the old saying, 'you can pick your friends…but…."

Steph grabbed the pillow and laid back on the floor, stuffing the pillow under her head. "Geeez, Dani…could your family have come from a further place or a more remote country?"

"It wasn't my choice—my mother fled her country right after Romania's emancipation from Russia. Communism had ended and western-based values were beginning to take over. I can't imagine what it was like living within a fascist government." Dani sighed. "I'm curious as to why she came to California instead of staying in New York where her boat had docked. Some of this stuff seems so strange. She never talked much about Romania. I used to think we were so tight and now I'm beginning to question that."

Steph sat up and looked at Dani. "I can't imagine being nineteen all alone, travelling across the world by myself and not knowing a soul...then setting up a whole new life inside a dramatically different country, especially with no help? Or did she have help? Coming to California seems premeditated somehow."

Dani turned her head and looked out the window. In a soft voice she said, "How did they know when I was born? Who was that benefactor?"

"Yeah, but the records are filled with such holes, it seems almost impossible to find what we are looking for! Had she come through Ellis Island Federal Immigration Station, we would have a better chance of finding out a lot more information. That's where all the immigrants passed through...their records are impeccable compared to the ones we've been searching through."

Dani sighed. "Well...Ellis Island closed in 1954 and she came to the states way after that. At least we know that much from her passport, her age, and my birth. Of course, providing her passport is correct along with her age. I'm beginning to question everything that was once real to me."

"Technology only came into being the past twenty-five years. Most of the ancestry records were manually recorded in their own language; and the availability of those records, including vital statistics, from other countries may be limited. A few times we ran into some pretty strict privacy laws."

Dani picked up her birth certificate lying on the floor and waved it at Steph. "Thank God the hospital records where I was born are accurate." She placed it back on the pile of papers and continued, "I'm not going to give up yet!"

Steph smiled and touched her friend's arm. "Okay. Next on our list is her wealthy employer."

"I know she was a nanny to three difficult children." Dani frowned.

"Maybe we should begin looking for the wealthy families in the surrounding towns and see what we can find! That shouldn't be too hard, seeing that most Romanians lived in poverty during those years."

Dani picked up another piece of paper and her eyes scanned it.

Steph stood up and stretched her arms above her head and rubbed her tummy. "What I would like to find right now—a big, juicy cheeseburger down at our favorite place down the street!"

"Sounds good to me!"

chapter seventeen

"THANK YOU, BETINA, FOR THE RIDE HOME. TAKING THE bus home this late sometimes scares me," Dani said as she climbed into the truck and sighed.

Betina started the engine and slowly left the parking lot. "You're welcome, sweetie."

"How are the boys? Jamel and Nico are getting so big—so quickly. I bet they outgrow their clothes every few weeks. Kids grow like weeds!"

"Yes, they do, don't they?"

"How's everything else going?" Dani asked. She knew that Betina and her ex-boyfriend were having a tough time.

"I just wish Jeremy would leave us all alone. He shows up to all their games and creates such a problem. I had to place a restraining order on him last week. I don't get it. Why he is so obsessed with me and what I am doing? The relationship is over and he needs to understand that. I don't know if I will ever step into another relationship. This has been awful!"

"Oh no. You don't think that idiot will do anything harmful to you or the boys, do you?"

"I never know what he's thinking in that crazy head of his or what drugs he is strung out on," she said, with worry in her voice.

Betina pulled up in front of Dani's apartment and along the curb.

"Well, you be careful. Too many crazy people out there nowadays." Dani hopped down from the truck. "Thanks for the ride. See you tomorrow."

Dani was exhausted as she walked up the stairs and entered the lobby to her building. It had been a long week. The restaurant was packed to capacity most of the week, leaving her with little downtime. In the middle of the week, she worked a second shift for Steph so she could take her mother to the doctor. Then the hospital admitted four new children and it was a little chaotic for a few days. Dr. Cal had been a little distant. At first she thought she had done something to irritate him. But the second night, all the nurses were complaining about his aloofness.

The night before, she had finally had enough and cornered him in the nurse's lounge. He was staring into space and sipping a hot cup of coffee. She poured herself a cup and sat down across from him.

"The nursing staff and I were wondering if you are okay. Or if something we did is bothering you." Dani was drawing imaginary circles on the table with her index finger, waiting for an answer.

"No. This is not about you guys. This is about me. I have lots going on and I'm just on overload. My mother had some tests taken today and I'm worried about those." He took another sip of coffee. "And...I leave in a few days for Washington D.C. Sometimes I become really angry and apprehensive about the tumultuous pendulum our government swings back and forth on. It's hard to get anyone to promise any allegiance in helping me get any kind of commitment from the pharmaceuticals. While they make billions of dollars from their crappy cold and allergy medications, they could care less about a few sick cancer kids. All I want them to do is just throw me a bone once in a while! Most of the time, I think I'm just beating my head against the wall and hoping things will change—but they never do."

Dani reached across the table and patted his hand. He looked down at her hand on his, then up into her eyes. She whispered, "Think about some of those times you do win. Think of all the progress you make, even if it's little baby steps. Always remember those tiny smiling faces would not be here if you had not forced those clinical studies. You can't give up. You have to keep fighting!"

He placed his other hand on top of hers, and smiled. "Thanks."

"Maybe someday I'll go with you to Washington and kick some ass with you!" She laughed.

"Washington D.C. would eat you alive!" He winked.

Her face grew serious. "Is your mother okay?"

A frown crossed his face. "I hope so. I'll know in a few days. I'm just hoping her cancer didn't come back."

"I'm going to keep my fingers crossed for her."

"Thanks...."

She patted his hand. "Well, I'm going, and on my way to the bus stop, I will throw a kiss to all my little stars in the sky!"

"Do you need a ride home?"

"No. I've just had my jolt of caffeine so I should be fine. But I will hold on to that offer for a rainy day!"

The next morning Dani turned over and snuggled into her covers, refusing to wake up. She had slept like the dead and was still in the same spot where she fell asleep. She took a deep breath and yawned at the same time, nearly choking on the air that was stuck in her lungs. She turned over and laid on her back and stretched. She and Steph were going to hang out today.

She was going to concentrate on the wealthy family she worked for. Dani remembered little bits and pieces of the conversations, but not enough to completely put anything together. She remembered the family lived near Budapest—about fifty miles from where Ema was born. They had servants' quarters that housed a complete staff. The one thing that always stuck out in her mind was that they had had an arranged marriage.

After lying in bed overthinking her situation, she slid her legs over the side and tiptoed into the kitchen to make some coffee. An hour later, there was a knock on the door. Refreshed from her shower, and feeling anticipation, she swung it open.

Steph was holding her laptop and two cups of Starbucks coffee. "Well, I hope you're ready... these prying eyes want to find it all!"

Dani laughed. "Oh hell yes!"

Steph blew by her and put the coffee and computer down on the table and plopped down on the couch. "That was one hell of a work week. Thanks for the cover, Dani. Mom said to give you a hug."

Dani sat down and grabbed one of the coffee cups. "How is Rose?"

Steph gave her a big smile. "The new meds are working great with her diabetes and she feels better than ever. Finding the right meds sometimes is worse than the disease."

"Okay, grab your laptop. We have some serious stuff to do today. We are going to Budapest!"

Hours later, they were sitting on the floor typing away on their laptops.

Dani sat up and stretched her arms over her head. "I'm really excited with what we found today," Dani remarked.

Suddenly, there was a knock on the door. Dani stood up and she opened the door with a big tug, nearly knocking herself over. Anton reached out and steadied her on her feet. "Whoa, young lady. That was a mighty strong pull on that flimsy door."

Dani began to giggle. "Hey, Anton, what's up? Come on in. Steph and I have found some interesting stuff."

Anton followed Dani in, and Steph could see the slight frown cross his face. Steph asked, "You okay, Anton? You don't look happy."

Anton pulled his brows together and gave her a gloomy look. Then he said, "Well, it was such a beautiful day outside and it stressed me to see you lovely ladies wasting your time looking for nonsense, so I thought I would come rescue you. How would you like to go somewhere special?"

Dani narrowed her eyes. "It's not nonsense to me, Anton. I want to find out why my mom left me a box filled with clues."

"Clues for what? A past that was insignificant?"

"It's insignificant to you...but a big part of who I am could rest on those clues. Besides, Steph and I found out something new today." Dani beamed.

"How about I take out for one of the best dinners you've ever had, and you can tell me all about your day over a nice glass of wine. You know how much we Romanians love our wine!"

"Great idea, Anton," Steph yelled from across the room. "I'm starving and it would be nice to have a change of scenery."

Both of the young women's eyes were open wide like saucers as they exited Anton's fancy car. He handed the keys over to the valet and took his folded sport coat off the seat. He slipped it on and began to walk toward the building. "Are you ladies ready?"

"Wow...I've never been in the Beverly Hills Hotel before! Don't you think we are a little underdressed to eat here?" Steph asked, looking down at her jeans and tank top.

Dani looked down at her jeans and oversized T-shirt. "I've always wanted to see what this place looked like, but I knew it would never fit into my budget. The nicest restaurant I've ever been in is the one we work at. Or maybe Crustacean in Beverly Hills, when we took Nicole out for her birthday a few years ago." Dani tugged on the sleeve of Anton's sport coat. "Are you sure they are not going to throw us the hell out of here for dressing so casually?"

He laughed as he looked down at his attire. "I look fine. They won't throw me out. Now, you ladies...." Anton stopped, and stared at the worried faces of his two dinner companions, then he started to laugh. "They would not dare take the chance of losing a large dinner ticket. Besides, in this place 'money talks.' Look at the crowd...." His head spun around in all directions, and he casually pointed to a few patrons. "Do you see anyone dressed up in formal evening wear, like they used to do in my generation? No! This whole world has gone ridiculously 'casual!' So follow me. I made reservations, and I'm getting hungry!"

The Beverly Hills Hotel, in the heart of Los Angeles, was one of the most widely renowned restaurants worldwide. Built in 1921, it served celebrities, dignitaries, world leaders, and anyone who could afford the opulent prices. The entrance was very intimidating as they strolled down the red carpet to the large glass doors. The young women slowly followed Anton, who seemed to know exactly where he was going.

Dani began to giggle, then she whispered, "I always was curious as to what it looked like inside this iconic hotel. I heard that only the A-list celebrities hung here."

"Me too," Steph whispered back.

Anton stopped in front of the empty maitre d' podium and smiled at his dinner dates. "Well, ladies, this is the infamous 'Polo Lounge.'" He swung his arm around and asked, "Is it was you expected, or not?"

Instantly the maitre d' appeared. He tipped his head and said, "So sorry to keep you waiting. Follow me, Mr. Petrescu. It's always a pleasure to see you. Do you want your usual table or would you like a larger one to accommodate your friends?"

Dani tapped Steph on the arm to see if she heard the maitre d's comment.

Anton nodded his head in acknowledgement. "Thanks, Pierre. A larger one would be fine. Somewhere not too close to the music—would be great."

The look on Dani and Steph's face was priceless. Their eyes were so wide that you might have thought they had seen a ghost.

"Follow me, ladies," the maitre d' said.

Anton pushed Dani forward and Steph followed as they went single file around the restaurant absorbing the grandeur. When they finally reached their table, the maitre d' pulled out a chair for each lady, and then again nodded to Anton as he pulled out his seat as well. He handed each woman a menu and looked directly at Anton. "You want your usual, or would you like a menu?"

"My usual would be great," Anton said.

Dani leaned forward and her jaw was still dropped open in awe. Then she whispered, "He actually knew your name! Do you come here often?"

Anton laughed. "Not often enough, nowadays! But I manage to get here once in a while. I like good food and good service."

"Yeah, but he even knows your usual," Dani whispered.

"You don't have to whisper, Dani. They won't throw you out if you talk in a normal voice. They are very good to their customers." Anton smiled. "Why don't you ladies tell me what you found today in your 'witch hunt?'"

Dani pouted. "It's not a witch hunt, Anton. And I think we found the family my mother worked for."

The waiter came over and Anton ordered a bottle of wine. Then he leaned forward and asked, "Where do they live and what's their name?"

Dani looked serious. "They live on the outskirts of Budapest. I knew their last name was Borsack, but not much else, nor which of the Borsacks they were. The master of this house we found was married to a younger woman and they had three children. He also had a twin brother, and then a younger sister who died at an early age. Theirs was old money. That's consistent with what my mother told me."

Anton handed a glass of wine to each of them and held his up in a toast. "Congratulations on your find today! I hope everything will lead you to a better place."

Dani looked puzzled. "Well, there are a few snags. The husband and wife are now deceased. They drowned in a boating accident over ten years ago. We're not sure who lives in the house now and if it's still even owned by the family. The business was bought out by a large corporation from out of the country, and I'm not sure how to find more information. But I know in my gut this is the family."

Steph took a sip and then said, "We have this feeling that her mother may have fallen in love with someone. The staff were all lodged in the same quarters behind the main house and I actually placed a call to the head of the staff."

Anton smiled. "That seems quite logical. She had to be involved with someone. Who…remains a big mystery."

"We are hopefully going find out the names of the staff. The problem is that it was such a short space of time. She was only there for just a little over a year. Actually, we hope the mistress had some documentation we can look at," Steph said confidently.

Dani watched Anton; she had never really seen him in this cultured and sophisticated level before. He seemed extremely comfortable in this prestigious environment and was looking more distinguished than she could ever remember. She wanted to find out more about him. It had been over the twelve years that he lived next door, and she just realized that she barely knew anything about him or his illustrious past. She knew he came from Romania, but that was the extent of her knowledge. He was never really open about his family or his lifestyle in Romania. Sitting here, she could see there was more to his past than he led them to believe.

Dani took a sip of wine and casually picked up the menu. Every once in a while, one of her eyes would peek over the top of the menu and observe Anton. After finally picking out her entree, she said to Anton, "Where exactly did you come from in Romania? I know you used to talk for hours with my mother about Romania, but I don't seem to remember."

He crossed his legs and sat back. He finally said hesitantly, "I lived further south…but I am familiar with Bucharest. It's such a big city, and my family and I visited there sometimes. We did enjoy frequenting some of the same places. Your mother loved the parks and more casual haunts in the city."

She lowered the menu and laid it on the table. You could see the curious look on her face. "Did you ever visit the family that she worked for as a nanny?"

"No, no, I never met them." He didn't blink an eye as he looked directly at her.

Dani leaned forward and Steph watched her every move. "Can you remember anything else my mother said? I mean, you used to have such lengthy conversations."

Anton plucked a hair from his sport coat and let it drop to the floor. "No, she was reluctant to let me know anything about her past at all. I'm in the dark just as much as you. I wish I could say or do something to help you find what you're looking for." He picked up his glass and swirled the wine around. "My parents have been dead for a long time, and I left Romania to find a better life—just like your mother. I don't feel connected to anyone there anymore. Those days are long gone. My friends and family are long gone, too."

Dani clasped her hands together and laid them in her lap. "What happened to your home?"

He lifted his hand to flag the waiter. "My parents once had lots of money and it's all gone now. That's what happens when a country's economy takes a downturn and all that was there is now wiped out."

For the first time, Dani was prying. "What about your brother? Didn't you say you had a brother?"

The waiter came over and took their order. That didn't stop Dani from her inquisition.

"He and I haven't seen or talked to each other in years. My sister passed away long ago with my parents. I'm afraid I'm quite alone in this world—just like you!" He winked. Then he picked up his napkin and leisurely placed it on his lap. "Maybe that is why I can relate to your circumstances. We seem to be in the same place— no family, nobody but ourselves."

Dani leaned forward. "But—"

Anton interjected, "I see you both ordered the lobster. That was a great choice! I used to love it, but I'm afraid my stomach can't deal with it anymore—they poach it in creamy butter and it's just too rich for my stomach. It's really not fun getting old!" He laughed.

Steph placed her napkin on her lap. "I haven't had lobster in over ten years. Thank you so much, Anton. This is a real treat to me."

The waiter rolled up with a serving tray. Three plates were covered with silver cloche domes. He took the dome off each plate and placed the huge lobster-filled dishes in front of Dani and Steph. Their eyes opened wide and Anton smiled. "Enjoy, ladies…I told you we were going to do something special on this nice day."

Nothing was said for the next hour as everyone feasted on the finest food in Los Angeles. When they had eaten as much as they could, all three sat back and sipped on the rest of their wine.

"Thank you, Anton. What an extraordinary meal. I only wish my mother could have been here to see it and share it." Tears began to well in her eyes as she rubbed her swollen belly.

"Life is not fair sometimes, little one. Be happy that she was bright enough to leave you with the bank account. Now you won't have to struggle. You might even decide to go back to school or seek a job more suited to your calling."

"I don't know what the future has in store for me."

"Well, the least you can do for yourself is to start indulging in those special little things you always dreamed of. That's what that money is for."

"I really want to find out who it is from before I spend a dime."

Anton placed his napkin on the table. "You may never find anything out. It would not be the end of the world. You've lived this long without knowing…."

"Yeah, but I know those pictures are going to tell me my story. I know one is my mother. I only hope the mistress of the staff will call back soon."

Anton stood up and smiled down at the women. "Would you like to take a walk around the hotel? The pool area is simply charming. I remember swimming in that pool as a child when I visited here with my parents. Come on…let's go explore!" He clasped each of their hands and began to walk toward the lobby.

chapter eighteen

IT HAD BEEN A WEEK AND DANI HAD NOT HEARD FROM the staff mistress. She left two messages and was starting to get edgy. Why didn't she return her calls? She decided she would wait a few more days and then she would call her again. She stepped out of the bus and started walking toward the hospital. It had been a long week since she had seen Dr. Cal. She missed his humor and funny antics with the children; and she wanted to know how his trip to Washington D.C. went. She looked up at the setting sun and the sky was filled with amazing shades of pink, blue, and purple. Sometimes sunsets reminded Dani of an oil painting she once saw in the new Getty museum. She loved to pack a picnic lunch and sit on the bench watching all the people who loved to visit the museum. Today was one of those days she could easily slip under the wave of her loss, but she wasn't going to let that happen—not today. She was going to try hard to keep moving forward.

As she walked toward the elevators, Becky yelled out and caught her attention. "Hello, Dani. Dr. Cal is back so be prepared for a night full of chaos!"

Dani smiled in acknowledgement of Becky's statement. "Thanks for the warning!"

When the elevator doors opened she stood there for just a few seconds and looked around. The ward seemed very quiet tonight, contrary to most other nights. She moved toward the front desk where Lola and Alva were quietly sitting. Lola was on the computer and

Alva was getting the evening medications ready for the children.

Dani slid up to the front desk and leaned her elbows on it. "Evening, ladies," her voice suddenly boomed out.

Lola nearly jumped out of her skin. "Oh, lordy be! You scared me, girl." She placed her hands over her heart.

"Scared from what? Me walking up or is Dr. Cal on the warpath tonight? I was given a 'head's up' from Becky downstairs."

"I wouldn't say that. I find him kind of mellow tonight," Alva stated as she counted out pills.

"Me either...." Lola said.

"Is he okay? What room is he in?" Dani asked.

Alva pointed to baby Cedar's room. "She's having a tough time and misses her parents."

Dani took off down the hall until she came to the designated room. She poked her head into the room and then smiled at what she saw. Dr. Cal was sitting on the bed with a Peter Pan book in one hand and a little vial of green shimmering fairy dust in the other. He stopped reading and put down the book. Then he opened the vial. With a gentleness that Dani was used to seeing, he said, "Peter Pan wanted me to sprinkle you with his sparkling fairy dust. He said, 'if you closed your eyes, he would come get you and take you to Never-never land....'" Dr. Cal's eyes opened wide in excitement.

Cedar sat forward, wonder and eagerness making her little body shake. "I've never been to Never-never land before," her voice barely squeaked out.

He took a little bit of glitter from the vial. "Well, lay back and get ready. When I sprinkle you with this magic dust, close your eyes and start dreaming about flying there with Peter Pan!"

"But Dr. Cal...I'm afraid of flying...."

"Close your eyes and Peter will come get you and keep you safe. Are you ready?"

Cedar nodded. Dr. Cal threw some glitter into the air and Cedar's eyes opened wide in excitement. Then she squeezed them shut in sheer anticipation. Dani backed out of the room and leaned against the wall, then she closed her eyes. She knew it would only take a minute or two for the child to fall asleep. And she loved the way the young doctor cajoled her safely into dreamland.

The tap on her shoulder brought her back into the real world. Dani, herself, wanted to go on that adventure with Peter Pan where she could hide from all her hurt and pain. But, life wasn't always what you wanted or expected.

"Did you want me for something... or are you trying to sleep standing up?" Dr. Cal said, towering over Dani. Each of his arms were flat on the wall on either side of her head. She was pinned in. It was a very intimate stance that caught Dani off guard.

Dani smiled timidly. Then her cheeks reddened. "No. I was watching you with Cedar. I think I might have to get a patent on my fairy dust! Seems I have a lot of competitors who are stealing my idea...."

Dr. Cal laughed out loud. "Might be a good idea. Then we can blame all the glitter that is showing up all over the floor on you to our housekeeping department."

Dani laughed as she playfully pushed his shoulder back, breaking the circle of closeness. "You wouldn't dare! I'm in enough hot water as it is."

Alva walked by and said impishly, "If you kids want to beat each other up, please go in the game room and use the boxing gloves!"

Dani groaned at the comment and then turned to Dr. Cal. "I was looking for you. I wanted to see how your trip to Washington went."

"They granted us two out of five requests for the clinical studies. And the big 'win' is that they are going to start funding a program to help the parents of these sick children so they don't lose their homes and everything else they have just trying to keep their babies alive. That big one made my trip and the past year worth those fights."

"I'm so happy for you! Nice job!" Dani held her fist out for a fist-bump.

"How has the past week been? How are you doing?" Dr. Cal asked.

"Okay...."

"I hear a hesitation in your voice. Are you really okay?" he questioned.

"Yeah. I made a decision to take five days off; I'm flying to Budapest with Steph for one final shot to see if I can find anything. I would like to see where my mother grew up and what she went through."

Dr. Cal looked surprised at her statement. "You sure?"

Dani shrugged her shoulders. "I've not nothing to lose. Right?"

The plane landed with a big thump—jolting Dani's nerves. Steph slept through most of the long flight. Dani's nerves were too tightly wound to even think about sleep. She leaned over toward Steph and pulled one of her earplugs out of her ears. Then she whispered, "Wake up...we just landed."

Steph slowly reached her arms above her head and leisurely stretched. "Thanks for letting me sleep. All this excitement caught up with me."

Dani couldn't contain her excitement. "I can't believe we're in Romania. Do you realize this is where I was conceived, not to mention I probably have a thousand relatives within this country's borders that I have no clue about?" Dani smiled broadly.

Steph brought her arms down and touched her friend's forehead, looking for a fever. "Don't get too delirious, we have a long four days ahead of us. And...don't go into this trip with high expectations. I keep having to say that because we may leave without finding out one damn thing about your mother or her family."

Dani sighed and looked like the wind had just been knocked out of her sails. "I know...."

Steph bent over and tickled Dani's side. "Come on, let's go explore this birthplace of yours."

Dani and Steph rushed through the architecturally resplendent airport. Three-story ceilings loomed high above their heads and metal scaffoldings and glass tunnels brought one or two 'oohs and aahs' from the girls.

Dani chose a five-star hotel that looked very European and traditional. It was something she would have never splurged on had it not been for Anton's input and persistence. He was adamant that she should make this a great experience, especially if she might never come back again. He also selfishly wanted her to see the city through her eyes and not those of others.

"I loved that city so much as a child, Dani," Anton said, handing Dani the brochures the week before the trip.

Dani looked at the brochures and said, "Then why did you leave?"

"I never got along with my father. He was so staunch and so uncaring. I wanted more out of life than to be like him. He was mean spirited and hated the common townspeople who had made him wealthy."

"When did you leave?"

"I was considered the scholar. I was sent off to the best private school for most of my childhood. At eighteen

I came home and was sent off to the best colleges Europe had to offer. After that I just floated in and out of Bucharest. But, I did love that city and all it had to offer!"

"Can you tell me about the woman you almost married?"

Anton paused and leaned back in his chair, folding his hands over his stomach. It was a minute before he replied. "Leaha died one summer when a horse threw her off his back. It broke my heart and taught me a big lesson in life. Happiness was not about finding that one person. Happiness was finding—yourself. Besides, I was not one to settle down and have a house full of kids. I loved traveling and experiencing life."

"Your brother married," she stated.

"He was unhappy in his marriage, and his kids were just like his wife—self-centered and spoiled. I had never met a woman who was so hateful. Her arrogance and cruel demeanor became so unparalleled, she nearly destroyed our family's integrity in the community. It got harder and harder to go home and watch what a big mess my family had become. Eventually, once my father and mother died, there was no reason for me to go home at all. That's when I came to the United States."

"Why did your brother allow her behavior?"

"He had no control. She was bent on destroying his life and everyone around him. He eventually fell in love and asked her for a divorce, but she would not grant him one. After he lost his true love, life had no meaning. A few years later, my brother and sister-in-law died in a freak accident. I don't even know if it was an accident or if my brother planned it. He had given up on life and everything he did turned into a big embarrassment to our family's name. Many times I had to bail him out of trouble. Had my mother been around, it would not have been tolerated."

"You think he planned their accident?" Dani looked shocked.

Anton shrugged his shoulders. "That's only my speculation."

Anton handed her a piece of paper. "Here, take a look at the list I made up. These are places your mother told me she would go on her days off. I thought you might want to visit some of them."

He also handed her some leaflets of places he valued that she should visit in and around the city. There was one special place she wanted to go to—as a small tribute to her mother. For years Dani had heard stories about the Cismigui Gardens. Ema had told Dani of this fairytale type garden where she would walk for hours, never seeing it all—nor wanting too. It was filled with thousands of varieties of native plants, grottos, floral carpets, bridges, and benches. The large fishponds and water paths were filled with fish, swans, and pesky pelicans. Ema would talk about the only secret place she could feel good about herself and feel free and young.

After the long flight, jetlag had caught up with the girls, but Dani refused to waste one single moment of their time sleeping when they could be searching for her Romanian roots. With a list of places to go and a map in her hands, the girls walked out of the lobby to find a cab.

Hours later, complete exhaustion had finally convinced them to settle in for the evening. With a bag full of junk food they had purchased in a small store, they sat on their beds in their nightshirts reflecting on the day.

Steph popped an M&M into her mouth and said, "Well, at least you got to see where your mom was raised." She popped one more into her mouth. "Going from neighbor to neighbor and inquiring about Maria was an interesting accomplishment in itself. Seems she didn't have too many friends or neighbors who liked or cared about her. Most thought she was already dead, or should be, the way she treated her children. How sad…."

"I'm glad we ran into that guy, what was his name? Igoriv-something. I hate to say it, but did you get a whiff of his breath?" Dani wrinkled her nose. "He was definitely drunk...and the convalescent home Maria is at was just awful. Probably just as well she's had a stroke and doesn't really know where she's at."

Steph dropped an M&M on the bed and was looking all over for it. When she found it, she held it up and laughed. Then she went back to the conversation. "Yeah. The whole neighborhood was creepy, wasn't it? Poor Ema. What a horrible childhood she must have had. And from what you told me, Maria was a nasty piece of work. Can you believe she made your mother sleep on a cot outside most of the time? Some people just get what they deserve in life. I so believe in Karma...."

Dani nodded her head. "Well, I'm glad that the nursing staff called her daughter to come in and talk to us...though she wasn't much help."

"Yeah, but she didn't really try to help us, did she?"

"Maybe she was skeptical of us and our story. I didn't want to push her," Dani replied.

"Skeptical or not, she was as mean as her mother must have been at her age," Steph hissed.

"Look, Steph, this was a different country, living under communist rule, and in financial crisis. Everything was tough then. My mother said it was hard to keep a roof over your head and food in your children's mouths. Nobody trusted anyone or dared to do anything to bring the government down on their heads. For cripes sake, Maria was married to a drunk who didn't work. Not that I am sticking up for her, but times in Romania were different than they are now. It was different over here."

"You're right, Dani. I shouldn't be so critical. She didn't know who we were or why we were there. She may have thought we were trying to start something, wanted something, or wanted to take something away from her family or her mother. Although, I can't imagine Maria and her husband ever had anything of value."

Dani sat up and said, "But she did have something of value! She gave us some information; and confirmed who my mother worked for, in her own way. She just couldn't piece anything together because it sounded like her mother didn't tell her much. It was past her comprehension to make sense of anything we were saying. She had very little recollection of who my mother was and where she had come from other than the family had taken her in as an infant. She was a young child herself. She was fifteen at the time and just a few years later, she had left home herself."

"Leaving at that age makes me believe she had it pretty bad. Oh, what her life must have been like. Other than giving us that little bit of information—I could see she was uncomfortable; and that's why she left in a hurry." Steph grinned. "I think she was just scared of the past."

"Or scared of us. I'm keeping my fingers crossed. Let's hope that we find some answers tomorrow." Dani laid back on her pillows.

Steph laid down and shut off the light. "Dani…? Promise me that when we leave Romania in a few days, you will be done with this need to look at your mother's past. I'm beginning to feel that it's her past—not yours—she didn't talk about it for a reason. Will you let it go once and for all after we leave?"

"I'll try."

The next morning the jetlag began to really take its toll. Dani and Steph had a hard time getting out of bed to get their full day started. The morning weather was miserable and cold. The day before their fingers had been numb to the bone, so they made a quick stop at a small clothing store and picked up some gloves, scarves, and knitted hats. There wasn't a lot of damp precipitation, just drizzling off and on during the morning hours. But a freezing wind sent an unpleasant chill seeping into their bones. The only thing that would take away the bitter cold was a hot shower. And now they were up again, for another bitterly cold day in this foreign country that had been so unforgiving to Dani's mother.

"Get up, Steph!"

"No!" she said, pulling the covers and comforter over her head.

Dani got out of bed and ripped the blankets free from Steph's tight grasp. "Come on, we have a whole day of hanging around this interesting old city, and I plan to make the best of it. I want to go out to the Borsacks' home and see if that staff mistress is there. I talked to her briefly, but she never returned my other calls. I'm hoping she'll be there and receptive to talking with us."

Pretending to shiver, Steph got out of bed and walked into the bathroom. Dani smiled when she heard the shower start.

Dani walked over to the large picture window and pulled the drapes back with her hand. The sun was coming up over the incredible outline of the cosmopolitan city. What her eyes absorbed had no or little reflection of the city that her mother loved and left thirty years ago. It was an interesting town filled with an overindulgent population continuously on the move. From what she saw the day before, the old buildings lined with ornate art nouveau were gorgeous, detailed, and complete with frosted glass, wrought-iron awnings, high ceilings, and carved archways. Sadly, many of these gems were faded and falling apart. Dani and Steph also noticed the still-cracked and bumpy sidewalks that emphasized the shadow of the past.

Dani could only remember that in the middle of the luxury shopping, sophisticated cafes and restaurants, nightclubs, and trendy stores—a whole different communist country had existed before she was born. The

Bucharest that her mother talked about with such awe now had the magic of Paris—but it had also acquired a lot of sleazy characters, insane drivers, and the aggressive self-preoccupation of a place that had been reborn over many younger generations.

Thirty years ago, when her mother had lived here, this 'Little Paris' was under Communist rule. It was liberated in 1989, close to the time her mother had left to find another life in a country she knew little about. Dani's mother rarely talked about it, but it must have taken a person of influence to procure the visa and passport needed for her mother to leave the country and come to the United States. Ema didn't have the financial ability to do this on her own. She had been a penniless vagrant at eighteen. Dani wondered who would have helped her and how politically endowed they were. Hopefully, she would find out some answers today, because her time was slipping away. With a return flight in three days, she needed some answers now.

Dani heard the shower stop and sighed. Am I really ready to seek the truth? Would I be disappointed or would it open up more wounds that I might not be able to handle? She knew deep inside she should let go of her mother's past, but it was gnawing at her to find out. There had to be someone who carried her blood—if not her DNA. She didn't want to be alone in the world. Ema could not have conceived a child all by herself. There had to be another responsible party who had got Ema out of Romania and gave them a new life.

After all, money was deposited into an account for Dani—lots of money. And yet, none of it was touched and no one had come forward to claim it. Ema didn't use one dime—she collectively saved it for her only child and her only family. Dani couldn't say that now. She had met a distant cousin…who didn't want to be bothered. It was strange seeing someone who would be considered a distant relative. She had certainly seemed unhappy that

Dani was asking questions about their past, for fear it might upset their future.

The cab slowly drove down the long driveway and circled until it came to a stop in front of an enormous mansion. The driver got out and opened the door for Dani and Steph.

"Thank you," Dani said.

"Do you want me to stay?" he asked.

"Yes, please."

Dani and Steph looked around with wide eyes. Although this large manor had the look of 'falling on hard times,' it was still imposing and reeked of wealth and prosperity. Every plant and shrub was in place and trimmed with precision. The grass and gardens were manicured to perfection; and ivy had crept across all the outer front walls of the house, giving it a haunted look. The huge building had the same architectural style that had filled the city. The impressive ornate art nouveau, large imposing pilasters, and carved archways were beginning to show their age, and the massive fountain in the middle of the driveway was empty.

Dani and Steph slowly walked up the stairs to the ten-foot-high front doors that lent an air of superiority to the vast entry into the house. With all the strength Dani could muster, she knocked on the front door. No sounds or movement came from within the house. Dani knocked again—this time louder.

Suddenly, the door opened and a small woman in a gray dress and white apron stood in the doorway holding her hand up to shield her eyes from the blinding sun. In a sweet, quiet voice, she asked in Romanian, "*Vă pot ajuta?*"

Dani had no clue as to what she said. "I speak English," was all Dani could think to say.

The little lady smiled and said in slow English, "OK. Can I help you?"

Dani smiled and replied, "Yes, I'm looking for anyone who knew my mother."

The little maid looked confused. "I don't under-understand...I be back." She gestured for them to stay there, and hurried off.

Dani and Steph looked at each other. Then before they had time to get really nervous, the door opened wider and a tall, beautiful woman in her early forties opened the door. She was casually dressed in a pair of black slacks, a starched white shirt, and wool blazer. Her expensive leather loafers finished off the attire. Her long, brown hair was parted down the middle and hung on each side with a shine that would blind many. Her green eyes were big and piercing. But her voice was harsh. "I'm Stefani, can I help you?"

Dani held out her hand and said, "I'm Dani Vaduva. I came here from the United States to see if I could find out any information about my mother who used to work here. In fact, I think she was a nanny in this home when she was eighteen. I was hoping I could talk to someone."

The woman did not extend her hand. "What was your mother's name?"

Dani looked at her with curious eyes. "Ema Vaduva."

With a coolness that could freeze a lake, Stefani said, "I nev-ver knew any-one of that name. She did not work here." Her brows drew together and she started tapping her fingers impatiently against her crossed arms.

"Does Emila Silivasi sound familiar?" Dani asked stubbornly.

"No! How man-y times do I have to say no?" she hissed, enunciating each syllable very precisely.

Dani paused, biting her lip nervously, then asked, "Could I talk to Crina?"

"What for?" Then she waved her hand dismissively and said, "Sure. She is in the back building with our staff. But don't keep her too long, she has plenty of work to do!"

"Thank you, I appreciate it. I will only take a minute or two." The door slammed shut and Dani and Steph stood there, mounting anger in their chests. Dani stomped her foot and was about to scream.

Steph took Dani's hand and said, "If we only have a few minutes, let's hurry back there before that witch is back with her broomstick to sweep us away!"

They followed the way her finger had pointed and walked as quickly as they could. When they finally got to the large, rundown building, they looked for an entrance. Dani found a door and opened it. They were in a small sitting room. There were a few chairs scattered around, but no one in sight.

They began to walk down a large hallway. "Anyone here? Hello...hello...." They continued down the hallway with closed doors on each side.

Suddenly, one of the doors opened and an old woman walked out. She was short, heavy, and looked to be in her late eighties. Her hair was curled up under a maid's hat and she was wearing a light gray uniform with a white apron on top. Her hands were red and blistered and looked to be in need of medical care. Her soft gray eyes were sympathetic looking and she said, "*Da?*"

Dani leaned forward and smiled. "I'm sorry, we only speak English. I'm...I'm looking for Crina."

The old lady smiled and said very slowly, enunciating each word and syllable with great care, "*Da*, tis me. What can I do for you?"

"I don't know if you remember, but we talked on the phone a few weeks ago. I was the one asking you a thousand questions. You were supposed to get back with me; and now, meeting your mistress, I can see why you didn't!"

Steph leaned forward and whispered, "She's not a very nice person."

"No, she...in my mis-tress's de-fense...she's had a *big*" Crina spread her hands out, gesturing as she spoke, and emphasized the word 'big' very dramatically. "...bur-den t' carry on her shoul-ders t'ese past ten years."

"Can you tell me about Master Florin and his wife?" Dani asked.

Crina paused and a wary glint shone in her eyes. "T'ey passed...a sail—how do you say? A boat...crash mannny years ago."

Dani needed to know, so she asked, "Have you been here long, Crina?"

"Long, lonnng time, dear-ie. I was...hmmm...a-bout your age when I came to t'is house. Back then...things were...not t'e same. Not t'e same...."

"Like I told you on the phone, I think my mother worked here for a little while as a nanny. I'm twenty-eight, so it would have been close to thirty years ago. Ema Vaduva was her name. Do you have any records or anything that might confirm that?"

"I don't know that name. When I got off t'e phone, I looked through what few records I have." The old lady was massaging her tender hands and Dani could see the pain in the tightness of her face.

"Silivasi...does that sound familiar?'

Crina perked up and smiled. "You mean Emila Silivasi?"

Dani's eyes opened wide and she quickly nodded her head.

"Oh, yes! She was here. We shared a room for a year. We used to...oh...*da*! We did lots of t'ings to-ge-ther. She was a *good* friend...*da*...a good *surată*."

Dani's eyes began to well with tears. Steph moved closer to put her arm around her friend. "Just to know her mother wasn't always alone and that she had a friend is worth so much to my friend. Thank you, Crina," Steph said.

Dani leaned forward and touched Crina's sleeve. "Why did she leave?"

Crina looked confused and shook her head. "I don't know.... One day said she had t' leave. She was scared...so we packed up her things and a car picked her up."

"Do you know who she left with?" Dani was beginning to shake.

"No, but ru-mors went around that she had been at-tacked and t'ey were sending her far away." The old lady had a very sad look on her face.

Dani whispered, "Attacked? Like...raped?"

Crina nodded her head, looking regretful.

Dani quietly asked, "Do they know who did it? Was he ever caught and punished? I need to know...."

Crina touched Dani's face. "No. She had a...a friend. He was our new sta-ble boy. He seemed very nice. But, one night he was gone, and a few nights later, so was Emila."

Tears poured down Dani's face. "My mother was put on a boat and sent to America. I was born six months later." Dani turned her head and laid it on Steph's shoulder. She tried to hold herself together, but sobs rose up out of her throat and shook her to her core. Steph held her up, holding onto her tightly around the waist.

The old woman shook her head, sorrow in her eyes. "I am sorry.... I wish...it had not been so. I always hoped Emila found new life, and peace."

Steph looked up and said, "Ema passed on last year and my dear friend wanted to see if she could find out who her father was. I guess we will never know. Florin Borsack is dead, and the stable boy is gone. Is there anything else you can tell us that might help...? Like the stable boy's name?"

"Beni Popascu. And t'at name is very com-mon in Romania."

Dani wiped her eyes and took a few seconds to catch her breath, and then she opened her purse and pulled out an envelope. She reached inside the envelope for the five faded pictures. Carefully, she handed them to Crina. She sucked in a large breath and held it in, waiting for any kind of acknowledgement or response. Her heart was beating faster than it had in a long time, just knowing some answers were about to come.... Steph held her hand and squeezed it.

"Take it easy, Dani. Exhale—take slow breaths. I don't want you to have a damn heart attack or stroke. Okay?"

Dani looked at her friend and exhaled. She squeezed her hand and waited patiently as Crina slowly brought her old eyes closer to the pictures. One trembling finger touched the top picture and the girls watched as her face filled with sadness.

Crina stared at each picture and then she slowly tucked one under the other and nodded her head with recognition. She took her time, and when she was finished, she lifted her head to speak to Dani. "Let me explain each picture—ex-cept one...." she said.

One picture...which one was that? Dani wondered as she watched Crina shuffling her shaking legs over to a chair to sit down. Dani stared at this old lady who had aged more than her years.

She pointed to a picture. "T'is man and woman...t'ey are Master Florin and Mistress Lucia. Lucia had a...a hard-ness in her. For some rea-son Emila took the brunt of her an-ger. If not for Master Florin, no one would have stayed." Crina sighed softly. "Master Florin trea-ted us with dig-ni-ty." Her finger touched the picture again. "We were all sad when he died."

Dani nodded her head in empathy, and said, "I'm sorry."

Crina patted her hand. "Don't be, young one...."
She sighed and held up her crippled hands. Then the
sadness left her face and she smiled. She held up the
picture of the woman and three children. "T'is is Emila.
She was kind, spoke soft-ly.... She loved Stefani and the
boys verrry much." Crina laughed. "T'ey listened to her.
An-y-one else...." She shook her head sadly. "Stefani
followed Emila like...like a pup. I t'ink Stefani and Andre
and Petre missed Emila e-ven though she was here on-ly
a short time."

Dani said softly, "She was the best mother."

"I t'ink...t'at is why Lucia hat-ed her so. But...we
did hear that Master Florin would sit in the garden with
Emila on occasion. Well...un-til Lucia found out...." She
sighed.

Then she flipped to the much older wedding
picture and held it up. "I don't know t'is one."

Crina lifted the final picture of two young boys.
"T'ese are the two brothers I loved so dearly. I have seen
t'is same pho-to in the study. What a long time a-go t'is
was taken. Right af-ter I came here."

Dani and Steph looked confused, and Steph said,
"I'm not sure I understand."

Crina touched Steph's hand. "Oh, see here, dear.
This is Master Florin and his twin, Antonios...when
they were young."

"Can you tell me about Antonios?" Dani inquired.

"He was sweet, but he wasn't of-ten home."

"Where is he now? Is there any chance I could
talk with him?"

"I doubt it, dear-ie. He moves from place to place.
The last I heard, he was in France."

"Does anyone know how to get in touch with
him?"

"No, dear. He's long gone."

"Is there any known address?" Dani insisted.

Crina smiled. "He did not know an-y-t'ing a-bout Emila."

"I just wish there was more information I could find out."

"I wish I could help you more. I won-dered man-y nights what ev-er hap-pen'd to Emila. It was…such a hush-hush t'ing here. Talk-ing to you…I know she has a love-ly daugh-ter. T'ere's naught in life more than that, child."

Dani wiped her eyes. "Thank you, Crina. I'm going to give you my number. If you remember anything else or hear anything, will you please contact me?"

The old lady placed her painful hands around Dani's shoulder and gave her a motherly hug. She whispered in Dani's ear, "Emila was my friend. Look at t'e young woman she raised—I am proud for her."

Dani blinked rapidly to dispel the tears that threatened again and whispered back, "Thank you."

There was nothing left to search for now. Nobody knew more than Crina.

chapter nineteen

DANI WAS SITTING IN THE CORNER OF HER COUCH sipping a hot cup of coffee. Her hair was wet and her robe tightly tied around her waist. The lamp in the corner of the room shed very little light and the other person on the couch could barely be seen through the darkness.

"So, what did you think of Romania?" the baritone voice cut through the obscurity of the room.

Anton was sitting in the opposite corner of the couch in his slacks and polo sweater. One leg was crossed over the other and his leather loafers looked similar to the ones Dani had seen in Romania. He looked casual and very composed with his arm resting along the top of the couch. His white hair was slightly longer and wavier, and he was beginning to look more and more like Omar Sharif, the handsome Egyptian actor back in the sixties. His blue eyes stood out with his white hair, making him look more like royalty than just Dani's neighbor from next door. Dani looked at him and thought he looked very European and extremely handsome for a man his age. The only change over the past years was that his tanned face showed more lines and wrinkles than she had previously noticed.

Dani broke the silence that had encased the room. "It seems like it was just a fairy tale. One minute we were there, and the next minute we were on our way back. I fell in love with that old city. It reminded me of all those modernized European towns I love reading about in magazines. But of course you know that, don't you?" She looked directly at him. She always felt he knew more than what he let her believe. "My mother began her life there. Even if it was only for eighteen years, I'm glad I got to experience Bucharest. I now know why you spent all those hours with my mother talking about your beloved country."

He started to jiggle his leg. "Of course I did, Dani. I lived there during my childhood and part of my adult life. Sometimes my comfort zone rests in the beautiful countryside where I got to enjoy an affluent upbringing that every child dreams of having—your mother included. Yet, she was never jealous or envious of me. She was by far one of the kindest, gentlest, and respectful people I've ever known." He smiled deeply and showed off his still perfect set of white teeth and the deep dimples on each side of his cheeks.

Dani held a pillow in her lap and hugged it tight with both hands. "Anton, why did you make United States your home and not go back?"

His eyes narrowed and he had a thoughtful look on his face, then began to speak slowly. "In 1989, the Romanian Revolution had just ended and there was a violent period of civil unrest throughout my country. Once they executed the longtime Communist leader Nicolae Ceauşescu, I thought it was time for me to spread my wings and see the world. Visas were being offered to dignitaries and affluent families, and I always had this need to travel. So, after I got into a big argument with my father, I knew it was time to leave. In 1984, I came to the United States for the summer Olympics and fell in love with New York and California. I wanted to go back again and see if I could make a permanent transition. A few of my friends followed me so I wasn't quite alone, but eventually they all went back."

"Why did you leave your family to live in a strange country?" Dani looked at him curiously.

"Thousands of people left their countries and came through Ellis Island for years looking to start a new life in America. It was the land of opportunity. Why am I any different than them? My brother was married with children and I just felt it was time for me to go." He grinned. "I've never regretted it. Besides, my great-grandparents and grandparents had left me a large endowment that has been very beneficial, and with my investments, I have done amazingly well. I've been all around the world experiencing life and looking for a place to call my own. Europe, Asia, South America—I have been to them all over the years. This was my final destination."

"Did you ever go back to see your family?" she asked.

Anton laughed. "Of course, silly one. I went back regularly for many years. But then after a while there didn't seem to be a need." He took a piece of lint off his slacks and kept his eyes down when he asked, "So, tell me about your trip."

Dani sat up and cocked her head to the side, closing her eyes for a few seconds, as though she were remembering every detail of the trip. "Well, it was really an eye-opening trip. I really enjoyed Bucharest. I found it a fascinating city that's changed with the times, but still has an old charm. I can see why my mother loved walking around on her days off, enjoying the magic of the city. The weather was a little cold, but that didn't stop Steph and I from appreciating some of those places on the list you gave me. Especially the ones my mother frequented when she had a chance."

Anton smiled. "Which ones did you explore? And which was your favorite?"

Dani sat back and smiled. "Even though we didn't see it in the spring or summer, I think the Cismigui Gardens. Even in winter, it was absolutely incredible. The design and wandering pathways were captivating throughout the entire park. The plants, grottos, grass carpets, bridges, and benches took my breath away, and I can truly envision it in late spring. We missed the exotic fish, swans, and pelicans, but I can imagine how it looks with them during the summer. Steph and I walked around for almost a full day—absorbing it all."

"I spent many of my days walking around those beautiful grounds. What else did you get to see?"

"Well, from our room you could see the Triumphal Arch. It's exactly what I had anticipated it to be from all the pictures and brochures I had at home. It seemed to be the 'hub' of where everything started and spread out from."

Anton brought his arm down and placed it in his lap. "Did you find anything about your family?"

Dani shook her head. "Not much."

He looked perplexed. "Nothing?"

Dani looked up with sad eyes and said, "Well, yeah, I did find something out." She paused and took an unsteady breath. "When my mother disappeared, rumors were passed around that she had been raped by an employee. Of course, Crina said they were just rumors and there seemed to be few suspects along with a lot of speculations." She bent her head down into the pillow on her lap. Just saying 'rape' out loud had such a profound effect on her. Learning she may have been born from a violent assault on her mother—made her feel ugly and dirty. She sat there silently.

Anton looked surprised at the statement and her emotional reaction to it. He slid over on the couch and put his hand on her back and rubbed it in a very fatherly way. "Don't go there, Dani. You don't know if what this Crina told you was the truth or not. Like you said, it was probably all speculation with no verifiable evidence. Don't judge or condemn anyone right now. Your mother wanted to start a new life and she did it with grace and dignity. Don't sell your birth short of what it was."

Dani lifted her head. Her eyes were damp, and troubled. She whispered, "My mother was a baby and only nineteen years old when someone may have violated her. If...if...."

"You don't know for sure that she was. She may have come to America on her own. You just don't know...."

"No, I don't! What little information I found out after seeing Maria and going to the Borsacks' manor— was enough."

He took his hand off her back and sat still as a statue during every word. He finally replied, "Was the family there?"

Dani's eyes narrowed into slits. "Stefani Borsack opened the door—what a bitch." Dani paused and her eyebrows creased as she considered something. "She looked very familiar to me, but for some reason, I can't think why. What I did find out was that she was the little girl in the picture, along with her two brothers." Dani paused, as if thinking about her again. Then she continued, "She said that she didn't know anything about Ema Vaduva. Then she looked directly at me and stepped forward, almost like she wanted to push me back. Instead, she slammed the door in my face."

"Did she give you any information about the Borsack family?" he inquired solemnly.

"No." Dani sat forward. "You could tell she was filled with an uncontrollable anger. It was pretty transparent that life had not been kind to her. Damn...she was nasty!"

"Oh, I'm sorry to hear that. How did the manor look? I heard it is a beautiful place."

"Steph and I slowly walked around until we came to the servants' quarters. The property grounds looked very well manicured. However, there was a lot of neglect of the manor and surrounding buildings."

He lifted his brows. "That's all you learned on the trip? Had Crina ever met Ema?"

"Yes, in fact, her and my mother stayed in the same room and were friends. Oh yeah—one more thing...my mother had a boyfriend when she lived there. Crina told me his name, but the next day Steph and I went to the Hall of Records and could not find a trace on him. We searched for hours."

"Did you look your mother up in the Hall of Records?"

"We used the name Ema Vaduva and didn't find a thing. Not a birth certificate or anything. Then we tried the name on her passport. Which, by the way, was the name she went by in Romania—Emila Silivasi. The only thing we found was the date of her birth and nothing known after that. Not even her passport was listed. I don't know why she took on a new identity when she came to America."

"Did Crina have any records on this young man in any of the household files?" he asked.

"She told me she didn't."

"Well, I came from a wealthy family and we held on to all the information about our employees just in case the government had questions. That's standard procedure in those situations."

Dani swung her head around and questioned, "Would she have a reason not to tell me? She seemed so sincere."

Anton laughed out loud. "Dear little one.... Loyalty goes the distance in a small country like Romania, especially to a family you have been employed with for over forty years. Do you think she would give you incriminating information about anyone in that house? Or, for some reason, maybe all his records were intentionally destroyed. Actually, I'm quite surprised she even mentioned the young boy your mother was seeing—if she was seeing him."

"Really? She also told me a rumor that had floated around the staff. They said that it was the young man who raped my mother. But I guess I will never know."

"No. It shouldn't really matter. You are a wonderful young woman who is very productive in life. You need to let this whole thing go."

"There are so many suspicious things that don't seem to add up. Like—who put my mother on that boat."

"Did she know?"

"No, Crina said a few days later my mother had left in the early morning hours. Someone must have wanted my mother silenced; someone was scared to death something would be found out."

"Let it go now." His finger tapped her small nose.

Dani stood up. "I promised Steph I would stop looking for answers. But I keep wondering about the money."

"Oh. I don't think you will find out about that. There are laws that protect the banks from having to divulge that information. Besides, what difference would that make, Dani?"

"I don't know."

"Let it go," Anton begged.

chapter twenty

DANI SAT ON THE GRASSY KNOLL. SHE GAZED AT THE SUN as it rose high into the sky. It was a beautiful California day, but in the distance she could see a large storm brewing. The dark clouds were slowly creeping toward her and a cold wind was pushing the leaves and dust around. It had been a few weeks since she had come to visit. And yet, it was the only place in her life where she felt safe and loved. Somehow her self-imposed ceasefire had brought calmness to her need for answers. Her only family was here and nothing could change that. Today, for the first time, she had placed two roses on Estelle's brass marker as well. She really missed that brash old lady and all her words of wisdom. She never let Dani sit alone or linger in a pity party too long. Her need to push Dani forward constantly rang clear through her words. While Dani sat there this morning, she wondered what Estelle would have said about her trip to Romania. Would Estelle, in her deep raspy voice, tell her to 'let it go' or would she tell her to 'dig deeper?' Dani didn't have to ask herself that question twice. She knew the answer. "Let it go…."

Dani stood up and took a deep breath. The last few weeks had made her think more about her future and less about her past. Maybe not finding out the big picture was her own private passageway into anonymity. Searching for her father didn't seem as important as finding out what her future had in store for her. She was born because of all the small events that led to her mother leaving Romania. Maybe it was time Dani looked at what she had and moved forward. After all, her short life had already dealt with enough pain to last a lifetime. Why create more by wallowing in it?

For the first time in years, Dani felt a weight lift off her shoulders. She was walking down the knoll and leaving behind everything that had been weighting her down for a long, long time. Why not learn from her mother's courage and create a whole new identity? It didn't matter that she had no one but herself. At least she had herself; she had her jobs; she had her friends; and she even had Anton next door. What more did she need? The money in the account was nice, but would it bring her happiness? That was yet to be seen. It had definitely left Dani with a comfortable feeling that she had something to fall back on. Maybe Ema was trying to teach her a life lesson through that brown box. A lesson that would make her strong—and not so susceptible to caving under harsh realities of life. She had been trusting, naïve, and had gotten pregnant—and that was okay—but then with the loss of her young son and then her mother, she had become desperate to find answers— desperate for a shred of peace. She was finally letting go. Now she could take control of her life and not let anything stand in her way. Not even the name of her father!

Dani made it to the bus stop just as it was pulling up. With a smile on her face, she waved at Harry. "Thanks for slowing down for me, Harry. I appreciate it."

"You're welcome, missy. Nice to see you again—I was worried about you."

Dani patted his shoulder as she reached the top of the steps and walked past. "It feels good to be out and about!"

"You going to work?"

"Yeah...." Dani took a seat and watched riders getting on and off of the bus. With a small smile, her hand was touching the small can of Mace in her pocket.

When she got to her stop, she walked down the two steps of the bus and turned around to wave. Dani felt good today and nothing was going to stop her. She walked down the street and went into the alley of her restaurant. Steph was sitting outside on the small bench.

"Hey, Dani. I've been waiting for you. How's it going?" Steph asked.

Dani sat down next to her and patted her knee. "I'm having a great day. I think I had a self-proclaimed revelation today." Dani started to giggle.

Steph rolled her eyes and started to laugh. "You mean you've had a divine intervention?"

Dani nodded her head and smiled.

Steph playfully grabbed Dani by her shoulders and began to shake her. "Oh, lordy...don't tell me you joined that born again Hare Krishna group playing those little finger chimes and dancing down the street?" Her eyes opened wide in mock surprise. "...or that God came to visit you in a dream last night!"

Dani was uncontrollably laughing. "No, you silly goose, I just had a nice, long talk with Ema today and we decided it was time for me to let go of the past."

Steph instantaneously released her shoulders. Dani nearly fell off the bench from the release of the centrifugal force. Grasping the back of the bench, Dani slowly pulled herself back into the upright position. "Holy cow! These old bones are pretty brittle and I don't need them broken! It's not a big deal, Steph."

Steph laughed. "I'm really glad you finally figured it out. It is a big deal! You are finally understanding that you can't change the past no matter how bad you want to." Steph brushed her fingers along Dani's cheek. "You are such a beautiful young woman with a smart head on her shoulders, and you deserve some happiness. You have so much life to look forward to—I'm beyond ecstatic you are coming to that realization." Steph bent over and kissed the same spot her fingers had just touched.

Dani looked down and humbly said, "Thank you, my dear friend."

Steph pulled her friend's arm. "Come on...we better not be late or the dragon lady will come after us!"

Dani smiled. "Is she in a good or bad mood today?"

"Don't know—don't care!" Steph said flippantly.

Their shift was over and both the girls were exhausted. Dani and Steph were in the bathroom changing out of their restaurant attire and into street clothes. Dani stepped closer to the mirror and could see the dark circles under her eyes. She took out her makeup bag and began to apply some concealer, added a little blush, and applied some lipstick.

Steph came up from behind and started laughing. "Oh...you getting all dolled up to see your little boyfriend?"

Dani blushed. "What? No! I just don't want to scare anyone in the hospital. I look like a damn raccoon!"

Steph smiled as she picked up her backpack. "How is it going over at the hospital?"

"It's going okay. Dr. Cal has been out of town since we got back so we keep missing each other. Probably just as well." Dani's face turned red again.

Steph stood next to Dani and tweaked her nose. "Methinks someone's crushing on a certain handsome doctor!"

"No. He's just a nice friend; and I respect him for all the hard work and long hours he puts in for those little ones. And he's...he's way out of my league."

Steph regarded Dani curiously. Then her brows drew together. "What do you mean 'out of your league?' He's just a normal guy who poops in a toilet just like us. He's not Superman or God, so who is it exactly that you're comparing yourself to? Besides, I think you could use some solid male distraction right now." Steph winked at her and bumped her with her bottom.

Dani picked up her backpack and lifted it over her shoulder, ignoring Steph's insinuation. She nudged her friend out the bathroom door, and continued to walk toward the back door of the restaurant. "I'm doing just fine right now. I don't need any distractions...." She stopped what she was saying as she opened the back door and noticed the commotion outside. Steph and Dani were frozen in the doorway watching what was transpiring right in front of their own eyes.

Betina was sprawled on the ground and Jeremy, her ex-boyfriend, was grasping a handful of her hair in one hand and was bringing his other fisted hand forward towards her face. After she got over her initial shock, Dani jumped forward with all her might as his fist come down, seemingly in slow motion. She grabbed his arm, trying to stop him. Betina's face and body was already broken upon the ground. Moans were coming from her lips, but they were too caked with blood and swollen to allow much sound out.

Dani yelled at the bystanders who were now starting to gather. "Someone call the fucking police! Just don't stand their gawking! Hurry up before he kills her!" Just as she had screamed, his fist connected with Dani's chin, knocking her to the ground. Waves of anger generated more strength than Dani could have ever thought she had; she jumped to her feet and onto Jeremy's back. Jeremy was beyond comprehending what he was doing. The drugs had taken over, along with his rage. Dani had never seen or experienced anything like this before—it was beyond frightening.

Betina had curled up in a ball on the ground, trying to protect herself. While Dani hung onto his back and was grabbing his arms, Jeremy swung his leg back and kicked Betina in the gut with a horrible force. Betina cried out sharply once and then only whimpered. Chaos, yelling, and hands were everywhere—everyone was trying to stop him.

Dani was tenacious and would not let go of his flailing arms from doing any more damage to her terrified friend. Steph was shouting into her cell phone and sirens could be heard coming down the street as they came closer and closer. Within seconds, squad cars pulled up and blocked the nearby street and an ambulance came to a stop as close to Betina as it could. Red and white spinning lights and blue police lights lit up the sky as a swarm of officers raced into the melee. They pulled Dani away, and then they all pounced on Jeremy, bringing him crashing to the ground. He was still fighting with all his strength and the officers struggled to keep him on the ground. At six-foot-five and two hundred and forty pounds of nothing but muscle, Jeremy was giving it a good fight and unwilling to stop.

With Jeremy finally handcuffed and forced into a squad car, Dani immediately bent down on the ground to check out her friend, who looked to be shivering in shock and tremendous pain. Blood was streaming out of the wound on her head, and one arm looked to be in an awkward position. Dani touched her face gently before the paramedics managed to move her out of the way. "It's okay, Betina, the police are here and we are going to get you to the hospital. You're going to be okay now. I'm so, so sorry, sweetheart…."

Betina's eyes were swollen shut and her escaped tears were beginning to blend in with the light rain that was beginning to fall. Dani had seen those storm clouds earlier, but now was not the time for the sky to break open with rain. The paramedics gently placed Betina on a gurney. Shock had set in and her silence was deafening to Dani. Once Betina was securely situated on the gurney, Dani turned around and slid into Steph's arms and began to cry.

Steph pushed Dani's hair out of her face and said, "It's okay, Dani. You saved her life. He would have killed her had you not interrupted him. She's going to be okay."

Dani looked up and whispered, "She will never be okay. I'm…I'm going to ride over in the ambulance with her. I don't want her to be alone. No one should ever be alone…."

Steph looked at Dani's face and saw her swollen eye. "Well, kiddo, that's quite a shiner!"

Dani lifted her hand and gently touched her face. She winced in pain. "I'll have it looked at once we get her situated at the hospital." She started to walk over to the ambulance and took a step up to get in. "Steph, can you bring me my backpack?"

Steph ran over and picked it up and brought it to Dani. "Be safe, my friend. I hope she's okay…."

The doors closed and Dani took a seat next to her friend and picked up her small hand. She held on tight. Nothing needed to be said. With the hospital only a few blocks away, Dani finally could take a deep breath, knowing help was here for her broken friend.

The ambulance stopped and the doors opened. A full staff of doctors and nurses were waiting to administer aid to the patient—knowing that time was valuable. Dani immediately climbed out and then they pulled the gurney out. Once the gurney was on the ground, it was covered with people like bees to a beehive. Many were shouting out orders and others preforming necessary precautions for trauma patients. Dani stood back and watched silently as her friend was wheeled off in a sea of chaos.

Dani stumbled through the automatic doors after them, tears running down her face and clutching her backpack. The drama of the evening kept rolling in her mind like an endless bad movie. All she could think about was the crazed look on Jeremy's face after he crushed her friend with blow after blow and Betina curled up in a ball, unable to defend herself, and past the point of trying. How had this happened? Why did this happen?

Dani knew the answers, but had refused to acknowledge it the past few weeks as Betina became more and more scared of Jeremy. Dani sat there thinking back to what had led up to this horrific event. There were signs, and yet, no one took heed. Whoever thought that Jeremy would snap and nearly kill their friend? He never portrayed the violent type. Nor had he ever exposed such vicious and violent behavior. For two years, Dani had spoken to Betina about a few verbal fights they had had, but nothing physical had ever been perpetrated nor had she ever really felt threatened. Why now? Why tonight?

Two hands grabbed her shoulders and gave her a little shake. "Dani, are you alright? You're scaring me. I think you're in shock and we need to get you to the emergency room. Besides, I want to get all your injuries looked at," Dr. Cal said, his voice reaching her as if from a distance.

Who was shaking her? Where had this familiar voice come from? Why was he yelling? Dani didn't respond. She just stood there in a trance replaying the continuous evening. Without even knowing it, she had dropped her backpack.

"Dani, answer me!" he yelled again.

His desperation broke through her fog and Dani whispered, "I'm fine, I don't need your help."

"You need help. Let me get you some help," he pleaded. He reached one hand into his pocket and pulled out his cellphone. Without letting go of Dani, he hit one button and barked into the phone, "Becky, look up Dani's personnel file and find the phone number for Stephenee Orman. Give her a call and have her come down to the hospital immediately."

"Dani, listen to me, you're injured and in shock."

Dr. Cal released one hand and slowly and gently touched her battered eye, then felt her neck, silently checking her pulse. Dani just stood there, weak in the knees, staring blankly at his face as he appraised her injuries.

Dr. Cal took a step backward and slowly bent down to pick up her backpack, reaching for her hand.

Dani raised a shaking hand to her swollen eye and winced. She whispered, her voice cracking, "I'm fine. Go take care of Betina." Dani turned around, wobbling, and tried to leave. She could vaguely hear Dr. Cal begging her to stop and yelling for help. His head was turned towards the emergency room information desk as he bellowed for assistance.

Dani's head was spinning in circles; and the need to run away in sheer panic was all she could think to do. When the automatic doors opened, she staggered outside as the pelting rain unleashed its wrath and soaked her, plastering her dark hair against her alabaster skin.

"Dammit!" Dr. Cal yelled, and wrenched himself past the doors and towards her, but he was too late.

Not thinking about what she was doing or where she was going, a feeling of alarm consumed Dani and she fell into the street, just out of Dr. Cal's reach. The rising cacophony, the screaming, screeching tires, horns, all of this was meaningless in Dani's world. The only thing left was sudden, unspeakable pain and then...everything went black....

chapter twenty-one

DR. CAL WATCHED IN SHEER AGONY AS HER TINY BODY was thrown into the dark night and finally landed on the asphalt street. His screams died in his throat and he felt like he was going to choke to death. He fell to his knees beside her and his hands hovered over her still form. He was completely at a loss. He bent over her, trying to protect her from the rain, and stared down at her bloody, broken face in silent anguish. Her limp and bleeding body was damaged beyond human endurance.

The car had tried to brake, but in the pouring rain, nothing could stop the tires from spinning and sliding. Doctors and nurses were pouring out of the front doors with a lot of equipment. Many were barking out orders.

Dr. Cal's tears blended in with the rain and the sound of his sobs was absorbed in all the commotion. Lance, a good friend of his, pulled him to his feet and made him step aside so that they could load Dani onto a stretcher. Her breathing was shallow and her pulse was hardly detectable. She was losing too much blood; and there was nothing they could do until the trauma unit evaluated her condition.

"Let's put her into a medically-induced coma. Her head has major trauma and swelling has already started," Dr. Jerold hollered, as he held onto the stretcher and helped push it into the hospital.

Dr. Cal didn't say a word. He shook his head and began moaning. "If I could...just take it back. If I could…just change places with her. If I could…just see her smile one more time…if I could just…."

Suddenly Lance was shaking his shoulder. "Come on, Cal." He looked really concerned. "Don't fall apart. She's…she's in good hands. They're taking her to the fifth floor. Can I get you anything?"

Cal shook his head abruptly, staring at the glass doors. Lance gripped his elbow and steered him inside and out of the rain. He let go and peered at Cal closely. "We need to call her family and let them know. Cal?"

Cal stood there shaking. Then he whispered to himself, "She has no one to call." For the first time, he really deeply understood what she had been saying since her mother's death. There was no next of kin. There was no family to rush to her side. She was all alone in this world. He stood there looking around as though in a dream. There were people and police everywhere, congesting the lobby.

He weakly walked further inside and sunk down on a chair in the waiting room. Lance followed, and Cal waved him away with his hand. "I'll be alright, Lance. Go on, I'll catch up with you in a bit." After Lance reluctantly walked away, Cal gave a shuddering sigh, leaned his head down, and raked his fingers through his wet hair, shaking it out. Searching for strength, he pulled his phone back out and barely noticed how wet it was. He pressed the first autodial key.

The speaker crackled a bit, like some water had gotten past his OtterBox, but Cal didn't have time to worry about anything as trivial as his phone. "Pediatrics, can I help you?" Lola announced.

In a low whisper, his rough voice laced with pain, Cal said, "Lola, I need a big favor. On my desk is a sticky note with the name Anton on it. Could you get me that phone number?"

"Sure. What's up? I heard there was a lot of commotion downstairs," she asked cheerfully.

Dr. Cal's voice broke, and he could barely get his words out. "Dani…was hit…by a car…in front of the hospital…."

Lola gasped. She listened to his unsteady voice and sternly said, "You had better keep it together. You're no good to her if you fall apart. I'll be right down. And anything we can do…we will do it."

"They took her up to the fifth floor. I'm…I'm on my way up there right now."

With everything he had learned over the years, dealing with the negative aspect of his job, he desperately willed himself to stay calm. He got up and raced to an elevator and kept pushing the button until the doors finally opened. Then he pushed number five. Once he was secure and on his way up to the fifth floor, he quietly begged, "Please, God, don't let her die. You took everyone else—let her live! I'll do anything…."

Dr. Cal was not used to making promises. He had been through too much and knew that sometimes you have to let life work it out—on its own. He knew death when he saw it, but he also believed in miracles. And if today was the day that God passed out a miracle—than let it be Dani. It was going to take a miracle for her to survive.

The door opened and pandemonium was everywhere. By now everyone knew Dani was the patient hit by a car in front of the hospital. Everyone was coming upstairs to see what they could do and if they could give blood.

Dr. Cal caught one of the emergency surgeons. "Is she still with us? What is the initial prognosis so far?"

Dr. Ted Silver grasped one of his shoulders and said, "She was injured pretty badly. So far we found a few cracked ribs with a punctured lung, fractured hip, lots of contusions, but what we are worried about is the spleen. She's lost a lot of blood and she has some internal bleeding. We're trying to get everything evaluated before we take her into surgery. We're running several tests right now. We don't have much time, so we are pushing it hard."

Dr. Cal was trying hard not to panic. "Is Joel doing the surgery? Could they get in touch with him? I know it's his day off...."

"He already knows; and he knows what this means to you. He'll be here in ten minutes. Meanwhile, we need to order blood to transfuse...we're waiting to see what type she is."

Dr. Silver let go of his shoulder. "I'm going back in to see how it's going. I'll keep you posted."

The elevator door opened and Lola and Alva stepped out. They immediately saw Dr. Cal and quickly walked towards him.

Lola handed him a piece of paper with the information he was looking for. "How is she?" Tears were slowly sliding down her cheeks, and she used a tissue to wipe them away.

"Not good. She's got a lot of major stuff going on. I'm hoping Joel will get here in time to stop most of the bleeding."

Lola exhaled the deep breath she was holding. "Thank God Joel is the surgeon...."

Cal took his cell out of his pocket and dialed the number Lola had given him.

"Hello," Anton quietly answered.

Dr. Cal looked relieved. At the same time, his unsteady voice spoke into the phone. "Anton, this is Cal. There's been an accident and Dani has been severely injured."

"What do you mean an accident? What happened? Where is she?" Anton's deep voice was suddenly filled with alarm.

"She is barely alive...but still with us. She was hit by a car...." Cal said, feeling sick.

Anton yelled into the phone, "Oh my god, I will be right there."

All Dr. Cal could yell into the phone before Anton hung up was "fifth floor!"

Dr. Cal looked at Lola, who was standing right next to him. He mumbled, "They have her in a forced coma right now because of a bad concussion and brain swelling…." His shoulders slumped and he stared down at his phone brokenly.

Alma stepped closer and said, "The girls and I are going to offer our free services to watch her around the clock. We'll take shifts. And if need be, we will use our vacation and sick days. We all want her to know that we care." Alma turned to Lola and buried her head in her shoulder, unable to say any more.

Lola held her tight, and with enough strength for all three, she said, "She's going to make it, Dr. Cal. I know she is. She's one tough cookie."

"I hope you're right, because I'm pretty scared right now." Dr. Cal looked at his two nurses and didn't know what to say. He finally managed, "Thank you…."

"The nurses want to set up a blood drive with the employees and some of our patients' parents. She's going to need lots of blood," Lola said.

Dr. Cal nodded his head. "As soon as I get some information about her blood type we will immediately get that going."

Nurses and doctors continued to float in and out of the surgical room in rapid procession. A few doctors paused by Cal, offering quick updates, and their faces didn't look encouraging. Time was precious and every second counted.

The elevator door opened and Steph ran out. Confusion was written all over her face and she turned in every direction to see if she could recognize anyone. Once she spotted Lola at the nurse's desk, she hurried toward her. Lola was looking at a chart. Steph gasped and tapped her on the shoulder.

Tears were spilling from Steph's eyes and her voice was overwhelmed with emotion, but she choked out, "How...is she?"

It took Lola a few seconds to recognize Steph, and when she did, she pulled Steph into her arms and let her cry. Steph stood there uncontrollably sobbing in the arms of the nurse that Dani adored. Dani would constantly talk about her friends at the hospital, but only on a special occasion did Steph every really get to see them. Why was this happening to her friend? Why Dani?

When Steph's crying calmed down, Lola put her finger under her chin and said, "It is touch and go right now. They might have to remove her spleen and everyone is panicking because she has the rarest blood type there is. Only one percent of the population matches her type; and they don't have enough reserves at the hospital's blood bank. The staff is on the phones now calling all the hospitals and blood banks in the area to get enough for a transfusion. We are two pints short."

Steph looked terrified. "Oh my god, I can't lose her! Maybe I'm a match? Can they test me?" she begged.

Lola nodded. "I doubt you are, but let's test you."

Lola called over her two dear friends who were considered the best nurses in trauma surgery. She wanted nothing but the best to give Dani a fighting chance. If only she could find more blood, they would be ready to prep for surgery.

Within seconds, Dr. Cal came up to the desk to talk to one of the nurses. His face exposed enormous strain. "Did we find any close donors or anyone close who has even a few pints?" His eyes darted to the side and he noticed Lola and Steph. He quickly walked over and gave Steph a hug. "We are trying our best to save her. We need blood desperately. We can't go into this operation short. I don't know what to do." Then he looked at Lola and whispered, "Thanks for all your help."

Steph started to moan. "Can I see her?"

Dr. Cal shook his head and touched her shoulder. "Sorry, Steph, she's in an induced coma."

The door to the elevator opened and Anton stepped out. His normally tall, sturdy body was now hunched over at the shoulders and agony was etched over every plane of his face. His skin was as pale as a ghost, and his hands were clinched together. He was frantically looking around when he noticed Dr. Cal and Steph standing at the nurse's counter. With a quick pace, he found himself standing in front of them.

Dr. Cal and Anton exchanged handshakes. Then with his deep, shaky baritone voice, Anton asked, "Can I see her?"

Dr. Cal shook his head and sighed. "Sorry, she's in an induced coma. We need to get her into surgery, but we need some blood."

Anton looked confused at that answer. "What do you mean, you need blood?"

Dr. Cal inhaled and exhaled in frustration. "She has the rarest blood type. No one in the area has a supply. We were able to secure a few pints, but we are short."

Anton panicked. His eyes darted in all directions and when they settled back on Dr. Cal, he demanded, "Take some of my blood!"

Dr. Cal watched as Anton began to lose it. "Do you know what type you are?"

"AB negative! I know my blood will match hers!" he yelled and slammed one fist against the counter, scaring the surrounding nurses and doctors. "I am family!" he yelled for the whole room to hear. All eyes darted to Anton as his body began to shake.

Dr. Cal held up his hand to calm Anton down. "What do you mean, you're family?" he demanded sharply. "Are you sure? We don't have a minute to spare on speculation."

Anton took hold of Dr. Cal's shoulders and pushed him off to the side. They were whispering back and forth to each other in a heated conversation.

Immediately, Dr. Cal called for a nurse. "I need a phlebotomist…now! I need this man tested for his blood type. STAT! And then I want him prepped to go into the surgery room."

Anton's back leaned against the nurse's counter and he covered his face with his hands. There was no backing out now. He could only move forward if it meant saving Dani's life. He knew he had the same type blood. On many occasions, he was told by doctors that his type was rare. They didn't need to test him. He knew exactly who he was and why their blood types were the same. It didn't matter why or how. He couldn't stand on ceremony and hide what he knew. Dani's life was in jeopardy and he needed to step up and deal with it.

A nurse showed up with a plastic case and right there in front of everyone and as quickly as she could, she took a sample. She ran off and disappeared into a room. Anton, Steph, and Lola stood there counting the seconds as they passed.

Dr. Cal was leaning his elbows on the counter and holding his head in his hands when suddenly Lola touched his shoulder and pointed. When his eyes looked up, he saw Dr. Joel step out of the elevator and toward them. Dr. Cal rushed forward and gave him a bear hug. Then they stepped to the side. While they were discussing Dani, a nurse came running out, screaming for all to hear, "He's a perfect match! We have the blood."

Dr. Cal cuffed Dr. Joel on the back with excitement. Then they both went up to Anton and explained what was going to take place in the operating room. The nurse requested that Anton follow her into a room off the corridor. The doctors disappeared into the surgery room.

Steph watched with apprehension. Then she heard Dr. Cal yell, "Say your prayers, everyone. This is going to be touch and go! We're heading into surgery."

Dr. Joel then asked loudly, "You sure you want in, Cal?"

He followed Joel into the room, an unmistakable and stubborn look of assertiveness on his face.

Ambulances could be heard in the distance and suddenly the elevator door opened and an attendant was carrying a small cooler containing the needed blood.

Lola nodded to Alma. Instead of seating Steph in the waiting room by herself, Alma took her downstairs to the quiet and peaceful sanctuary where she could gather her thoughts.

Steph stood there taking slow even breaths as the enormity of the past few hours sunk in. Steph loved this small sanctuary that was filled with so many memories. She had spent many days and nights in the hospital holding Dani's hand and praying when her son was dying. No matter how much they prayed or how much they begged God to spare Levi, nothing had been able to save him. The disease had taken its course. There was nothing that they could do to stop the inevitable. Steph now sat there praying that Dani's life would be spared.

Steph was never raised around a family that practiced a specific religion—neither was Dani. Steph's parents had blamed God for the loss of their son, without as much as a thought to the surrounding circumstances that had caused his death. It was a rainy day and a dense fog had set in. He was happy to be off work and was meeting some of his friends at a local bowling alley. He was traveling faster than he should have been in his fancy car and when he turned a corner and hit a curve on the slick mountain road—he lost control and was killed instantly as he crashed into an electric pole.

It was a tough time for Steph and her family. Words could never take away the pain or replace the loss. It was hard for them to get back on track with normal everyday living. Blaming God seemed like the only likely catalyst in exchange for their son's carelessness. After all, impugning God was a normal reaction to death.

Dani had been there for her friend. Then, months later, life again repeated itself and it was Steph's turn to pull Dani through the pain and destruction of death—not once—but twice. And now here she was back in this room trying to make sense of what happened to her dear friend—moments ago.

Steph took a seat on the front pew. She placed her hands in her lap and stared at the rows of flickering candles. Nothing made sense to her tonight. She needed this space to try to deal with the unexplainable reality Dani was now facing.

In this room, the confusion and turbulent atmosphere from the fifth floor was gone—in its wake was a peaceful silence. The front table had a flower arrangement Dani would have loved. The wildflowers filled the room with a fragrance that brought Steph's thoughts back to Dani's favorite flower shop. Steph closed her eyes and continued to take slow, even breaths. She needed to slow down her fast-beating heart; it was pounding out of her chest. As she sat there, she tried to make sense of the evening. Nothing had been clear from the moment they opened the back door of the restaurant to the call she received an hour ago. Nothing! And now two of her two friends were both in this hospital fighting for their lives. Two innocent women who didn't deserve to be here.

Steph folded her hands together and closed her eyes. Then she began, "Dear God...."

Hours later Steph was sleeping on the couch in the waiting room. A slight noise woke her up and she refused to open her eyes. She couldn't remember how long it had been since she felt this need to never wake up. She laid there for another few minutes, and gradually she opened one eye. Anton was sitting at the end of the couch with his head resting on the back and his eyes closed. His face was relaxed and his arms were crossed and resting on his chest.

Steph didn't know how long she had been sleeping or when she had come up to the waiting room—everything was a blur. Now she was laying here wondering if Dani was alive or dead. With deliberateness, she laid there perfectly quiet and motionless, listening to her heartbeat as she stared at the ceiling. She didn't want to get up and find out. She just wanted her friend sitting next to her on the couch with a big smile on her face. That would have been a perfect scenario to this dreadful day. That was not going to happen, so with slow, easy movements, she brought herself up into a sitting position.

When she turned her head again to look at Anton, his eyes were open and he was looking at her.

"How are you feeling, Anton?" Steph finally broke the silence.

"Tired and worried." He didn't move.

"Have you been sitting here long? Have you heard any news? Is Dani okay?" She turned towards him.

He pulled himself forward and ran his fingers through his hair. "I was in the surgery room a few hours ago. She needed my blood. A few times I heard her heart flatline, but then they seemed to miraculously bring her back. They worked on her fractured ribs and punctured lung. I'm not sure if they removed the spleen."

Tears welled in Steph's eyes. "Did she make it?"

Steph was afraid to move or walk over to the counter where some of the staff had gathered. There seemed to be a lot of talking. No one was crying, so Steph took that as a positive sign. She could only manage slow and even breaths to keep herself from going back into panic-mode. In slowly, out slowly, she kept repeating to herself.

All of a sudden, Dr. Cal entered the waiting room. He looked at Steph and Anton and hurried over to take a seat between them on the couch. He rested his elbows on his knees and hung his head. "Just give me a moment and I will tell you where we stand." He sucked in a deep breath and let it out slowly. Then he pushed himself back against the couch and said, "She pulled through the worst. We are just waiting right now to see if she can make it the rest of the way. We don't want any clots or bleeders." Again, he inhaled and exhaled slowly. "She was in pretty rough shape and we don't know why or how she survived, but she's still here."

Anton held out his hand to shake Dr. Cal's. "Thank you, son."

Dr. Cal looked at Anton and then looked away. "Thank you for stepping up and letting the past go…we could not have done it without your blood. I don't know what to say…."

"Please don't say anything. Let's just leave it where it is for now. Do you know how thankful I am to have her rare type and to be here right now? Or how thankful I am to you and this hospital for their cooperative staff and keeping her alive. I know I have a lot of explaining that I will have to do. But right now, I am only concentrating on Dani and I'm so thankful she's still alive."

Dr. Cal took his surgical cap off his head and wiped his eyes and forehead. "I'm beyond thankful you got here—when you did. Everyone has worked so hard. Most of all, Dani must have a deep-seeded will to live because a few times she flatlined on the table and scared us all shitless!"

Anton said, "Let's just say 'I was meant to be here.' I think I've always been meant to be here. It was a promise I made and one I have honored for years."

Dr. Cal looked at him curiously. Then he nodded his head in acknowledgement.

"One day when the timing is right, she will know everything...I promise you," Anton quietly whispered.

Steph had watched the interchange between the two men and didn't even try to figure out what was going on. She just wanted to know how Dani was doing. "When can I see her?" Steph asked.

Dr. Cal looked at Steph and held up his crossed fingers. "Let's hope in a few days. We have to keep the room sterile; and we need to keep her sedated and in a coma because of the swelling in her brain."

Steph sighed. "Well, I hope that hit to the head knocked some damn sense into her. I thought, today, when she got back from the cemetery that she had finally let everything go and was turning over a new leaf. Then shit hit the fan when we walked out the door of the restaurant. I have no idea why she would pull something stupid like running into the street."

"I take the blame for not handling it better. She was in shock and I turned away for just a few seconds...." Dr. Cal admitted and his voice trailed off. He cringed and his shoulders slumped as he confessed his guilt.

"You're not to blame, son," Anton said firmly, his eyes kind.

Cal shook his head and then lowered it into his hand, shielding his eyes. "I could have prevented it. I was right there. I turned away and when I turned back, she was already out the door."

"It's not your fault," Anton repeated solidly.

Cal didn't reply, he just sat silently as he quietly dealt with the pool of guilt that had been tying his stomach in knots ever since Dani fell.

Steph stood up to stretch her aching muscles. "I don't put any blame towards you, Dr. Cal. Honestly, if it wasn't for you, she wouldn't still be here. Please don't blame yourself.... What...what do we do now? Is there anything I can do or should I go home?"

Dr. Cal stood up too. He shuffled his feet for a second and then switched over to his professional manner. "She is in ICU with around-the-clock nurses and some extra nurses who refused to leave her bedside. She has the staff all over her like white on rice." He smiled feebly. "I will personally be sleeping in her room for the next seventy-two hours. Go home and get some rest. There is nothing else you can do right now."

Anton stood up and shook hands again with Dr. Cal. Then he turned to Steph and said, "Let me take you home. I don't want you taking the bus in the rain."

Steph nodded.

chapter twenty-two

THREE DAYS LATER, ANTON ENTERED THE HOSPITAL. IT was early in the morning and he had not slept for days. He had come every day and sat for eighteen hours in the visitors' room, just hoping to get in to see her. So much of his past was spinning around in his head; and it was igniting emotions he had not felt in a long time. The night he got the call from Dr. Cal was one of the worst nights of his life. He had barely shrugged into his coat, when he was desperately flying out the door in fear. All the way to the hospital he had prayed that she wouldn't die—not before he had a chance to talk to her. He had so much to tell her and so many lies he had to make right. His regrets for never having the chance to confront Ema had almost eaten him alive the past year. Her heart attack and death had left him filled with remorse and shame. And now all those promises he had made to himself would become worthless if he lost Dani.

Anton quietly stepped into the room and watched the nurses as they took Dani's vitals. One was adding a medication into her drip and another was taking her pulse. Machines and equipment were everywhere and odd sounds from the technical devices filled the room. Dani had tubes and wires attached all over her small body. Her face was pale and her frail arms were lying on her chest. Small sections of hair had been shaved and you could see the staples that held her scalp together. Her dark and swollen eyes were closed and a peaceful expression suffused her face. Anton stood and stared at

Dani. He had never been afraid of anything in his life. He was a man who was used to being in control. But that night while they were taking blood from his body, to save her life—all he could do was silently beg for forgiveness...and mercy.

In the corner of the room was a small cot occupied by a sleeping man. Anton took a closer look and realized it was Dr. Cal. He had large, dark circles under his eyes and his wrinkled scrubs looked as if they hadn't been changed in the three days since Dani's accident. Anton listened to his deep breathing and stepped a little closer toward the bed. All of a sudden, he tripped over the corner of the wheels under the hospital bed and grasped onto the footboard to break his fall.

The slight commotion alerted the nurses he was there, and immediately brought Dr. Cal to his feet.

His eyes darted around the room looking for where the noise came from. When he noticed Anton, he shook his head and said, "Jesus...I thought the team of trauma doctors were back!"

Anton's cheeks turned red, and he held out his hand. "Don't you ever go home, Doctor?"

Dr. Cal glanced down at his scrubs and it was his turn to blush. "Not lately. Hopefully we are now out of the woods and I can finally breathe easier. She had her turning point late last night. She is going to make it— providing there are no complications."

Anton smiled. "She's too tough to have complications. Besides, she had the best of the best taking care of her. I want you to know that I am eternally grateful."

Dr. Cal looked at the machine flashing her vitals, then he turned and looked directly at Anton. "I don't know exactly who you are in regards to Dani, or why you are in her life, but something tells me you're going to have a lot of questions to answer."

Anton nodded his head. "It's a long story and one that started twenty-nine years ago. I need to talk to Dani first."

Dr. Cal put up his hand like a stop sign. "Give her time to heal, both physically and mentally. She's very fragile right now. I know she can't take any drama right now."

Anton spotted a chair and went to sit down. Dr. Cal returned to the cot and had a seat.

"Will she have any long-term injuries or problems?" Anton asked.

"She was very lucky and we made a decision not to take out her spleen. We know it was smacked around like a punching bag when she was hit, but it seems to be healing. Our biggest worry then was the hairline fracture of her skull and the swelling of her brain. We won't know the extent of those injuries until she wakes up. We took her out of the coma early this morning, so now it's up to her."

Anton leaned his elbows on his knees. "How is her friend?"

"Pretty beat up. Charges were pressed and a restraining order is in place. She left the hospital yesterday." Dr. Cal ran his fingers through his unruly hair.

"What's next with Dani?"

Dr. Cal stood up and said, "We just wait." He walked out of the room.

Anton sat for the next few hours watching Dani as her chest rose with every shallow heartbeat. Crossing his legs, he sat back and started to evaluate why he was sitting here, and how he came to this exact moment in his life....

Since he was old enough to leave home, his life had been about him—his wants; his needs; his desires. Even at a young age, his rebelliousness against his parents had him drifting meaninglessly—without looking back. Nobody could slow him down, or interfere with his burning need to endlessly wander around the world looking for a meaning to his life. His affluent upbringing had only given him the gift of choices, but somewhere deep inside he was still searching for that meaning of existence. He had been everywhere and had done almost everything humanly possible. His incredible experiences were beyond anyone's comprehension, including his own twin brother, Florin. And yet, life had passed him by and he had nothing to show for it—except a promise. It was a promise until this day that he had honorably kept. And one that tore his insides out from the betrayal to the two most significant women in his life the past twelve years. It was a betrayal so deep; his lies and deceit and his fears of losing them became an endless nightmare.

He had watched his brother from a distance as he made a mess of his life. Florin had tried to please his controlling father to no avail. The deeper he plunged, the harder it became. With constant criticism and cruel abuse at the hands of his parents, Florin continued down the path of self-destruction. Then he took over the family business, only to run it into the ground. He married a much younger woman whose vicious and spiteful character was set on destroying not only Florin, but their three children. Unfortunately, nothing in Florin's life had given him any reprieve—he just continued to stumble forward. His wife had crushed any self-esteem and confidence he had and she had reduced him to a deflated man. He was dead on the inside—a shell of a man.

Then one summer day, Florin found the only safe place he could hide. It was a place that had offered him peace from a world of painful regrets and loneliness. Her name was Emila Silivasi. For that one year he had found a deep-rooted contentment that pulled him out of his dark abyss. Those few stolen moments they had left him with a feeling of euphoria and being truly loved. Emila was his ray of sunshine. She made him feel alive again. It had been love at first sight and she never asked for anything in return. She became an addiction he couldn't let go of—until one day—a day that changed all of their lives and emotionally broke him—forever.

His wife, Lucia, found out about the affair. Her heart filled with unfathomable hate and spite, Lucia made plans without him knowing and executed them with precision. Within a few days, Emila was on a boat sailing to a country she knew nothing about, thousands of miles away. Unable to fathom this depth of loss and her despair, she had placed her hands in fate and walked the path alone. Once she was settled, Daniela was born, and her life took on a different meaning. Unable to forgive or forget a man who never even said goodbye, she closed herself off from those around her, only focusing on becoming the best mother she could.

Anton had only seen Emila once in Romania and that was from a distance. He had come home for the holiday to find out his brother was acting irresponsibly and foolishly. They had talked for hours. His wife would never divorce him, nor would she let him continue his affair with a young servant. Anton had tried to talk some sense into Florin, but he was too smitten to listen to anyone. Anton knew nothing good could possibly come from this affair, but Florin saw it differently. He was going to walk away from everything and live in peace and happiness with Emila. Anton didn't know what to do, and it wouldn't be long before Lucia was told of the affair by the stable boy, who had seen them.

Lucia paid handsomely for the tidbit of information, and the stable boy took off in the middle of the night.

When his brother told him there was a child coming, Anton didn't know what to do. How could his brother impregnate an innocent eighteen-year-old servant? What kind of shame would it bring to his children and family? Before Anton could figure out a way to take care of things, and before his parents found out, Lucia had taken the matters into her own hands. She secured a false passport, booked the tickets, and confronted the young girl. Emila was young and naïve. She begged Lucia to let her to stay in the country. She promised she would not see Florin again. But it was not enough and her cries fell on deaf ears. Emila never saw Florin again. Lucia's plan worked perfectly and three days later Emila was on a train to eventually catch a ship bound for America.

Anton had always been a man of honor and integrity. When he found out that Lucia had shipped Emila away, he was enraged. He went to Florin and confronted him. Florin didn't know what to do. He made Anton promise he would always keep a distant eye on Emila and his child. Florin was never the same after that day.

Anton was beyond anger. How was that innocent young woman going to survive alone with a child, let alone in a new country? Someone had to take responsibility. Someone needed to make sure they made it okay. And so, Anton set up a trust account from the date of the baby's birth, to insure Emila some financial stability. He anonymously wrote a note on a piece of paper embossed with their family crest and enclosed the passbook. Then he mailed it to her with the bank's instructions. He took special precautions that it could not be traced or she would never know exactly where this monthly pittance came from. She could only surmise it was from his brother who did not step forward and had cowardly abandoned her and their child. It was Anton's final promise to himself to never let that child feel alone, unwanted, or go hungry. After all, she was family....

When he continued to contact the bank and found out that the money was left untouched, he decided to move to California. He took up residency in the Beverly Hills Hotel where he could watch the small family from a distance. For years, he watched as Dani grew into a beautiful and kind young woman. Never did he intrude on their lives or acknowledge himself as any form of beneficiary or family. It wasn't until twelve years earlier, when Dani had turned sixteen and they were financially struggling, that he made a choice. Rather than confront Emila, an opportunity came up and the apartment next door was up for rent. Against his better judgment, he rented the place and soon his façade began. His secret betrayal turned into his own living hell as he became a lonely old Romanian man living a quiet, secluded life— next door to his niece.

He got to know Emila and Dani, and truly enjoyed the time he spent with them. He and Emila became friends, and the hours they spent talking about Romania became the highlight of his existence. He never exposed who he was or talked about certain areas of his past. After twelve years, they had become close and his enjoyment was watching Dani grow up. When she became pregnant, he rejoiced with them. At Levi's birth, he accepted the honor of becoming his godfather. At Levi's death, he felt the pain so deeply, he finally realized and found what he had been searching for his entire life—a family. Then when Emila died, his heart was broken and he tried his best to console Dani. She was lost—she was alone—she had almost given up on life. But he wouldn't let her. He kept fighting to make sure she pulled herself out of the depression that nearly consumed her. He wanted her to think of him as her family.

He was almost there when she found the box that contained her mother's clues to her past. He worried that she would find out the real reason of her existence and everything her mother had endured at the hands of his selfish family. He also knew she was not going to give up until she found her father. Then when he found out about her trip to Romania, he was deathly afraid her world would come crashing down. He knew he had to tell her the truth. It was just finding the right time. He also knew there was a large chance she would never forgive him and this could be the beginning of the end.

When she came home from Romania, she was crushed. The time had come and Anton knew he had to tell her. She deserved to know that she was not alone in the world. But did he want to expose her to the miserable family that had ruined her mother's life? Her biological dad was dead. His selfish children would never accept her. She was always going to be an outcast.

When he talked to his attorney, the advice was always the same. "Tell her the story and let her know that you are sorry. Tell her that you will always be here for her. That's the best you can do. Let her know everything, including that you are leaving her your estate."

"What if she never talks to me again?"

"Then there is nothing you can do. But she deserves the truth," his attorney reiterated adamantly.

Here he was sitting in this hospital terrified she was going to die, and now his anxiety was replaced with the fear. Telling her about his duplicity was tearing him apart. Anton laid his head back on the chair as the shame of his betrayal consumed him.

Dr. Cal gave Anton a little nudge. He had been sleeping in the chair for over an hour since he came back into the room.

Dani blinked her eyes for a few seconds and tried to lift her hand.

Anton jumped out of his chair and followed Dr. Cal to the bed. A few of the trauma doctors and nurses were gathered around in anticipation.

Dr. Cal grasped her hand and bent down close to her face. He whispered, "Dani...can you hear me? Open your eyes."

Everyone held their breath, waiting to see her response. He whispered again, "Dani...this is Cal. Squeeze my hand."

Dani's eyes twitched a little. Then Dr. Cal squeezed her hand. A big smile came on his face when he felt the slight pressure of her hand as it clutched his. He looked around the room at all the smiling faces and said, "She did it!"

Dani felt like she was coming out of the clouds. Her head was pounding and her mouth was too dry to open. Noises were surfacing and she didn't know where they were coming from—nor what they were. She couldn't move and it was beginning to scare her. No matter how hard she tried, her body would not respond. She tried to take a deep breath, but even that was impossible. Where was she...and what was happening? All she wanted to do was go back into those clouds where she felt safe from pain and noise. It happened again. Only this time it was a voice.

"Dani...can you hear me? Open your eyes," a male's voice said.

She knew that voice. It sounded familiar and comforting. She wanted to see who it was. With a tremendous amount of effort, she saw some bright shapes through the slits of her eyes and tried to focus. She opened her eyes a little wider and eventually could see the smiling face of Dr. Cal.

Dr. Cal touched her forehead and ran his finger along her nose and onto her lips.

In a low, hoarse whisper, she said, "Stop it."

Dr. Cal and the group began to laugh. He leaned closer and said, "Go back to sleep, Dani. You need more rest."

Dani closed her eyes and went back into the clouds.

The next day Dr. Cal, Anton, and Steph were sitting in the room. Dani had woken up twice since the first time. Both times with a slight bit of improvement.

She was beginning to move her fingers and she quietly whispered, "Water...I need...some water."

Everyone rushed to her bedside. Lola produced a small cup of water with a straw and placed the straw to her lips. Slowly she let a few drops at a time run through her lips. "How's that?" Lola asked.

Dani slightly lifted her hand up and down. "Thank you."

Lola gave her another sip.

Dani's eyes scanned the room. "Where am I? Why am I here?" she whispered.

Everyone was leaning over her. Dr. Cal said, "You had an accident. We've been so worried about you."

Dani looked down at her body. "Am I missing anything?"

Everyone laughed. "No. You have all your parts...you are just pretty beat up."

Dani closed her eyes as a painful look crossed her face. "Did he beat me up, too?"

Steph reached for her hand. "No, Dani. You were hit by a car."

Tear began to well in her eyes, and they spilled over the corners and dripped onto he pillow.

Steph squeezed her hand. "Go back to sleep...we'll talk later."

It had been a week and Dani was just starting to remember everything that happened. Dani's body was on the mend, but the signs of her struggle were everywhere. Her staples still remained in her head and her bruised and battered body was black and blue all over. A flimsy nightgown barely covered the remnants of her near-death nightmare. A handful of tubes still remained to administer medications and hydrate her body, along with a catheter. She was alive…and that was all that mattered.

She opened her eyes one afternoon and Betina and Steph were sitting next to her bed, talking quietly to each other. In a small whisper, she called out their names. They both walked to the side of her bed and smiled down.

Betina's battered face was barely any better than Dani's. Half of her face was black, purple, and blue, and some of it was a faded yellow color. Bandages covered her cheek and along her chin line where she had received stitches. Betina bent over and clasped Dani's hand. She bent lower and smiled. "Hi, Dani. How are you feeling?"

Dani whispered, "Uhmm, pretty…awful. What about you, Betina?"

Betina's eyes filled with tears. One tear fell on Dani's face. Betina bent closer and wiped it away. "I don't know what to say or how to thank you. I know you took a few punches for me and I'm so sorry."

Dani tried to reach Betina's tears on her face, but her arm would not lift up enough. She whispered, "Let me wipe those tears away. I'm so sorry, Betina. I wish I would have been there sooner, or I would have been quicker, or that bastard wouldn't have done what he did. I hope he's in jail."

Betina bent down and kissed her friend's cheek. "He is. I'm just sorry you were in the middle."

Dani grinned. "I was right where I wanted to be. Protecting my dear friend…."

"Thank you, Dani. I was so worried about you and I'm so happy you made it through. The boys send their love."

"Looks like we are two pretty bruised up old broads!" Dani laughed.

Steph started to laugh. "I don't know why I'm laughing. Lawrence is now bald after pulling out his hair because three of his waitresses are out."

Dani looked at Steph. "Aren't you working?"

"Triple shifts sometimes. But it is worth it since he fired the drama queen."

Dani's eyes opened as wide as they could. "Really? He fired her?"

Steph crossed her chest. "Swear on my life!"

Dani's eyes started to close.

Steph bent over and kissed her cheek. "Okay, princess, Betina has got to go pick up the boys, and I can only stay a few minutes more. You need your sleep; besides, they have booted me out enough that I know when my time is almost up."

Betina walked out the door as Dr. Cal walked in. He winked at Steph and then he strolled over to check Dani's vital signs and opened her chart. He glanced over at Dani and shook his head. "You look tired. Do I have to limit your visitors?"

"Don't you dare!" she growled.

He walked over to a chair and pushed it next to the bed. He placed his hand on hers. "Okay, I'm going to sit here until you go to sleep."

"Why?"

"Because I'm the doctor and you need to sleep! And just in case you can't get to sleep…I brought my fairy dust!" He took out his little jar and sprinkled a little glitter on Dani.

Dani smiled and closed her eyes.

Dr. Cal had the stethoscope on her chest and was listening to her heart. Steph was sitting up in her bed.

Dani whined, "When am I going to get out of here?"

He rolled his eyes upward. "Never...if you don't keep your mouth quiet and let me hear your heart!"

Dani moaned like a little kid. "But you listen to it all the time! I've been here for weeks; can't I go home? I promise I will listen to what you doctors say...if you just let me go home!" she pleaded.

"I think I'm going to have to enroll you in the whiners club. For pity's sake, give this old doctor a break!"

Dani huffed but remained quiet until he was finished.

There were flowers everywhere. Most of flowers were Dani's favorites. Their smell permeated the room with the fragrance that Dani loved in her little florist shop. Get well cards hung all over the walls, along with pictures from all the little children in the oncology pediatric ward. No space went untouched.

"You know, for a woman who thought she was alone in the world, this room is a testament to how wrong you were and how loved you are!" Dr. Cal's eyes gazed around the room.

"I can't thank everyone enough for their support and their love. It's meant the world to me."

Dr. Cal was looking at her chart. "You know you wouldn't be here if it wasn't for Anton."

Dani looked around and didn't see him. He had been at her side every day since she came out of the coma. "Where is he?"

Steph got up and leaned over to kiss her goodbye. "Sorry, kiddo, I have to go do a double shift. One of my dear friends couldn't make it in, so I promised I would cover!"

Dani frowned. "I don't want you working so hard, especially to cover for me."

"Oh, go blow! You are such a pain in the ass!" Steph giggled. "I need the money anyway...." Steph picked up her purse and went out the door.

Dr. Cal sat down on the bed next to Dani. He picked up her hand, and said, "I feel so guilty sometimes when I think of that night. I wish I could have stopped you."

Dani squeezed his hand. Then she pulled him closer and gently gave him a hug. She laid her head on his shoulder for a few quiet moments. She could feel his heartbeat with her hand on his chest. "It wasn't your fault. Quit beating yourself up. It was my stupidity that caused me to go out the door and into the street."

"I should have stopped you; handled it better." His voice was choked up.

Dani pulled back to look into his face. Their gazes locked and for that single second, time stopped. They could both feel the attraction, like a moth to light. Dani wasn't sure she could ignore it anymore.

Unexpectedly, the door opened and Anton stepped in, carrying more flowers. He smiled at them. Dani blushed and Dr. Cal moved off the bed and stood up. His face was red and he began to shuffle his feet in embarrassment.

Anton looked at Dr. Cal's reddened face and smiled. "I just met Dr. Orsini outside. Is she related to you?"

"Yes, she's my mother. I hope you stayed clear. She can be quite cantankerous."

"On the contrary. I found her to be quite charming. She was teasing the nurses and giving them a hard time over all the vases of flowers. I was just happy I was on this side of the nurse's desk and she didn't see these!" He held up the flowers in his hands.

"I'm warning you—stay clear."

Anton laughed and then turned his attention toward Dani. "How are you feeling today?" Anton said, looking around for an empty spot. "Where should I put these?"

Dani laughed. "At the nurse's station! This room looks like a damn florist shop! You have got to stop this, Anton. You can give them to one of the nurses to take home and enjoy."

Anton laughed. "Okay. But I will miss that young girl in the florist shop!"

"Yeah…Paige is a sweetie!"

Dr. Cal walked toward the door. "Have a good visit. I probably should go see my mother before she stirs up all the nurses beyond endurance. I'll catch you later, Dani. I think you might want to pack up your stuff. Looks like you're going to be released tomorrow." He grinned.

Dani looked surprised. "Why didn't you tell me that when I asked you?"

Dr. Cal winked. "Because I wanted that hug!"

Dani picked up one of her pillows off the bed and threw it at him. But, not before he ducked out the door. It hit the closed door and Anton bent down to pick it up.

Dr. Cal popped his head in and blew Dani a kiss. "See ya later."

Anton shook his head. "I can see you are in good spirits. I guess they want to get you out of here before you take over this floor."

Dani laughed. Then she patted the space next to her on the bed. "Come sit over here. I can't stop thinking about everything we talked about the other day. I have a thousand questions, but I'm not sure I want to hear the answers anymore. I found out all I needed to know. I was a child conceived from love, not rape. And I am so blessed to be surrounded with all this." She circled her hand around the room.

Anton looked down and inhaled a deep breath. Then he exhaled and looked up. "Twenty-eight years of carrying around such a secret nearly killed me. You don't know how many times I wanted to tell you, but was terrified your mother would run. Or you would hate me. So, I did the only thing I could think of and moved in next door. I set up that bank account the day you were born and your mother never touched it, for what reason, none of us will ever know. Pride, I suppose. I wanted you both to have everything you needed. Instead, I watched what the strength of love between a mother and a daughter could create. And a bond that was unbreakable and worth more than anything money could buy."

"But why did you do this? I wasn't your daughter. And my mother was only a servant." She looked into his face.

"I made myself a promise after my brother broke your mother's heart and left her all alone to survive. When his vicious wife put Ema on the boat, I had to do the honorable thing. Duty is what bound me to it—my brother's spinelessness was an embarrassment. But he was a broken man. I don't have any excuses for your father. I can only hope you forgive me for my deceit. I will try to make it up to you the rest of my life."

Dani searched Anton's sad eyes. Then she reached up and let her fingers travel along his cheek. "How can I be mad? I love those brown bags at my door every morning. I'm not alone anymore. I do have a family—you."

Anton's eyes began to well, and with her finger, Dani wiped off his tears. He looked at the young woman sitting in front of him with pride in his eyes. Then he smiled and bent forward to give her a hug.

Dani smiled.

chapter twenty-three

THE NEXT MORNING DANI WAS LYING IN THE HOSPITAL bed with her eyes closed. All she wanted to do was go home. So much had happened the past few weeks and she had a lot to be thankful for. The chain of events that night of her accident had happened so fast and furious, nothing could have stopped it.

Her future now had so many positive possibilities. With Anton constantly doting on her, and her friends all nearby, she didn't feel alone at all anymore. With all her money in the bank, she sat in the hospital bed thinking of the endless ways she could donate it to the children in the oncology ward.

Even Dr. Cal had surprised her. The stories she had heard about those first few weeks of her recovery were touching. He never left her side and he slept in her room while she was in the coma. His need to be around her had him permanently living in the hospital and driving all the nurses crazy. Many times during the day, Lola had come down to drag him out of the room to take a break or a shower.

Dani heard the door open, but she kept her eyes closed. She laid there perfectly still, pretending she was asleep. All of a sudden, she felt warm breath caress her forehead, along with a pair of lips.

Dr. Cal ran his finger down her cheek. "Okay, I know you're awake. I can see your fast beating heart. Is that because I am here or is it because today is your lucky day?"

Done with the pretense, Dani's eyes opened wide and she sat up as quickly as her injured body would let her. She winced in pain, and then she squeaked out, "My lucky day! They're going to release me, right?"

A concerned look crossed his face. "Whoa...you're not going anywhere if you don't slow down and take things easier." He tapped her nose. "Your body has been through hell. I got them to release you early, because you promised to take it slow and easy. If you don't think you can do that...let me know, now!"

Dani swung her legs over the side of the bed and then looked up into his face. Her hands were at her side, and when she started to get dizzy from getting up so quickly, she grabbed onto his strong shoulders to steady herself. "I promise to be good."

Dr. Cal put his arms on her shoulders and looked deep into her eyes. The affectionate attraction he had for her was hard not to see. He leaned in closer and Dani began to panic. She whispered, "I think I'm all packed."

The moment was broken and Dr. Cal cautiously pulled away. His sad eyes reflected his disappointment and Dani looked down. She knew what he was asking of her, but she wasn't sure she could be in a relationship. She had been wounded so deeply once. Her feelings for him scared her.

He pulled the wheelchair up and asked, "Do you want to sit on it yourself, or do you want to sit on my lap and I can take you for a ride down to the car? I know Levi would love that! He went crazy popping wheelies with me!" He placed her bag on the handle of the wheelchair and turned around to look at her.

Dani gazed at him with her big blue eyes. Slowly she nodded her head shyly. With one swift motion he grabbed her and pulled the chair closer. Then she burst into laughter. She realized that they needed to start somewhere on mutual ground. Especially if he was going to actively pursue her. "I think I want to sit on your lap, providing you are careful and don't do some of that crazy stuff you did with Levi."

Dr. Cal gave Dani the biggest and most childish smile he could produce. Without giving her a chance to change her mind, he sat down in the wheelchair. "I'll be careful. If anything happens to you, I have to answer to Anton and I don't need any more trouble in my life."

Dani started to giggle as she nestled into his lap. Suddenly she realized that this wasn't so scary, Cal was one of her best friends. Without another second of hesitation, she placed both her arms around his neck and held on tight. If he wanted to play—she was going to play with him.

"Hold on tight!" he said.

When she looked down into his smiling face...their lips finally met!

if you've finished reading, please leave an honest review at Amazon and Goodreads. thank you so much!

I LOVE TO GARDEN, TRY NEW RECIPES, TAKE LOTS OF pictures and occasionally I enjoy a glass of wine with dear friends. I've never jumped out of a plane, climbed Mt. Everest, or seen the Northern Lights of Alaska. But, I have danced in the rain, sent a message in a bottle and I've ridden my motorcycle down the Pacific Coast Highway on sunny California days!

My passion of writing has led me on the most amazing journey. I thrive on developing strong storylines that showcase today's contemporary lifestyles. Rags to riches, Robin Hood, and surviving the odds, seems to be my one common denominator that showcases my fascinating and diverse characters.